DEATH WIND

To Sara,

Beware the long grass...

DEATH WIND

Travis Heermann (signature)

TRAVIS HEERMANN

&

JIM PINTO

WordFire Press
Colorado Springs, Colorado

ISBN: 978-1-61475-470-1

Cover design by Duong Covers

Art Director, Kevin J. Anderson

Cover artwork images by Forrest Imel

Book Design by RuneWright, LLC
www.RuneWright.com

Published by
WordFire Press, an imprint of
WordFire, Inc.
PO Box 1840
Monument CO 80132

Kevin J. Anderson & Rebecca Moesta, Publishers

WordFire Press Trade Paperback Edition August 2016
Printed in the USA
wordfirepress.com

PREFACE

On December 28, 1890, on the Lakota Pine Ridge Indian Reservation, a detachment of the U.S. 7th Cavalry intercepted an armed band of Lakota led by Chief Spotted Elk and forced them to camp near Wounded Knee Creek in southwestern South Dakota.

On the morning of December 29, supported by four Hotchkiss guns, the troops went into the camp to disarm the Lakota. A scuffle over the weapons resulted in a firefight, which escalated into the wholesale slaughter of approximately 350 Lakota, the vast majority of them women and children. The corpses of fleeing women and children were found shot as far as two miles from the fighting.

The Army suffered twenty-nine dead and thirty-five wounded—most of them from their own bullets and shrapnel. Twenty Medals of Honor were awarded after the battle.

Although a handful of minor skirmishes continued for almost two more decades, the battle that became known as the Wounded Knee Massacre was the last major conflict of the Indian Wars.

PART 1

"I want to say further that you are not a great chief of this country, that you have no following, no power, no control, and no right to any control. You are on an Indian reservation merely at the sufferance of the government. You are fed by the government, clothed by the government, your children are educated by the government, and all you have and are today is because of the government. If it were not for the government you would be freezing and starving today in the mountains.... The government feeds and clothes and educates your children now, and desires to teach you to become farmers, and to civilize you, and make you as white men."

—U.S. Senator John Logan to Sitting Bull, last of the great Lakota chiefs, August, 1883

I

Oliver McCoy scraped the remainder of his beans back into the now-cooling pot. He knew he couldn't cook. His ability to reheat beans was somewhere near the capabilities of the blind village idiot; he would rather starve than take another bite of his own burnt paste. Besides, his guts had been cramped up all day like a boot-stomped snake. "Better in the morning," he muttered, only half-believing it.

He spared a little water from his canteen to rinse the plate. Unlike some men, he could not abide a dirty plate come morning.

He had learned long ago to clean it now lest you be eating bugs in the morning with your breakfast. Reclaiming his spot by the fire, he huddled close for some warmth against the relentless wind. What a long day. He was too young to feel this damn old. Felt like he'd been riding for thirty years continuous.

"That was some piss-shit supper, Oliver," Reese said. "You better have some of that booze left." He fixed his rheumy eyes on Oliver and scratched his grizzled stubble.

Oliver tried to grin, but Reese's inscrutable eyes made it impossible to tell if he was joking. Emmett Reese had spent more time in the saddle than Oliver had been alive. Even though Oliver was supposed to be in charge, since the herd belonged to his pa, most of the time he just felt like a fool around Reese.

"Yeah, booze or whores!" Dawson grinned and spat a tobacco-brown stream into the fire. Dawson's teeth looked like an unpainted picket fence, and he had a scar across his lip that made children cry—the result of a close shave with a newly shod hoof. "How do you bugger up beans anyhow? They practically cook themselves."

Reese laughed at this too.

Oliver's ears burned, but he shrugged and allowed himself to share in the laugh with the other two.

Dawson called into the encroaching darkness toward the horses. "Hey, Ferrell! What are you doing out there, nuzzling up to your horse?"

The three of them laughed. When Oliver had announced that the beans were ready, Ferrell had passed, saying that he was going to check his tack. Strange, Oliver thought, because Ferrell had been grumbling all day about how hungry he was. But he had said something that Oliver was still trying to wrap his ears around. "There's a black _____ coming." Oliver had not been able to make out that word. *Mouth? Mouse? Mount?* Ferrell's accent gave him fits sometimes. Couldn't fellers just talk normal English? None of the words made much sense, and Ferrell had been quiet out in the darkness for a long time.

Oliver pulled a half-finished bottle of Tennessee bourbon out of his jacket and tossed it to Reese. "Make it last."

The wind grew chill and cut through his wool jacket like it was kerchief.

Reese grunted, yanked out the cork, and took a pull while Dawson held out his hand expectantly.

The fire guttered as a gust of wind washed over their campsite, rustling the sea of grass surrounding their camp. Not far away, one of the herd released a tremendous fart.

Dawson laughed. "Sounds like you in the morning, Reese."

Reese gestured toward the pot of beans. "That'll be you in about an hour. On second thought, give me that bottle back. I need to pass out before it starts."

Oliver relaxed a little. His shitty cooking had already been forgotten.

Dawson leaned back against his saddle with a groan of relaxation, then called into the night. "Come on now, Ferrell. Don't be no New York Nancy. Join us for a drink now. Since when does an Irishman forego whiskey?"

Oliver could hear Ferrell somewhere just outside the firelight fussing with leather and buckles.

Reese took another long sip. "That's some smooth whiskey. Where you been hiding that?"

"Pa likes the best," Oliver said.

Reese nodded in appreciation.

Dawson said, "I like the best, too. Too bad you ain't got a sister."

Oliver laughed with them, until a sudden chill gust laid the flame sidewise for a moment.

Dawson said, "Goddamn wind is like to carry you off."

Twelve hours in the saddle watching Pa's herd for late calves didn't make much opportunity for conversation, but Oliver still noticed that, except for the grumbling, Ferrell had been quiet and withdrawn all day. After all the trouble with the Indians over the winter, he was jumpy enough to be grazing the herd so near the reservation. Word was that Sioux were practically starving, and Pa had admonished him to be on the lookout for Indian cattle rustlers. Stories of their abilities at sneaking around like ghosts were well known. And it wouldn't be unheard of for some wild, young buck, itching at being cooped up on the reservation, to sneak up to camp and count coup on the white man.

Oliver called out, "What are you playing at, Ferrell? Get your ass warm before it's too cold to thaw."

Dawson took a long pull of whiskey.

Oliver said, "Hey, easy! It gots to last us."

Ferrell emerged from the darkness, firelight glowing in his ash-gray eyes. He was perhaps twenty-five, the same age as Oliver, but bigger, with a wild shock of red hair when his eagle-feathered bowler was not clamped tight over it. He was Pa's newest hire, had only been working at the Bar-M since the drive last fall. Ferrell once said he always counted himself lucky to get a job at all, being Irish. He spoke little of his past except to say that he came from some New York Irish slum.

Dawson shoved the whiskey bottle toward Ferrell. "Drink it while it's still hot."

Ferrell sat down, ignoring the bottle, staring into the fire.

Dawson gave him a long look, then shrugged. "That look on your face reminds me of that madam back in Valentine. One too many miles of dick come her way."

Reese laughed, but Ferrell did not react, as if he had not even heard.

Oliver had heard the story a dozen times. As Dawson's voice droned on, he found himself transfixed by the strange look in Ferrell's eyes, like he had just danced on his own grave. Ferrell licked his lips.

Then a frigid slash of wind through his jacket made Oliver shiver, and Dawson's voice reached him again. "So then she says, you broke it, you bought it."

Oliver laughed like he was supposed to, but it felt hollow. He could not take his eyes off Ferrell. Ferrell just stared off into the night, one hand locked around his other quivering wrist.

The wind moaned, and the grass rustled again. The cowhands' small fire was an island in a vast sea of dark, rustling grass.

Reese took another swig of bourbon. "I hope she tasted better than those beans."

Ferrell mumbled something, his eyes flicking out into the darkness. For a moment, Oliver thought he had not understood because of Ferrell's Irish accent.

Dawson sniffed. "For all I know she tasted like a dirty horse's ass, but by that time I—"

"Don't it never stop?" Ferrell voice rose just above a whisper. "Don't you all hear it?"

Reese was quick to get a jab in on Dawson. "Hell, Bill, that night you'd a fucked your horse if'n she winked at you."

"Maybe if I was tall enough—"

The sound of the wind grew, and embers leaped from the campfire. They all pulled their jackets tighter and edged closer to the pit, except for Ferrell.

His voice quavered, body rigid. "Last night I saw a face so black, I thought the sky was turning to ash."

They stared at him.

Oliver said, "What did you say?"

"My mouth was as hot as the sun, and as dry as this Godforsaken land."

The laughter subsided. All they could hear was wind now. Wind and Ferrell's voice.

Dawson looked sideways at Ferrell. "You gonna come to sense anytime soon?"

"I tell you, death was in me mouth. I swallowed it whole. And now it's in me belly."

Dawson said, "Hell, I swallowed death just a little while ago, and pretty soon you'll be smelling it!" He laughed, but just a little too long.

Oliver could not take his eyes from Ferrell's taut face.

Reese took the bourbon bottle and tried to hand it to Ferrell. "Maybe you need this more than I do." Ferrell stared off at nothing, as if they weren't even there.

Oliver tried to follow Ferrell's gaze, but there was nothing out there except darkness and grass and wind.

"Maybe that Injun witch put a spell on him back in Valentine." Dawson said. "He don't look right."

Ferrell doubled over, clutching his belly.

The three cowboys traded worried looks. Ferrell curled up like a dry leaf, groaning like a wounded animal.

"Christ!" Dawson said. "You all right?"

Oliver and Reese jumped up. Oliver froze in place, a chill that was not from the wind washing up his back.

In the darkness, the horses began to fuss and whicker.

All of them stared, transfixed as Ferrell's body spasmed and twitched. His mouth opened wide and unleashed a primal, incomprehensible string of nonsense.

"Holy Mary's Tits!" Dawson said.

Ferrell screamed. "It's got me! It wants to breathe! Oh, God! Oh, God!"

Oliver wanted to reach for him, to help him, but his entire body felt like it was made of dry cottonwood.

Ferrell tore at his clothes. "It wants to breathe!"

Reese snatched up a firebrand, raising it like a club. A tongue of flame licked the wood.

Ferrell spewed a deluge of black vomit that splatted across Dawson's chest and face.

"Ah, fuck! Fuck! Jesus Christ!" Dawson threw up his arms.

The wind moaned louder around them. The fire threatened to go out. A rhythmic susurration followed, sounding almost like speech.

Dawson wiped the black puke from his eyes, spitting and gagging. "Goddamn, Ferrell! What is going on?"

Oliver stood motionless, quivering, his guts wrenching inside him at the sight and stench of the black vomit, not like the smell of regular vomit at all, not unless Ferrell had been eating a week-dead buzzard. Time dragged to a crawl. The wind slowed to a gentle breeze. Ferrell collected himself. Dawson wiped the puke from his eyes. Reese placed his hand on Ferrell's shoulder.

In one swift motion, Ferrell pulled his pistol, planted the barrel against the bridge of Reese's nose, and set loose a fiery explosion of powder and brains. Reese dropped like a puppet with the strings cut.

The horses screamed and jerked their tethers.

Dawson scrambled back. Ferrell's thumb drew the hammer back once again. Dawson rolled onto his hands and knees, scurrying away. Ferrell fired a lead ball squarely between Dawson's shoulder blades. The force drove Dawson against the cold earth.

Oliver's body turned to wood and his heart stampeded. He had never seen a man shot before.

With agonizing slowness, Dawson's arm reached out, trying to crawl away, but it was no use. Ferrell stood over him, cap-and-ball Colt smoking, and fired another shot into the cowboy's body.

Oliver's gorge threatened to spew out of him, but he could not move.

Ferrell stood over Dawson's body. Dawson's last breaths gasped in and out of him, wet and desperate. Ferrell looked at the pistol, counted the loaded cylinders. Then he looked at Dawson's body, and a smirk trickled across his lips. He turned the pistol in his hand, knelt, and hammered Dawson's head like a farmer nailing wire to a fencepost.

The image of crushed melon found its way through the haze of fear into Oliver's mind. A wreckage of bone and blood.

Ferrell lifted the bloody pistol to his mouth and licked blood and brains from the grip. A gentle moan escaped from inside his throat.

Oliver had always thought Ferrell a decent sort, but this gore-spattered thing was not even a man anymore. Oliver didn't know what it was.

Ferrell stood and turned to Oliver, his eyes bleak but full of intelligence. "It wants to share its grace, Oliver. Embrace it."

Suddenly, Oliver's wooden body became water, and his legs threatened to collapse under him. He broke and fled toward the horses. "You stay away from me! Stay away!"

Ferrell's boots came through the grass.

Oliver pulled his Colt .45 from its holster, his hand shaking, and spun to face Ferrell. His father had given it to him on his seventeenth birthday, and he had never had cause to do aught but shoot a few bottles with it.

Ferrell came toward him as calm as a man crossing the street.

Oliver raised his pistol, cocked, squeezed. The shot went wild.

Unfazed, Ferrell came.

Oliver could feel his blood rising up in his throat, as though his heart was rejecting it. He struggled to steady his hand and fired again.

He missed.

Ferrell smiled. "So hard to shoot with your britches full of shit."

Warmth flooded Oliver's trousers, and he smelled piss. He took the pistol in both hands and fired a third time from six feet away. Another miss.

He was moving quicker now, but still stumbling. His boots felt like they didn't fit, and his hands were heavy. Oliver wanted so bad to be home again.

"Fuck you, Ferrell. Fuck you!"

Ferrell smiled, raised his blood-drenched pistol, and fired.

A lead ball the size of a locomotive slammed into Oliver's belly, knocking him off his feet and tearing deep through soft parts. Breath whooshed out, and blazing white pain ripped in.

Ferrell fell upon him.

The pistol butt slammed into Oliver's head, and bright lights exploded in his vision. He covered his head with his arms. Blows fell upon his arms, glancing off his head. Their arms tangled, but he felt weak as a child against Ferrell's relentless strength. Ferrell's fetid breath flooded his nostrils. Their hands clasped at pistol wrists, struggling, straining. Ferrell's mouth opened, teeth reaching for the soft parts of Oliver's face, bestial white chisels.

Oliver moaned under his breath, then cried out, "Ferrell! Goddammit, don't do this! Ferrell!"

Ferrell pressed the weight of his body against Oliver, pinning him. Oliver's wrist was trapped now, his gun pressed against his own belly. Metal dug into his own stomach, grinding into the wound Ferrell made.

Oliver tried using his free hand to push Ferrell off of him, but the pain stole all of his strength. He could do nothing but count the moments of life he had left before Ferrell killed him too.

But with a sudden twist, Oliver's gun hand came free. He cocked and shoved the barrel up under Ferrell's chin. A .45-caliber explosion, and Ferrell's head fountained brain and gore.

Oliver gasped and moaned for an eternity, then fought back the pain long enough to heave Ferrell's twitching corpse off of him.

The cold, distant blanket of stars glimmered over him. Horses nearby jerked and reared at their tethers, their screams fading with the sound of the shot, all swallowed by the wind. Cold whipped the air, as if seeking him.

He shivered.

Oliver looked down at the dark, wet stain on his belly. "Oh, God. Oh, Goddammit."

Coyotes yipped and howled in the long, cold dark. "Goddammit."

II

Dr. Charles Zimmerman's eyes felt raw, full of sand, and in the mirror earlier this morning they had been scarred by red. He wondered if he would weep again as he placed fresh handfuls of spring wildflowers over the two dirt mounds. Dew glistened on the fresh, wooden crosses at the head of each mound. At least some tears would fall on the graves today.

He tried to pray, as he had every morning for the last several weeks. But his thoughts of God still felt hollow and bitter, like begging mercy from an unjust tyrant who sentenced two little girls to death.

Did measles obey the will of Heaven? How many others in the town of White Pine had prayed and prayed? How many special prayer services at the town churches had been called to beg for the end of the outbreak? Now that it had ended, petering out in the weeks since these graves had been dug and filled, the Reverend Caldwell said that their prayers had been answered. But why had they been answered too late to save Eva and Josie? How were Charles' daughters somehow unworthy to live?

The interior of his torso was a vast cavern. What kind of doctor could not even save his own children? How many times since December had he written a Death Certificate? Pulled a shroud over a dead child's face? Offered his hollow condolences to grief-shattered families? And every single time coming with a stab of guilt that he could not save them.

How many? Too many for a newly hatched frontier town like White Pine to easily withstand, or forget, or forgive.

Moreover, those tragedies were not only among the white population. The graves before him called forth the memory of the great mounds of funeral earth, the mass graves and blood-stained snow near Wounded Knee Creek. The succession of fear and horrors of the last six months would never leave him.

The prayer snagged behind his lips.

His children not yet one month in the ground. Was the ground still too cold for the worms to have taken them? The earth looked as if the graves could have been filled yesterday.

Charles had carved the inscriptions himself in the crosses. "In loving memory. My beautiful daughters."

From the kitchen window, Charles felt Amelia's eyes like cold spears on his back. This morning had begun like most others, with tears and silence. All he felt nowadays from her was resentment and blame, and he wondered when he would reach his limit of sufferance for that or when he would cease to notice.

His eyes instead meandered over the grass, and the fence, and the patches of bare dirt, and the swing he had made from a rope and plank and hung in the old cottonwood. The plank swayed gently in the morning breeze.

The girls' voices scampered through his memories—their laughter, the sounds of their play. "Not very lady-like," Amelia would remark whenever they took off their Sunday dresses and played in the prairie dirt. "Josephine! Eva! Stop that!"

But Charles had never cared to stop them. There were enough dour, unhappy people in the house without trying to turn angels into two more.

What could he have done differently?

He remembered his words to Amelia. "I can save my daughters."

And he remembered how her face had turned to granite when he could not.

Two pale little girls, lying in their beds under mounds of covers, their faces splotched by raging red freckles, too sick even to ask questions anymore or to ask for reassurance.

Eva had managed a tiny voice near the end. "Will Josie be all right, Daddy?"

"Of course, sweetheart."

"Will I?" The eyes of an old woman should never reside in an eight-year-old face. They glimmered with fear. And then the glimmer died.

That was the image he could not shake.

Finally, there it was, the trickle.

Like a baptism.

He wiped his cheek.

A flicker of motion behind him bespoke the kitchen curtains falling closed. Doubtless she was wearing the same black dress again.

He jammed his hat on his head, tugged absently at his vest, tucked his medical bag under his arm, and walked to the livery stable to prepare his wagon.

III

Red Horse's jaw tensed as he stepped up to the quartermaster's table on the front porch of the commissary. A stiff wind rustled the papers on the table, and the quartermaster slapped them flat with a plump, hairy paw. The planks of the porch creaked under Red Horse's moccasins.

Behind him, the line of Lakota women stretched around the building, and he heard Quiet Clouds' hoarse cough. She was a kind and gentlewoman, but a cough had come upon her during the long, hard winter, as with so many others in the scraps of the tribe that remained after the massacre.

Only a few hundred Lakota lived here at the White River Agency camp, most of them women and children, and most of those ravaged by sickness, or starvation, or still recovering from wounds taken in the fighting at Wounded Knee Creek and elsewhere. They huddled now in the muddy spattering of tents next to the Bluecoat headquarters of the White River Sioux Agency. Most of their dwellings were not even proper lodges anymore, but canvas Bluecoat tents, their lodges having been destroyed or confiscated.

Quiet Clouds' cough turned Red Horse's heart into a gray coal.

The Bluecoat sergeant called Smith stood behind the quartermaster, rifle in his hands. Three other Bluecoats stood guard along the line of Lakota stretching behind Red Horse. Smith's pale eyes bored into Red Horse's. Red Horse looked down at his own arms, grown so thin from hunger, felt the tightness in his sunken belly and the way the woolen coat—a "gift" from the white man's government—hung loose on him. He had once taken the scalp of a Bluecoat with hair the same color of dry prairie grass. For several years, as a gift of honor to his wife, he had kept the scalp in his lodge, and with it the spirit of the warrior he had defeated on the battlefield. It was among the many prizes that had been stripped from him, one by one, until nothing was left but the white men's version of his name.

He imagined burying a warclub in Smith's face, but would he even have the strength now for a killing blow?

Almost forty winters now behind him, and he could not have foreseen this fate. He had been a warrior since his sixteenth year. Now, the buffalo were gone. All but a few scraps of Lakota land had been stolen. All the horses that the Lakota had possessed, great majestic herds, now all slaughtered or stolen by the Bluecoats, the white men, and the iron-road companies.

Chief Red Cloud had submitted to life on a reservation, too old to fight anymore. Crazy Horse was dead. Spotted Tail was dead. And now, the last of the great Lakota leaders, Sitting Bull, in the last Moon When the Wind Shakes Off the Leaves, had been killed by Indians working for the white man, and Chief Spotted Elk's entire band had been butchered at Wounded Knee Creek in the Moon When the Elk Shed Their Antlers. Of all the leaders, there was no one left.

All lay in the hands of the Father now. Soon the grass would be knee high, the time when the Father had foretold. The time when white men would be swept from the land, and the Earth would be renewed. Talk of the Son of the Great Spirit's coming had diminished since the slaughter near Wounded Knee Creek, but Red Horse had not forgotten the Father's words, or the dances in the Moon of the Brown Leaves where he had seen—

"Are you going to stand there all fucking day?" the quartermaster said.

Red Horse's awareness returned from the land of ghost dreams. "Medicine," he said.

The quartermaster twisted the bushy hair on his face. "Look, Red Mule. Born-with-a-Tooth got her ration of medicine. I can't give you no more."

Red Horse had refused to go to the white man's schools. He had refused to take on their ways. He had refused to become a farmer in this land where crops did not grow. His poor skill with English meant that he sometimes did not understand the words of the Bluecoats, but there was no mistaking the contempt in the quartermaster's tone. He restrained the anger from his voice. He had had enough beatings, for now. "Her name is Born-with-a-Smile."

The quartermaster's eyes narrowed. "What did you say?"

"I say her name is Born-with-a-Smile. I am Red Horse. She is my wife." His English name tasted bitter in his mouth. He was not the English sound, "red horse." No matter how the white man tried to rip away even his name, he would always be Sunka Wakan Luta. And his wife would always be Kici Iha Tunpi, at least for a while longer, until she joined their ancestors.

The quartermaster leaned forward. "And I'm telling you, Red Mule, she got her medicine. She ain't getting no more."

The sting of a red-hot arrow shot through Red Horse's breast. He glanced at the guards.

The quartermaster waved his hand. "Next."

Red Horse stood stiff as the trunk of pine tree.

The quartermaster met his gaze, unflinching. "I said *fucking next!*"

Red Horse clamped his teeth together and stomped off the porch, careful to avoid the tense guards. Two children coughed as he passed. Mud covered their bare legs.

He stopped there and held up his useless, helpless hands—the hands that had once carried a rifle, a warclub, a bow. These were not the hands of the Sunka Wakan Luta. They were the hands of "Red Horse," the White Man's dog.

A two-horse wagon rattled up the trail that ran between the shabby tent-village and the hastily made army post.

Red Horse squared himself. Maybe there was still hope. "Doc Zimmerman!"

IV

Charles Zimmerman surveyed the squalid tent camp where the Lakota were interned. The last of the spring snows had melted and turned much of the camp into a bog of cold mud. Wisps of smoke rose from fires of dried horse dung, and the air surrounding the camp held a vague, sour stench.

He reined the wagon toward the commissary shack, where a long line of Lakota women waited for rations of food or medicine.

Red Horse came alongside the wagon, his face grim, supplicating. "Doc Zimmerman?"

Charles tried not to think about how ragged Red Horse's clothes were. Buckskin trousers, moccasins, nothing else under a stained, torn peacoat. "Red Horse. How is Born-with-a-Smile?" He stepped down and grabbed a satchel from the seat.

"She is very sick. Army man not give medicine." Red Horse pointed to the commissary.

Charles moved to the back of the wagon and opened the gate, revealing crates of medicine and bags of grain. He pulled out several packages of medicine and a bottle of laudanum from a crate and handed them to Red Horse.

Red Horse's face was solemn. "Thank you, Doc Zimmerman."

"I'll check on Born-with-a-Smile in a few minutes." Charles glanced at the soldiers standing guard. "Get out of here with that before they shoot us both."

Red Horse hurried away and disappeared among the tents.

Charles strolled to the quartermaster shack, tipping his hat to a passing soldier. His patent leather shoes struck a hollow sound against the planks as he passed gloom-shadowed Lakota women. He bypassed the queue and stood before the quartermaster. Behind the quartermaster stood Sergeant Smith, a hard-eyed veteran with a nose like a hatchet, fingering his carbine.

The quartermaster smelled like an outhouse. "Everything there this time, Doc?"

Charles caught himself staring at the sweat on the fat man's lip. "Pardon?"

"I said, is everything there?" The quartermaster's eyes narrowed.

"Yes." Charles handed him the bill of lading.

The quartermaster paged skeptically through the paperwork. A grunt escaped his bloated lips. "You know we're gonna count everything."

"You do what you think best, Sergeant."

Sergeant Smith stepped forward. "If everything is in order, Major Wilson has been waiting, Doctor. The Major shouldn't have to wait."

Charles said, "Is it urgent?"

"He's in his office."

"More urgent than a dying woman?"

"The Major is in his office. Sir."

Charles knew the meeting with the Major would be unpleasant regardless of when he visited. "Then I will see him later."

Numerous eyes followed him away. He grabbed his medical bag from the wagon and headed into the tent village.

V

As Charles walked through the squalor of the Lakota camp, his feet grew heavier with each step, and it was not from the mud. Downtrodden, starving people hung their heads and would not meet his eyes. It was as though death had followed him here from home. It pulled at him like a tether. Among the tents, the air reeked of human waste, smoke, and disease.

His heart clenched at the suffering around him. And yet these soldiers, these "good Christian men," many of them little more than boys themselves, were party to degradations, torture, and persecution. Indians of all tribes were barely human beings in the eyes of the law. The White Man had brought medicines, and advancements, and civilization, but whenever Charles began to think about the costs, his mind went gray and numb.

The entire countryside, the reservations of White River, Rosebud, and Pine Ridge, the town of White Pine, were still recovering from the wounds of the Wounded Knee massacre and the unrest that had led up to it. Charles could hardly blame the Lakota for their actions. The government had egregiously violated every treaty it had signed with the Sioux nation: land stolen and given to railroad companies and white settlers, promises of cattle that when they were delivered were half-starved themselves, their meat wasted away to nothing, promises of foodstuffs and supplies in perpetuity only to have their rations cut by a third and then cut again, promises of winter clothing that never materialized.

The agent installed at Pine Ridge, October last, bore a significant share of the blame, one D. F. Royer; he had clearly been the beneficiary of a new government administration and found himself in a position for which he was destitute of any qualities necessary to succeed—experience, courage, force of character, or sound judgment. Within a month, the Lakota had begun calling Agent Royer "Young-Man-Afraid-of-Indians." As the aftermath of the massacre continued to rumble through the newspapers and halls of Congress, Charles dearly hoped there was a reckoning in store for that spineless buffoon whose actions had contributed to so many needless deaths.

Early last year, the emergence of a mysterious new cult had spread throughout all the tribes, terrifying the white population across the West, fueling rumors of unrest and rebellion. Its origin was unknown, but there were rumors of the Lakota gathering in remote places to dance some secret ceremony. The Indians refused to speak of it to whites.

Red Horse waited beside a dilapidated canvas tent. The Lakota at the White River camp possessed few of their traditional lodges; most of them had been destroyed by the Army. They lived in Civil War-era canvas tents, likely dragged out of some government storehouse, designed to be used in the mild climes of the South, ill-suited for harsh prairie winters. Even most of the Lakotas traditional clothing had been confiscated or supplanted by government handouts. They were forced to live like beggars, interned prisoners, wearing cast off clothes to keep back the cold. South Dakota winters were not to be taken lightly.

Red Horse opened the tent flap for Charles.

Charles entered the shadowy interior, stepping around the mound of ragged blankets and half-rotten hides that stirred and breathed. He knelt beside the woman. Red Horse's wife was so pale and thin that she resembled a corpse. She lay feverish and delirious, clutching a battered Bible to her chest, struggling not to cough. A crucifix hung prominently over her head. The Bureau of Indian Affairs had done its level best to beat their ancestral heathen religion out of them, but nowadays Charles could not see that his own ancestral religion offered any solace or hope of redemption.

He said, "Born-with-a-Smile? Can you hear me?"

Red Horse spoke from behind. "She sick long time. Not talk or she coughs."

Born-with-a-Smile's eyes opened, bleary. Her voice was dry, raspy. *"Mitakuye oyas'in."*

Charles could not be sure she knew he was there. "What?"

"Mitakuye oyas'in."

"Red Horse, what's she saying?"

Red Horse shook his head. "Don't know English. Maybe 'all my family.'"

Charles sighed and felt the glands on her throat. "Family is everything."

Her eyes fluttered with recognition, and he gave her a smile. She gave him one back, however feeble. He put on his stethoscope and listened to her breathing for a moment. Charles did not like what he heard. He backed out of the tent, and Red Horse followed.

Charles said, "She's been taking her medicine regularly?"

"Yes."

"I'll talk to the major about getting her a space in the infirmary."

"He say 'no' many times."

Charles sighed again and rubbed his chin.

Approaching footsteps caught his attention, and he turned in time see a familiar face. Little Elk's eyes reflected maturity, wisdom and intelligence, shadowed by dark circles under them. Her hair had been raggedly hacked, an expression of mourning that gave her a wild appearance. Her dress was less ragged and had once been more elaborately decorated with beads and ribbons, but those adornments had been stripped away. Her only remaining piece of jewelry was a bracelet of wood, beads, and a dark, polished stone. She said, "You care for our sick like your own children. You are so kind, Doctor."

Charles did his best to conceal the stab that went through him, unable to meet her steady gaze. "Hello, Little Elk." Even in her disheveled, bereft state, she was a handsome woman. He handed another bottle of laudanum to Red Horse. "This will help her rest."

Red Horse took it with a solemn expression.

Little Elk said, "Can the white man's medicine help her?"

Charles said, "Can yours?"

"There is more to living than laudanum and powders. We need food and water. Real food. People will get sick more."

Charles took Little Elk by the arm and led her some distance away. "I know. She's getting worse." When he noticed a patrol of two soldiers nearby looking his way, suspicion crossing their features, he realized that his hand was still on her arm. He removed it. "If she doesn't get proper rest in a proper bed, isolated, she's going to spread her sickness to the rest of the tribe. The old will die first."

She cast the guards a scornful glance. "I know you want to help us." Her gentle, calloused hand fell upon his arm, her bracelet delicate and beautiful around her slender wrist. His gaze fell upon the truncated lengths of her two smallest fingers. The scars on the stumps were fresh.

Suddenly Red Horse was there, snatching her wrist, glaring at her.

Charles drew back. "Red Horse, what are you doing?"

Red Horse kept his hard, glittering eyes on Little Elk.

Little Elk pulled her hand gently away from Red Horse's grip. Their eyes locked for a long moment, then Red Horse stomped away.

Charles said, "What was that about?"

"He is my husband's brother. They were warriors. Red Horse was not … with us, with Spotted Elk." Her face blanched, and her eyes went dead.

"You were there?" Charles stepped back, unable to contain his shock. So many bodies, all of them frozen solid by the blizzard that had kept the burial party away for three days, bodies that had to be pried from the frost by iron crowbars and pickaxes. So many ravaged faces and contorted, frozen limbs. Such a thing would melt a man's heart even if it were made of stone, all those little children with their bodies shot to pieces, women young and old, some of them pregnant, all tossed naked into the pits like rubbish. Had his hands touched Little Elk's husband at the side of one of those mass graves? His voice was thick. "I was there, too. On the third day. How did you—?"

"I ran, and I hid, and I ran." Her voice was tight and clipped, her fists clenched, her eyes fixed to the ground. She stood silent for several pregnant moments, tears glistening in great bulging droplets that refused to fall. "I came to White River because I was ashamed. I could not be at Pine Ridge anymore. And Red Horse was here."

The bodies of fleeing women and children had been found two miles and more from the site of the camp where the violence began. After the warriors were all dead, soldiers had hunted the women and children like vermin.

"His hatred for white men runs deep," she said, her eyes flicking to him. "Even if he is grateful to you, Doctor, he can never truly trust you." Her gaze fell away into a dark distance, and the tears finally trickled down.

"I'm sorry for what happened to your husband. It was a terrible thing the Army—"

She cleared her throat. "Red Horse thinks it is too soon for me to touch another man."

Silence hung between them for a long moment, her words sinking deep into him. Somehow, for a just a moment, the fog of pain around her parted, and she stood there as warm and lovely as any woman Charles had ever seen. Her anguish dispelled, her eyes bright and brimming with life, he saw her as she had once been. And he imagined that she turned that warmth upon him, and how lucky he would be if he were its recipient. He could not remember when last he had enjoyed a woman's warmth. Then his ears warmed, the spell retreated, and it was his turn to clear his throat. "Why are there so many guards today?"

"You have not heard? I thought you are here for that."

"What do you mean?"

"Last night there was shouting and screaming from the barracks. Then many gunshots. For several hours all the soldiers were awake, angry, and afraid."

Charles drew back in surprise. The Major was the kind of officer to frown upon indiscriminate use of ammunition. "Gunshots?"

Her expression was grave. "I have heard that they buried something."

VI

Marshal Hank Zimmerman adjusted the brim of his old felt cavalry hat, so faded that it almost looked Confederate gray, and squinted into the midday sun, scratching the grizzled stubble along his jaw. His horse stamped and fussed about being reined up so harshly. A few rocky buttes and stands of brush and cottonwood were the only irregularities in the endless sea of grass.

Except for the lone, distant figure silhouetted on a hilltop, a figure moving unsteadily.

Hank turned his horse toward the figure.

Beyond it, in the distance, the brooding outline of a larger, rocky butte loomed over the prairie, Sentinel Hill, crowned in pines and cottonwoods.

What was somebody doing so far from town or homestead, on foot, and this close to the reservation? Relations were tense with the Sioux after what had happened in December. The Army gave them a good beating, but the homesteaders and even some of the folks back in White Pine were still nervous about another uprising. All that wild dancing they were doing last year, days of it at a time, gave white folks the shudders.

The wind whipped over the grass and tugged at his hat, forcing him to jam it tighter on his head. His eyes were still sharp, even at his age, and he kept them on the figure. A lone man, no hat, a white man, carrying something in one hand.

Then the figure collapsed out of sight.

Hank spurred his horse to a canter, keeping track of the small impression in the grass where the man's body lay. Reaching the spot, he reined up and dismounted, cursing his stiff old bones as his boots hit the sod. A slow, steady, metallic, rhythmic clicking reached him from where the man had fallen.

He approached, hand on his Colt. On the wind, he smelled blood, and his shorthairs spiked like a porcupine. The man lay on his face. Hank rolled him over, and drew back. "Goddamn!"

A horrid groan escaped the man's blood spattered face, like a man already reaching for the hereafter. He clutched an empty revolver, thumb and finger cocking and squeezing the trigger in rhythmic succession. His abdomen was a crusty wet mass of caked blood. Clots of brain and skull clung to his face and stubble.

The man's eyelids fluttered, and Hank recognized his face.

"Oliver McCoy! That you, boy?"

Another groan, barely intelligible. "Marshal?"

"It is. You gutshot?"

A faint wheeze came back. "Yeah."

Hank peeled his eyes and swept them around the area, pulling his six-gun. "What happened?"

Oliver's broken, raspy voice forced Hank to lean in. "Camped. Ferrell. Crazy. Crazy. Killed ever'body." His free hand snatched Hank's coat. "Saw god!"

Hank clutched Oliver's hand and tried to pry it free. Even gutshot, the kid was stronger than he looked. "What the hell?"

The whites of Oliver's eyes blazed. "God! Saw the face of a black god!" Then Oliver's eyes rolled back, and his head lolled.

Hank grasped the empty pistol and found Oliver's fingers glued thick around it with dried blood. "Christ!" Prying it away, he thrust the pistol into his pocket, blood and all, then looked down at Oliver with a swell of pity. He knew what a gut wound was. He knew what bleeding out looked like. He knew all too well that getting Oliver help was nearly impossible.

His thumb tickled the hammer of his Colt. One shot, through the head, would end Oliver's misery, like shooting an injured horse or a man too far gone from Confederate shrapnel. One quick shot. His hand shook a little, seeing creased blood funneling over Oliver's lips, down his neck. Hank remembered all too well what young, wounded faces looked like. Thirty-five fucking years and he still remembered.

Common sense fought with common decency. They were miles from anything. White Pine was half a day's ride. Oliver would never make it.

"Damnit to hell."

But Hank was going to try today.

He eased the pistol back into his holster. "Pain in the ass." In one swift motion, Hank slung Oliver over his shoulders. He approached his horse, knowing this boy should have been dead hours ago. "I'm gonna get your stupid ass to a doctor, son." As he reached for the reins, the horse shied away. "Christ, Daisy, settle down! He ain't gonna hurt you." He reached for the reins again, but the mare shied back again. "What the hell is wrong with you?"

As his hand reached again for the bridle, the animal bolted for the nearest horizon.

He could do nothing but watch the horse's rump grow smaller with distance. Who was the horse's ass now?

"Son of a bitch."

The McCoy boy was already getting heavy.

In a heartbeat, Hank took stock of his situation. Nothing to see in any direction except the grim gray butte of Sentinel Hill and those thunderheads in the distance. No way he could get back to White Pine now, not carrying a gutshot man. The White River Agency was the closest habitation. His jaw tightened at the thought of going among so many redskins, but he wasn't going to change his mind now about saving Oliver's life. It was a few miles to the reservation, but whatever was keeping Oliver alive might just kill him in the next hour. If was going to go, he had better get to it.

"Well, Oliver, how do you feel about walking?"

VII

The odor of cigar smoke reached through the door of Major Wilson's office before Charles knocked.

The major's voice grumbled through the wood. "Enter!"

Charles steeled himself and did so.

The major sat behind a well-appointed desk, uniformed in dapper blue wool and golden buttons, fashionably trimmed hair and waxed mustache. He held a thin cigar between two fingers and fixed his steel-gray eyes on Charles. A portrait of the major hung on the wall behind him, next to a handful of medals glinting in a glass display case. On the desk was a decanter of brandy amid a tossed sea of paperwork.

Charles marveled for a moment at how thoroughly the presence of Donald Abercrombie, the civilian agent formerly in charge of White River Reservation, had been removed from this office. The uprising had resulted in all of the civilian agents on every reservation in South Dakota being removed temporarily and the agencies placed under command of the Army. Agent Abercrombie had not been a decent man; he had been nothing more than an ambitious politician looking for the next step to a more prestigious government appointment, with as much knowledge of Lakota ways as Charles had of South Pacific cannibals.

Sergeant Weatherly stood beside Major Wilson, fidgeting with a sheaf of papers.

Charles said, "Major."

Major Wilson rose and extended a hand through the haze of blue smoke. Charles took it, noting the absence of any calluses.

"Brandy?" Major Wilson motioned to Sergeant Weatherly. The sergeant poured Charles a drink from the fine crystal decanter.

Charles accepted it, looking into the potent amber liquid, but all he could think about was how many doses of laudanum the cost of that bottle would buy.

The Major sat down, gesturing for Charles to do the same. Charles remained standing.

Major Wilson drew a long drag from his cigar and blew a cloud of smoke. "As you can see, I am deep in Army paperwork. Luckily for you, you took your time and arrived today instead of yesterday."

Charles waved the smoke away. "We have things to discuss."

Major Wilson sniffed. "Indeed. Last night, a weapon discharged accidentally, and now three of my officers are dead. I'm still trying to discern the whys and what-fors. As you can imagine, the men have been in quite a state today."

Charles said, "I've been around the camp. They still are."

"As I say, we are all shocked by these events."

"And naturally saddened by their deaths." Charles had not meant that to sound so sarcastic, but his mind had tripped over the details of the major's words. "Three officers dead from one weapon discharge?"

"Four, actually."

"And what does your surgeon say about this?"

"Sadly, he is the fourth. A most calamitous affair. I fear this incident will further delay our redeployment. My men are already restless at having to nursemaid a bunch of heathen savages for so long. There has been some friction."

The military presence on the Pine Ridge, Standing Rock, and Rosebud reservations had already been redeployed, and the Nebraska National Guard troops massed at the border had been mustered out, mostly to ratchet back the pressure and allay the Lakota fears that the Army was preparing to exterminate the rest of the tribe. The current cessation of hostilities balanced on the edge of a knife. Charles wondered how those people out in the camp, those people beaten down so badly, could have much fight left in them.

"So, what do you need from me?" Charles said, "In lieu of your surgeon, am I inspecting the dead?"

"I would be most grateful if you just examined the bodies and signed a statement. Then you can be on your way."

Sergeant Weatherly offered some paperwork to Charles, which Charles accepted.

Charles shuffled through the forms. "I will not sign off on four dead men without a proper inspection, Major. Give me until the end of the day."

"Very well, Doctor. You may go."

Charles tossed back his brandy, letting the warmth of the liquor suffuse the sizzle of anger in his belly. He paused to survey the room. "One of the women in the camp is dying. She needs a proper bed. And food."

Major Wilson fixed him with a harsh glare and crumpled a piece of paper under his hand. "Quite the Indian lover, aren't you, Doctor." He flattened the paper again. "If I make one bed available, I must make them all. I don't make the rules."

The major's dismissive tone set Charles' teeth on edge. "The disease in this camp is going to spread unless we give them proper food and medicine."

Major Wilson tapped away a column of ashes. "I am doing the best I can with what I have, Doctor."

Charles looked at the fine crystal decanter of brandy. "I know you are, Major. Soon enough they'll all be dead and you can go elsewhere."

"Sergeant Weatherly will escort you to the infirmary. The bodies are there."

The sergeant stepped forward, eyes downcast, the corners of his mouth weighted downward. "This way, Doctor." He opened the door for Charles.

As Charles stepped outside, the major called after him, "And, Doctor. Say nothing of your findings to anyone."

The door closed.

VIII

Katie Delacroix hitched up her britches and crouched low when she spotted the jackrabbit over by the barn. All winter she had been itching to try out the slingshot she had made from a stout oak branch and two pieces of rubber she had found in town behind the wagoner's shop. It had taken her some time and trial to get the bands just right, strong enough to put some good zing on a pebble, but stretchable enough that her almost-nine-year-old arms could pull them.

There it was with its big old ears and big, lopey back feet, sniffing around the corner of the granary. The granary section of the barn was mostly empty now after the long winter, but there were still a few dusty kernels of corn and wheat that might keep a rabbit occupied, while she got herself into a good shooting range.

Reaching into her pocket, she felt for a stone of a good size and shape, one that would fit nicely in the slingshot leather, one that was round and smooth and would not curve much in flight.

Slipping an acceptable stone into the leather pad, she crept along the corral fence, slow and quiet, using Bessie the sow to screen her from her prey's vision. Jackrabbits didn't miss much, and once they got spooked, they were nothing but ears, feet, and a cloud of dust.

She was mighty tired of gristly pickled pig's feet and corn dodgers. Ma had been using the same ham bone to make soup for a week. Katie did not have to ask why. Pa never let them forget. The Delacroix family had homesteaded this plot of ground when Katie was five, and for last two years their crop and their garden had turned to dust by harvest time. A scant few onions, a handful of leathery potatoes, some twiggy carrots, and a corn crop "not worth a Pharisee's word." All they had to do was pray harder for rain, and the Lord would turn their place and the whole countryside into a new Eden, bursting over with fruit and grain. But that apple tree Pa had planted looked a little peaked.

Emily had said to Ma just last week, in a long, yearning talk about sweet, juicy apples, that she would be bearing her own fruit before that tree ever did. Ma had shushed her.

Katie's mouth watered, and her belly growled. The taste of a good rabbit stew—Ma made good rabbit stew—formed on Katie's tongue as she watched the rabbit sniffing, nibbling, its long ears bobbing. Then quick as a flash it was standing on its hindquarters, motionless, alert for danger. Katie froze, holding her breath.

She had been practicing with the slingshot for weeks for just this moment, until she could plink a tin can off a fence rail nine times out of ten. Yesterday, she had spotted rabbit tracks over by the barn, so earlier this morning, she borrowed a few of handfuls of corn from the granary to scatter outside, hoping to lure something in. The jackrabbit went back to sniffing for corn kernels.

Here was her chance. Her heart thundered, and each of her careful footsteps sounded like a stampede, as if her own ears were as big as a jackrabbit's. A quick glance between the corral boards told her the jackrabbit was nosing close to the foundation of the barn.

Reaching the corner of the corral, Katie gauged the distance. The shot would be a long one, but if luck and Jesus were with her, they'd be having rabbit stew for supper. She braced the slingshot against the corral post to steady her arm, drew back on the stone, closed one eye, and drew careful aim.

Hold still, critter.

Release.

The stone flew straight and true and struck the jackrabbit on the side of the head. Instantly it flopped onto its side, legs flopping and thrashing like it was trying to run away, but it didn't know it wasn't on its feet.

A thrill of victory shot through her, and she ran toward it, jumping with delight. It was a big one, stretched out as long as her leg. Its skull cracked open, droplets of scarlet bubbled at its nose, in its ear, and one eye bugged from the socket. A pang of remorse shot through her, a lump of sadness shooting into her throat. She hoped it wasn't a mama rabbit with babies.

For long transfixed moments, she watched its death throes subside. It had spun itself on its side through two complete circles.

She sniffled, sickened at the smell of blood, sad at the way that bugged out eye seemed to stare at her with accusation.

Nevertheless, the thought of rabbit stew with carrots and onions and potatoes made her mouth water. She grabbed the jackrabbit by the back foot. It was warm and soft and wiry, and the whole animal was almost too heavy for her to lift off the ground without using both hands.

Now to find Pa, so he could skin it. Had she seen him going into the barn? Their homestead was not much—just a sod house, a wooden barn with a granary attached, a corral, and a chicken coop—so he should not be hard to turn up.

Dragging the jackrabbit by the foot, she circled the barn, her smile returning with the thrill of success, and a skip found its way into her feet. She imagined Pa giving her a good pat on the back for putting food on the family table, and Ma cooking it up, and even Emily would have to say Katie done a good thing. Of course, in that special I'm-so-much-better-than-you way Emily had, she would accuse Katie of being too much like a boy, and Katie would wonder again if all older sisters everywhere were as annoying as hers.

She caught Pa's voice echoing in the barn and followed the sound, practically bouncing higher with each step. Who was he talking to? Emily? Ma was out back of the house washing clothes.

"Papa, what—? No, don't!" came Emily's half whisper. "Please."

"You'll do as I say, missy, or you'll like to get switched." Pa's voice sounded strange, thick.

"Ow! Please, I didn't do nothing!"

Katie leaped out to surprise them, a huge grin on her face, jackrabbit foot held aloft. "Hey, look what I got!"

Pa had Emily by the wrist. Emily's face turned the color of fresh cream, and Pa's turned the color of a roasted beet. Emily stood against the wall like she was trying to shrink plumb away from him. He leaned toward her, other hand on the wall.

Both of them looked fit to jump out of their britches. Emily's eyes bulged in horror, but she was not looking at the rabbit. She pried her wrist out of his grip.

Pa's eyes were cold and flinty in his narrow face. "That's real nice, Katie Jane. Now you run off now and give that to your ma. You hear?"

"But, Pa, I—" The excitement that had been surging through her turned cold and sour.

"You hear me, girl?" He glanced back at Emily, who had slipped under his arm and darted for the opposite door. As he watched her go, his jaw clenched over and over like he was chewing on something.

What was Emily running off so quick for? She liked rabbit stew.

Katie felt her eyes starting to tear up, but she bit those tears back, squeezing her hurt into the rabbit's foot. She threw the rabbit down at her father's feet. "I got us a rabbit, Pa." The cold and sour inside turned hotter with each word. "All by myself! But I ain't gonna clean it alone!"

Pa cast one last look at Emily's disappearing skirts, put his hand in his pocket to adjust his trousers, then turned back to Katie with a sigh. "That's real nice, Katie Jane. Come on, I'll show you how to clean it." His voice was almost back to normal, without that huskiness. "I got a new knife from the heathens I been hankering to try out. It's powerful sharp. The more I think about it, the more the sight of that rabbit is making me hungry."

The anger in her simmered off then, but the cold sourness came back, and it would not go away.

IX

Hank had to pause for a breather, lowering Oliver to the earth as gently as could, but he would be gutted and damned if he ever gave old age an inch. Ten more steps and he might have had to drop the poor kid. Good thing Oliver was a half-pint. Skinny, nervous types needed to learn how sit down and eat a goddamn potato. Nevertheless, Hank's arms and shoulders and legs burned with the exertion. His back would pay him an even harsher recompense tomorrow.

In the skillet-flat expanse of endless prairie grass, he spotted the agency buildings and attendant Indian tent camp, still about a mile and a half away.

In the distance, a thunderstorm roiled dark against the infinite sky, growing larger from the last time he looked.

Hank took his hat off, wiped his brow, and looked to the heavens.

Directly above him, three dusty, black shapes made lazy intersecting loops. Beady, black eyes in naked, scarlet heads peered down with otherworldly patience.

"You bastards go look somewhere else," he grumbled.

The tops of the grass rippled and floated with the brush of the wind, but his eye caught a movement that went against the flow, something moving low through the grass. Several somethings. A glimpse of mangy, grayish-brown fur through the grass, quiet and slinking low through the deepest grass.

Stalking toward him.

"What the hell?"

By the movement of the grass, he counted at least eight of them. If they were coyotes, he had little to fret about. Coyotes never attacked people. Maybe if they were starving, they might try to snatch a baby away. On the other hand, in all his sixty-five years, he had never seen more than two of them together. Coyotes were lone scavengers; they did not hunt in packs like wolves.

Nevertheless, a pack of somethings was converging on him. With a cold chill, he looked behind him and saw several more passages slinking through the grass. A bushy, tawny tail. Yellow eyes and lolling tongue and grinning fangs.

"Goddamn."

He trained his Colt at the movement of the nearest, perhaps forty feet away, cocked, aimed at the location most likely to be its head, and fired. The thunder of the pistol echoed with the sound of the bullet tearing through the grass. His target stopped moving, but still he could not see it. It was right there, close, but still invisible.

He cast about him.

None of them were running away.

Coyotes always fled for the horizon at the sound of a gunshot. Always.

Patches of grass started moving again, quiet and slow. "Goddamn it." How close did he dare let them get before he started shooting? He could not pick up Oliver and shoot at the same time, and there was no question now that he and the McCoy kid were their intended prey.

He spun, and they were close enough now that they were beginning to emerge from the grass. Coyotes for sure, slinking low, slavering, fangs bared. At least ten of them, more like fifteen, with him at the center of a shrinking circle.

Five shots left in his pistol. If one shot did not scare them off, would five more? Would he have time to reload if they attacked en masse? Unlikely.

The closest one, perhaps the largest coyote Hank had ever seen, perhaps as large as a wolf, locked eyes with Hank, grinning, growling, with an intelligence in its eyes that startled him.

He raised his pistol and shot it between the eyes, and it dropped like it had been clubbed.

The rest of them charged forward. In a heartbeat, a rush of tawny shapes swarmed toward him, snarling and yipping and snapping. Four more times his pistol barked, and four coyotes tumbled in mid-charge, but still the rest of them came.

They were all over Oliver, going for his hands, his legs, his throat. Oliver moaned and feebly tried to defend his face. Hank lunged at them, kicking, flipping his pistol in his grip and using it for a club. The beasts snapped and yipped in pain. Some fled a short distance and returned, some lunged at Hank, snapping at his hands, at his pistol.

Hank roared with fury, feeling bones crunch under his boot, skulls collapsing at the butt of his pistol, swinging blindly, blood spattering his face, teeth tugging at his boots, at his trouser legs.

Oliver cried out in pain and terror. Clothes tore and teeth tugged and dragged at him.

Hank pummeled and kicked, with one hand dragging a beast by the scruff of the neck from Oliver's boot, and crushed its face with the butt of the pistol. It died instantly, spasming and spraying blood.

In a red haze of rage and battle fury that he had not experienced since 1863, he seized the dead coyote's forelimbs and swung the carcass like a weapon at the others, smashing and trailing blood in great spinning arcs until the remaining coyotes finally started to back away.

Hank roared at the top of his lungs, "Get the hell out of here, you mangy devils!"

They flinched back and fled.

Ten of them lay dead around him, one forty-pound mass hung limp in his hands, and six or eight more dashed away through the grass.

Hank roared again and slammed the carcass against the ground, driving a fresh gout of blood from its ruined head. He snatched his pistol back up, eyes scanning for returning threat, and started to reload. His mouth was as dry as sandstone, his thundering heart shooting pain through his entire chest, each breath a tearing ache.

Oliver groaned beside him, half-weeping with pain and fear.

As Hank loaded his pistol, he gave Oliver a quick appraisal. He expected to see nothing more than a mass of savaged limbs, but Oliver seemed to have suffered only a handful of real bites. His clothes and boots, on the other hand, had been damned near shredded.

Oliver's voice was pained wheeze. "What was that, Marshal? Coyotes don't go after people!"

"That was the goddamnedest thing I ever saw." Hank snapped the loading gate closed, cocked the pistol, and scanned the area. He spotted two shapes moving away through the grass. Taking stock of himself for a moment, he realized that there was barely a scratch on him. His hands, however, were caked with blood and fur, and his pistol was slick with gore.

Why had the coyotes focused their attack on Oliver, not the one who could fight back? Was it because they sensed a wounded man? Easy prey?

He knelt beside Oliver and looked him over more closely. "Anything worse, boy?"

"Still gutshot, Marshal, but them bastards didn't do me much more harm. Except maybe my arm here." Oliver raised his left arm feebly. Fresh blood soaked the torn shirtsleeve.

Hank peeled the sleeve back, surprised that the kid had much more blood to lose. The bite looked superficial. Maybe a couple of stitches were all that was necessary.

"You ever seen anything like that before?" Oliver said.

"I ain't even heard of anything like that before, except maybe in dime novels."

"The black god sent them. It wants me."

"Lay off the talking nonsense. Are you ready to move again?"

"Just leave me here for the coyotes, Marshal. I can't take the pain no more."

"Getting ate alive ain't no way for a man to die. Now, shut up and just let me catch my breath a piece. We'll be there soon. It's only another mile and a half or so."

Oliver's eyes closed with dread, but he nodded.

Hank looked up into the sky, and saw the buzzards had circled lower, anticipating a feast of dead coyote. Too bad these coyotes had shed their winter fur. He might have been able to come back to retrieve the pelts, but they were worth nothing at the furrier with their winter fur falling out in chunks.

Why had they attacked at all? These did not appear to be starving. Coyotes always lived on the fringe of life, scavenging mostly. They did not run in packs.

How long these thoughts would trouble him, he could not guess.

X

The infirmary smelled like death pickled in rubbing alcohol. Charles stepped around the screen and saw the examination tables laden with four shrouded corpses. He glanced over his shoulder at the two sick privates occupying beds on the other side of the room, discomfited at being forced to share their room with the dead.

Sergeant Weatherly hovered just behind him.

Charles pulled back the linen shroud on the nearest of the bodies, revealing a face with a gaping bullet hole just under the left eye. The rear of the skull was collapsed, pulpy wreckage. This wound did not look particularly accidental.

"All like this?"

"Uncanny." Sergeant Weatherly shifted uncomfortably.

Charles bared the faces of the other three corpses, peeling back just enough sheet to expose their faces. All but one of them with bullet holes in the face. The one with the face still intact, the third corpse he examined, sent a chill up Charles' neck. Even amid all the death and visceral agony he had witnessed in his profession, especially in recent months, he had never seen such a look of horror, much less one frozen like a sculpture into the face of a dead man.

The last of them had two bullet holes, forehead and eye socket. With the shots fired at such short range, little remained of the rest of the man's skull.

Charles turned to Weatherly. "How does a single weapon discharge, accidentally, and strike four officers? Did the bullet make some left turns?"

"Can't say, sir."

"Who can?"

"They were dead by the time my men arrived."

Charles pulled back the last man's shroud fully, revealing an officer's uniform so crusted with dried blood and pocked by bullet holes that only the rank insignia were recognizable. He counted. "This man was shot ten times! Did the weapon reload itself?"

"Will there be anything else, sir?"

"Only if you intend to tell me the truth, Sergeant."

Sergeant Weatherly snapped his heels and left, his hard leather heels punctuating each footfall on the rough wooden floor.

After Weatherly had departed, one of the two sick soldiers cleared his throat and said, "How does it look, Doc? Think they'll pull through?" He grinned awkwardly.

Charles said, "I highly doubt it, Soldier …"

"Private Aaron Spalding, sir," said the first.

The other began to laugh quietly, the laughter slowly gaining strength and speed like a loose wagon wheel rolling downhill, until the laughter dissolved into a fit of coughing.

Charles crossed the room. "Well, Private Spalding, were you here in the infirmary last night?"

"I was," Spalding said.

Charles checked Spalding's pulse. The warmth of the man's skin indicated a low-grade fever. "Care to tell me what really happened?"

"Woke me up from a dead sleep. I heard this yelling and screaming. A bunch of voices."

"Saying what, Private?"

"I don't rightly remember, sir. Sounded like nonsense to me, gibberish you might say. Sounded almost like one of them fiery tent preachers, but no language I ever heard before."

"It wasn't the Lakota tongue?"

"No, sir, I hear plenty of that. Even picked up a few words."

The other man voice was ragged as torn linen. "Yeah. Then the fun started." Dark circles ringed his bloodshot eyes, and the desolation in them somehow seeped in and turned Charles' stomach to lead.

Charles tried to shake the feeling away, pouring some water into a tin cup and offering to the second man. "What's your name, soldier?"

"Garrett, sir." He took the cup and slurped at it, then winced.

Charles felt Garrett's pulse. The soldier's wrist felt like a stick left too long near a campfire. "Take it easy, Mr. Garrett. Mr. Spalding, tell me about the shooting."

Spalding slid up to sit higher in bed. "I heard three shots. One. Two. Three. Slow, like he was taking his time, you know. Then it got quiet for a bit until I heard a bunch of the boys going to see what happened. I heard Sergeant Weatherly's voice. Then things got all strange. Sounded like Lieutenant Cox's voice, but strange, like he weren't himself. Then a bunch more yelling, and then more shooting, like a goddamn firing squad. What I don't understand is why they took Captain Lawson's arm off last night after they brought 'em all in here."

"Took his arm off?"

"Cut it right off with a hacksaw. I think they went to bury it somewhere."

Charles returned to the bodies for closer scrutiny. Lawson was the man with the frozen, contorted face. Charles peeled back the shroud fully and found that Lawson's right sleeve was missing. The arm had been severed at the shoulder. Ivory-yellow bone peeked out, half-buried in dried blood and crusted flesh.

"What on earth?"

The door of the infirmary burst open.

Two blood-spattered apparitions filled the doorway, along with a soldier supporting the shoulder of a badly wounded man.

An instant later, Charles recognized his father. Their eyes met for a long moment. "What's this?" he said.

His father's face was always haggard, but now he looked taxed beyond his limits, a manifestation of violence, his blood-spattered face fringed by sweat-stained salt-and-pepper hair, leathery face flushed under days of gray stubble. "Oliver McCoy. Found him wandering a few miles south of here. Gutshot." Hank's voice was a hoarse rasp.

"What the hell happened to you?" Charles said.

"That's a story for later. This boy needs help."

There were no surgery tables left, all occupied by the dead. "Get him on a bed. How long?"

"Can't say. Maybe last night."

Hank and the private hefted the wounded man onto the nearest bed, and Charles hurried around the infirmary gathering instruments.

Charles set his tray of instruments and supplies beside the bed. "Fetch some fresh water, soldier." The soldier took up a bucket and went away to the well outside. Charles used a scissors to cut away the stiff, blood-crusted shirt.

Oliver lay on his back, stirring faintly, his torso naked, while Charles sponged the dried blood away from the wound. Hank stood nearby, watching.

"At least you'll help a white man," Charles said, without looking at Hank.

"Well, that didn't take long. My back will have me laid up for a week. Now mind your tongue and do your job."

Oliver convulsed in agony, squeezing out an anguished moan.

Charles pressed Oliver's shoulders back down. "You just going to stand there, or are you going to lend a hand?"

Hank's face tightened, but he stepped forward.

Charles said, "Hold him down. Put something between his teeth." He picked up a pair of forceps and examined the bullet hole. The smell of the dirty wound escaped when Charles pressed open the flesh.

Oliver's eyes snapped into focus. "What? What are you doing? You can't! You can't take it out of me!"

Charles did his best to keep his voice calm and dispassionate, but that smell was still in the air. "Hold still, Mr. McCoy. I need to get the bullet out." He turned to Hank. "Are you going to hold him down or not?"

"No. No! You can't cut into me!" Panic turned Oliver's eyes into empty teacups.

Charles said to Hank, "You've been around this sort of thing before. Why are you—?"

"Don't remind me." Hank leaned over Oliver, placed two hands like gnarled leather over the young man's shoulders. "I'm surprised he's still alive. This runt can't be more than a hundred-fifty pounds with pockets full of rocks. He's been wandering around out there in a daze for the good part of half a day. Blood coming out both ends." He tried to place a strip of leather in Oliver's mouth, but had to pry it between clamped teeth. "Damnit, boy, open up! We're trying to help you!" Finally, he managed to wedge the leather in place.

"You look like you shot him yourself." Charles' gaze traveled over the plentitude of smeared and splattered gore covering Hank's face and clothing.

"We had a run-in with some coyotes."

A question rose in Charles' mouth, but Oliver lurched under him. "Hold still, son," Charles said. He took a deep breath and probed the bullet hole with the forceps. Oliver convulsed with a sharp cry. Black and red blood seeped from the wound.

Charles dug the forceps deeper into the dark wound. "Come on. Damnit." Blood and something not blood seeped to the surface, hiding the tips of the forceps. What was this black fluid? He had never seen blood or bodily fluid take on that color or viscosity. He had treated gunshot wounds before; some of those patients had survived. This one, however—the wound was likely in the liver. With the tip of the forceps, he felt for the hard irregularity of the bullet.

Oliver screamed and lurched, teeth clamping hard into the leather, forcing Charles to withdraw the forceps.

Charles snapped at his father, "You're not helping!"

Hank shoved Oliver's shoulders down, teeth gritted.

The leather strap turned Oliver's words into gibberish.

"Dad! Please! Hold him down!"

Charles dug deeper with the forceps. The bullet had gone deep, deeper than he expected. Maybe deeper than he could reach. He was an adequate doctor—or so he had once believed—but he felt like a clumsy blacksmith pulling hot screws from a raging forge.

Moments stretched on forever. Charles became vaguely aware of Oliver's continuing screams, but his entire attention was focused on feeling for the hard rasp of lead against the tip of his forceps, the forceps disappearing little by little into Oliver's abdominal cavity. Oliver screamed and screamed, until, finally, mercifully, he fell silent and still.

In that instant when Oliver's body went limp, Charles gave one last deep probe.

There it was.

Moments later, he withdrew the lead ball, and dropped it into onto the pan with a .44-caliber clank.

Charles slouched and released his breath.

Hank released Oliver's shoulders. "Like shoeing a mean stud."

Charles sagged back, exhausted.

Oliver stirred and spat the strap from his mouth, blood trickling down his cheek and into his ear. "Ferrell. Ferrell shot me. That son of a bitch. He was crazy. I think he tried to bite—god— I don't even know. I think he's dead. I think I killed him. Oh, god! Oh, g—" His head lolled to the side again, eyes rolling back.

A moment of calm fell. Charles put down the forceps and massaged his cramped hands. The silence stretched like a hanging rope between him and his father.

Finally Charles said, "What happened to his arm?"

"Bitten by coyotes. Like I said, we had a little scuffle."

Charles examined the wound. "I may as well put in a couple of stitches while he's out." The strangeness in Hank's voice, the unusual reticence, the ensanguined, exhausted specter that his father looked right now, stirred the unease in Charles' belly. He took the needle and thread again and quickly sutured the lacerations on Oliver's forearm. "Were you bitten?"

"No. The kid got the worst of it."

Sergeant Weatherly strode in, glowering, Private Anderson at his side. "Doctor. A word, please."

"A word, indeed." Charles wiped the sweat from his forehead with the back of his forearm and felt his resolve harden.

Sergeant Weatherly motioned for Charles to follow and the two walked outside. Weatherly thumbed over his shoulder. "Who is that man?"

Hank stepped into the doorway and leaned against the jamb with one hand, the other on his pistol. "His name is Oliver McCoy. His pa owns the Bar-M. I found him walking a few miles south of here, gutshot and mostly dead."

Weatherly glared. "What's his condition now?"

Charles growled through his lips. "Still gutshot and mostly dead." How much callousness could he withstand in one day? "He might make it. He might not. He's going to need a soft bed for a few days."

Weatherly looked back and forth from Charles to Hank. "Major Wilson might have a problem with that."

Charles kept his voice as even as he could. "Major Wilson might."

Weatherly's mouth tightened. "If the Major says he goes, he goes."

"Like the Indian woman?" Charles said.

Sergeant Weatherly and Charles locked eyes. Charles hated blind submission to authority, hated it especially when the authority was just as blind and stupid. Weatherly chewed on a plug of tobacco.

Charles stepped closer. "Before you run off to tattle, perhaps you can explain to me why Captain Lawson is missing an arm?"

Weatherly's eyes widened, and he stepped back. "I don't—"

"Someone removed it last night. Post mortem."

"You really need to ask—"

"Nonsense, Sergeant. I know you're under orders, but don't lie to me." Charles felt the anger brewing like black coffee. The idea that they wanted his help, but would still lie to him, galled him to the verge of rage.

Weatherly chewed and swallowed. "I—"

Hank said, "You had better tell him, boy. He's stubborn that way."

Charles stepped closer again, sensing that Weatherly's resolve was weakening. "If I'm to help you, I need to know everything."

XI

Amelia Zimmerman knelt on the moist, spring grass, careful to keep her dress out of the area where the grave dirt lay naked. The very idea of one of her daughters' grave dirt on her dress twisted the familiar knot in her stomach even tighter. She tucked a wisp of blonde hair—or was it one of the gray ones—behind one ear and ignored how thin her hands had become.

This morning the White Pine Gazette had come out with the fresh headline, "Dr. Zimmerman Declares Measles Outbreak Over: Urges Vigilance and Early Treatment." There had been no new cases in roughly three weeks, but the town and surrounding countryside were as taut as the sinews keeping Amelia's neck rod straight.

Charles had left this morning—again—without speaking to her, not one word. His utter indifference had become commonplace. If he hated her, that would be easier than behaving as if she did not exist at all. Indifference was so much crueler. Someday, perhaps, she would no longer care. But then, how could she blame him? She could hardly stand to look at herself in the mirror anymore; how could she expect him to want to look at her?

Her fingers traced the hard corners of the small, gold cross in one hand, while the other caressed the textured, leather cover of her family Bible. The corners of the Bible had grown more worn in recent weeks.

She took a deep breath and thought about what she should say in her prayers. These days, most of her thoughts and emotions were such a dark, pitiful chaos that she could hardly grasp individual feelings. It was all she could do to muster enough composure to teach school every day. The students all sensed that something was amiss with her, and they knew the reason, but she could not help it. This morning she had tried to walk the children through arithmetic and reading lessons, only to find herself at the end of the lesson having shambled through it all like a sleepwalker. How many times in the last month had this happened? Perhaps tomorrow would be better.

Another deep breath. Yes, she must get this over with, the daily prayers, a habit instilled in her by her father, a Lutheran minister back in Philadelphia.

"Dear Lord, I know you must have a reason for taking my babies. You killed Your own Son, so why should You hesitate to take mine? But You took Jesus home to save the world from Your own rules. I grew up believing in those rules, in Your Word. I swallowed everything Daddy taught me, terrified of fire and brimstone. But why would you send these angels to me and slaughter them? If you're there at all, explain this to me."

The Almighty would have to forgive her anger. Thus far, there had been no one to assuage her sorrow. No comfort. All she could think about was her two girls' frail little bodies among the worms.

She gathered herself and stood, feeling like a spring that had been only slightly released. Without understanding why, she hung the cross on Eva's grave marker.

Cupping her hand over her womb, where the bulge would soon begin to show, she said, "If you intend to take this one, too, you might as well send me to Hell now. I haven't told Charles yet. If something happens to him now, I don't know what I'll do, so please keep him out of harm's way."

But that was a lie. She knew very well what she would do. The Almighty would have to forgive her for that too.

XII

Sergeant Weatherly squirmed under Charles' gaze. "It weren't no accident!"

Hank spat and crossed his arms. "I think we ciphered that out already, Sergeant."

Charles pressed forward. "The arm, Sergeant!"

"Well, you see, Doc. When we went in that barracks ... I ain't never seen anything like it, and I pray to the Almighty I never will again. Lieutenant Cox, he stood up, and he ... he ... We put a dozen holes in him, but he didn't fall. It took a shot to the head to, to take him down."

Charles crossed his arms. "So you shot him because he murdered the other officers?"

"It weren't just that. Cox had blood all over his face, his mouth ... he was ... he was eating Captain Lawson!"

Charles said, "Eating! You can't be serious!"

"Serious as my eye teeth! He was still chewing, and Lawson's arm had the bites torn out and—"

Major Wilson's voice roared over them, "Sergeant! That is quite enough!" The major stalked toward them. "Sergeant, you recall my direct orders, do you not?"

"I do, sir, but—"

"Consider yourself fortunate if I don't court martial you for insubordination. How would you feel about a month in the stockade?"

Charles interposed himself between the major and the sergeant. "I need a full explanation, Major. How can I help without knowing the full story?"

Major Wilson clenched the slender cigar between his teeth and blew smoke out his nose toward Charles. "With all due respect, Doctor, you're a civilian. I cannot, under any circumstances, allow the truth of what happened here to spread beyond this camp."

Charles waved the smoke away, heat rushing through his body. "You ordered Lawson's arm removed post mortem? Since when does the army mutilate the dead? Unless you're taking scalps, that is."

Major Wilson drew back, and his eyes narrowed. "Indeed I did order it. His family need never know that he had been cannibalized, nor will Lieutenant Cox's family have to deal with the stain of such a heinous dishonor. This was all merely a terrible accident. I asked you for a medical examination, but what you find is for my ears only. Understood?"

Something clicked in Charles' thoughts like gears meshing. "Wait a moment. That man in there was shot by one of his friends, last night, by a man who just went crazy. The fact that this same kind of thing happened in two places on the same night tells me they're connected."

Major Wilson sniffed. "Nonsense! How could they possibly be connected?"

"Oliver McCoy said something," Charles said, "something about one of his friends trying to bite him. It almost sounds like rabies."

Hank stepped down from the doorway and approached. His face was grim and gray under the spattering of blood. "I hate to admit it, Major, but the boy might be right. My instincts are doing a war dance. When I was carrying that kid here, we were attacked by a pack of coyotes. A whole mess, maybe twenty of them."

Charles' mouth fell open.

Hank shook his head. "That boy might already be a goner."

Wilson scoffed, "*Attacked* by a *pack* of coyotes."

"Wilson, I don't appreciate your tone. You don't need to tell me they don't come after people, much less in a pack. You want me to go fetch them and throw the carcasses on your fucking desk?"

Wilson bit down on his cigar.

Charles said, "Something doesn't fit there. Rabid animals are not social. A sick animal would want to be left alone."

"Before you ask, I didn't see any frothing at the mouth," Hank said.

Charles scratched his head. "Major, could your man, Lieutenant Cox, have had any possible contact with the dead cowboys? Could he have been bitten by an infected animal?"

"Impossible. My men have been on post for the last month."

"No one leaves? Ever? Have there been incidents among the Sioux?" Charles said.

"As I said, there has been friction among the men. But among themselves …" The major shrugged and spat a bit of cigar. "You must ask the Indians about their own affairs."

"Then let us speak to one of them," Charles said.

XIII

Little Elk found herself back at her tent, rubbing her once-injured hand. The stumps of her severed fingers were sometimes overly sensitive, other times numb. They had only recently healed over, but they still ached, the little one severed for the death of her husband Running Wolf, the third finger for the deaths of Dances-Like-Grass and Chasing-Two-Horses. The one the Ghost Dancers called "Father" had preached that they abandon the old ways of mourning, that there should be no more cutting or self-mutilation, but she did not follow the Ghost Dancers, however much her husband had wished it.

Guilt washed through her at having been so brazen with the white doctor. Red Horse's reaction had been understandable; it mirrored her own. She had not intended to touch him and now wondered why she had. She and the doctor had spoken often since she had come to the White River Agency in January, most often with her serving as interpreter when the doctor was interviewing the sick and infirm.

Could she ever call a white man "friend" after—?

No, she must not cling to hatred, lest it blacken her spirit, close her path to the spirit world.

As she walked through camp, the women greeted her with as much respect as could be expected through the pall of despair. So many of them had lost their husbands, their fathers, their children. So many men were dead of all the tribes. Even though Little Elk still felt like an outsider, she shared the bond of tragedy with all these women. Many of them had lived here on the White River Agency for years, but Little Elk had been with Running Wolf in a camp on Pine Ridge, until the Ghost Dancers came and Running Wolf fled with her and the children into the Badlands when the troubles started.

In her canvas tent, she carefully closed the flap behind her and pulled out the leather satchel that held all she owned. Her herbs and ingredients were long gone, left behind in her panicked flight from the carnage, blown apart by artillery, or lost in the blizzard that followed. Not that she had had much left. Her stores had been long since depleted by the sheer number of sick and injured from the winter, from starvation, from years of heartsickness at their unending plight.

As well-meaning as the white doctor was, his medicine would not save Born-with-a-Smile. Her spirit was sick, beset by despair on the inside and starvation on the outside; she needed the medicine of her people.

Little Elk gathered up her last few bundles of dry sage. There was no way for her to replenish them, cut off from trade with other tribes, trapped here so close to the white men, who raped the natural world wherever they went.

All Little Elk could do was go to Born-with-a-Smile and sing for her, entreat the spirits to give her strength, but the Old Ways had been outlawed. The sage might serve to give Born-with-a-Smile some ease by keeping evil spirits at bay for a time. But Little Elk had to be careful; the white soldiers were so anxious, many of them hateful and afraid, that they might simply shoot her for ignoring their regulations.

Nevertheless, she had to try.

She took up a bundle of sage and went to the tent of Red Horse and Born-with-a-Smile.

Red Horse sat out front of the tent, cross-legged, eyes closed. She stopped before him, sat, and waited until his eyes opened.

She said, "Has there been any word about the children?"

"No," he said.

Two children had been missing this morning, and much of the camp had been enlisted to search for them, but the Army's regulations would not permit them to look far. No one had broached the news of the disappearances to the army. It was hoped that the children would be found without having to ask for help.

His voice was low. "You like that white doctor, do you?" He used the English word "doctor."

"No," she said, "I do not. I was merely overcome by fear for your wife's life."

"She sleeps now. Her pain is lessened. Her spirit grows weak."

"Soon she will meet her ancestors unless you let me help her."

"The Old Ways are forbidden. If the Bluecoats come here and see, they will take both of us away, and she will die."

"Since when do you fear the soldiers?"

He stiffened, and glared at her. "I fear nothing! But if they take me away, she will die alone."

"She has friends and relatives here. None of us are ever alone." A pang shot through her. *Except for those who died this winter alone in the snow fleeing the white man's bullets.* She swallowed the burr of anger. "Let me help her."

He shrugged. "You can do nothing for her that the Father cannot do. I have been praying to him."

She nodded, having expected Red Horse's response. "But there is no one left Ghost Dancing now. Sitting Bull is dead. Spotted Elk is dead." She chose her words carefully. "After all the troubles, no one dares now. These soldiers will kill anyone wearing a ghost shirt."

He stiffened again. She could see that her words lodged deep in him. His lip curled down. "You never believed."

"No, I did not. Running Wolf believed in the Ghost Dance. I went with Spotted Elk because Running Wolf followed him. He is dead now and the Messiah has not come."

"Running Wolf and I were brothers. We shared our thoughts. When we were young we shared our horses and our victories. And when the stories of the Son of the Great Spirit came, we shared those, too."

"You are his elder brother. Of course he followed you." Blame crept into her voice, which she had not intended. Nevertheless, it was there. Running Wolf had listened to the stories of Red Horse and the others who had met the Messiah's emissaries, and he had believed.

Red Horse's voice grew thick. "I should have shared his death, too. At least it would have been a warrior's death." His chin fell, and a long shuddering sigh crawled out of him. Then he straightened. "But we will see him soon, all of them, all of us, together again forever."

"Red Horse, we have known each other since I wedded Running Wolf. We have always gotten on as brother and sister should. I have been a Dreamer my whole life. Often those Dreams come true." But not always. All of her dreams lately tortured her from the moment she fell asleep, dreams of terror and meat and strife, but all so vague and disjointed that she could glean no meaning from them.

"I held the buffalo meat in my hand!" he said, eyes growing wide, "It was real! When the Father's disciples came from the west, we heard his message, and it was true. They taught us the Ghost Dance, and for five days we danced, and I saw wondrous things. I saw my parents living in a great buffalo-hide lodge with thousands of our relatives in a land rich with game. I saw … I saw Quick Strike waving to me, smiling, telling me that we would meet soon in a new world when the grass was thigh-high, and then I heard the Father's voice and—"

"But this 'messiah' is not Lakota! He is a Paiute from the beyond the mountains and desert!" Her nephew Quick Strike had been a brave, quick-witted boy of ten winters until sickness took him two winters ago.

Red Horse continued, "His message is for all the people. He came down from the sky in a great cloud and told us that he was the Son of the God, and that if all people dance the Ghost Dance, the ground will tremble, and the sky will go dark, and all the white men will be swept away in a great storm, and all the ghosts will come back, and all Lakota people will live again, healthy and young, and the world will be remade as it once was, with great herds of buffalo and plentiful game.

"During the dance, many dancers collapsed and went to the Happy Hunting Grounds, and when it was over they came back to life. When I came back, I found a piece of buffalo meat in my hand that Quick Strike had given me."

She listened politely, even though she had heard the story many times, or stories like it, from her husband and others.

Red Horse leaned forward. "There are no buffalo anymore, and I know buffalo meat! Quick Strike gave it to me!" His lips worked as if the very thought had brought a burst of water into his mouth. "The Father's words are for all people except the white men. If we dance the Ghost Dance, all will be made new. Everyone listens to the Father: the Cheyenne, the Arapaho, the Kiowa, the Apache."

"But many times, you and all the others danced the Ghost Dance, and there was nothing. For a year, you all danced, and the time of the prophecies came and went, but nothing happened. It is spring now, and the ground does not tremble."

He sniffed. "The grass is not yet high enough. The Father's prophecy will yet come true. There is a storm in the west. The Father comes soon."

Anger rose higher in her with each heartbeat of silence between them. Prophecies were mere words, and words were wind.

Finally, she took a deep breath and opened her memory. "When the soldiers caught us, they made us camp by the creek." Her voice trembled at the memory of how terrified the children had been, with a force of soldiers on horseback and artillery not far off. "That night, while the rest of us waited, the warriors met with Spotted Elk and Yellow Bird, but Running Wolf would not tell me what they spoke of. When the soldiers came that morning to take our weapons away, Spotted Elk, Running Wolf, and all the warriors wore their ghost shirts like your Messiah told them to do! Did Wovoka not say that if they wore their ghost shirts, the white man's bullets would not be able to harm them? All of them sat on the ground before Spotted Elk's lodge as if expecting something momentous to happen." Perhaps they believed that the Messiah would aid them in wiping out the soldiers. Perhaps the Messiah would strike down the soldiers' artillery with lightning from the sky.

Red Horse's lips drew tight.

Her voice turned hard and sharp. "But only one thing happened. The warriors in their ghost shirts were all shot dead at the very first! The women in their ghost shirts were shot in the back as they fled across the snow carrying their babies! Children were … shot to pieces—"

His chin thrust out like a boulder in a river. "When the Father comes down from the sky, everyone will see. You will have your children again, and I will have mine. Running Wolf will come back, and the white man will be gone, and everyone will be young forever and fat with buffalo meat."

She could rail at him for a fool, but Red Horse was as stubborn as Running Wolf had been. She wanted to jump up and tell him that if he was so certain Born-with-a-Smile would return in the spring after her death, she would thank him to kill her now and save her misery.

Not even Born-with-a-Smile had believed the stories of the Ghost Dancers. When the Old Ways had been outlawed, she had become friends with Christian missionaries, who soon converted her to their ways. If Born-with-a-Smile could muster any strength to speak now, would even she think him a fool?

Little Elk said, "So you will not let me treat her with the Old Ways?"

"She is in the hands of the Father."

The sound of heavy shoes on the earth grabbed her attention. Two soldiers stalked toward her with purpose in their eyes.

She looked at Red Horse one more time and sighed. He cast a contemptuous glance at the oncoming Bluecoats before lowering his eyes. "Ask me again tomorrow," he said.

XIV

Little Elk stood before Major Wilson's desk, with the doctor, the marshal of White Pine, and Sergeant Weatherly in the wings. The doctor's eyes lingered on her appraisingly, if not openly, and the attention annoyed her, even as she let Major Wilson's arrogance wash over her.

Wilson said, "Speak, witch. What do you know? Answer the man!"

The doctor stepped forward. "Little Elk?"

Little Elk focused her eyes on the wall above the major's head. The memory of Born-with-a-Smile's rasping cough did not encourage her to cooperate with a man such as Major Wilson, who had stampeded his military might across her people's heads since he arrived here during the troubles. "My people are sick, and they are starving. Such people do strange things."

"This is not the time for a saucy lip, witch." The major leaned forward, punishing the tip of another cigar with his teeth.

The doctor said, "Have any of your people turned violent within the last few days? Did anyone leave camp and do harm to someone else?"

Little Elk's voice was even, almost bland. "Lakota men are warriors, hunters. Sometimes they are filled with rage." The Lakota were too hungry. Many of them left camp to forage for food and small game. But her people had not fought among themselves since the Ghost Dance had divided them last autumn.

A zephyr whistled across the office window, rattling the panes, dusting the glass with grit.

Major Wilson slammed his fist against the desk top. "One more circumlocution from you and I'll have you flogged."

She had looked down the barrels of distant Hotchkiss guns. This bully's anger did not faze her. "The Major's men do not let us eat or breathe. We are scared, but not foolish." She looked at the doctor for the first time. "There is something else, Doctor. Two children are missing. They went to sleep last night in their parents' tents, and in the morning they were gone. We have been looking for them all day, but there is no sign."

The doctor said, "Did you know of this, Major?"

The major shrugged. "The first I've heard of any such thing. Besides, they probably just wandered off and got lost in the dark. She's evading your questions, Doctor. As I said she would. She's now wasting your time *and* mine."

The doctor said, "Two children would not simply leave their parents in the dead of night." He turned to Little Elk. "How old are they?"

"Seven and five winters. Their names are New Moon and Two Otters, a girl and a boy."

"Were they sick?"

"No. We have searched as best we are able, but we are barely allowed out of our tents. We cannot extend our search, and the soldiers will not listen to us, so we do not speak."

Major Wilson sneered at her. "Of course not. You cannot be trusted."

Little Elk suppressed a bitter laugh at the ridiculousness of a white Army man saying that her people could not be trusted. The number of treaties and agreements the United States government had broken in the last fifteen years alone would fill a book the size of a Bible.

The doctor's face reddened. "Major! For God's sake, there are parents out there who have lost their children!"

Wilson gave the doctor a long look, a smirk flickering for an instant at the corner of Wilson's mouth. "They are still heathens, Doctor, despite the progress we have made in civilizing them. Heathens die every day, and God does not care. He is quite happy to send all their souls into the fiery furnace. However, for as long as they are in this world, they are my charges, and I won't have them wandering across the hills. Sergeant, initiate a search for the missing whelps."

Sergeant Weatherly saluted. "Yes, sir. Right away, sir." He spun on a heel and departed, clearly relieved to be leaving.

Major Wilson gestured vaguely, dismissively at Little Elk. "Go with him."

Little Elk held her tongue and followed the sergeant out.

Then a distant scream echoed over the wind.

XV

Hank was the first out of the Major Wilson's office as all of them ran outside. Soldiers converged on the infirmary in ones and twos, their faces confused and shaken. Hank spotted the one called Red Horse and two other braves gathered in conversation, near the tent village, their eyes dark and furtive.

Major Wilson snatched a nearby soldier's arm and pointed toward Red Horse's group. "Corporal, go break up that little pow-wow."

The soldier peeled away and stalked toward the group, carbine brandished.

The braves dispersed before the soldier could reach them. Red Horse's expression of sullen hatred swept over the entire group of white men.

The medicine woman and Sergeant Weatherly paused. Wilson pointed at her, "Sergeant, get her out of here."

"Yes, sir." Weatherly took Little Elk by the arm and led her toward the Indian camp.

Hank reached the infirmary door first, pulled his six-gun and flung open the door.

One of the sick privates, Garrett, stood over Oliver McCoy, hands clamped around Oliver's throat. Oliver gurgled and thrashed, but his struggles were diminishing quickly. Private Spalding curled up against the wall, his eyes bulging, mouth open, clutching his blanket to his chest.

Hank trained his pistol. "Get off him or I'll put a hole in you, Garrett!"

The soldier leered at Hank, his eyes bleak but cognizant. "The black god wants this one. He's heard the call."

Hank cocked his pistol. "Let him go!"

The full intelligence in the private's eyes, as if he *knew* things that Hank could never imagine, sent a chill down Hank's spine. A chill he had not felt in decades. "The sun fades and your final hour nears," the private said through gritted teeth, "The storm is coming. The sky will cleanse you all."

"I didn't carry that runt all this way for this!" Hank took aim and shot him in the arm, a mere graze, but the private did not relent. "Goddammit!" He cocked again, and sent a bullet squarely into Garrett's torso.

Garrett staggered, but maintained his grip on Oliver's throat.

A cold hand settled over Hank's chest and squeezed fingers through his ribs. He took careful aim. His next bullet blasted through Garrett's skull. The body fell like speared buffalo, convulsing, twitching.

Oliver gasped for breath, clutching at his throat, hacking, coughing, sobbing. Charles shouldered past Hank and ran across the room to Oliver's bedside.

Hank holstered his pistol and crossed the room to stand over Garrett's twitching corpse. His lips were tight, teeth clenched. A dark pool of blood spread from the apple-sized hole in the back of Garrett's skull, seeping into the rough planks of the floor. There was a stain that would never come out.

Major Wilson strode in, surveyed the scene for a moment, and then approached Spalding's bed. "What happened, Private?"

Spalding's face could have been fashioned from the same linen as his sheets. "I ... It's just ... Clete woke up like he had a nightmare. He was talking gibberish. You heard him, sir!"

"I'm not sure what I heard," Wilson said.

Charles said, "Something about a black god."

Spalding's tongue darted out to moisten cracked lips. "Right! Right! And how the black god is coming. A black sun, chosen people, it was all crazy talk, sir. I ain't never seen madness like that! And he just got up, all calm like, and walked over there, and started choking that poor feller."

The corners of Major Wilson's mouth turned downward, and his eyes narrowed.

Spalding said, "He told me yesterday he's been having some powerful bad nightmares. Ain't been sleeping well, he said."

Charles said, "What kind of nightmares?"

"Wouldn't say, sir. But he remembered 'em. I saw that much."

Hank nodded toward Oliver. "He gonna be all right?"

Charles cocked his head skeptically. "He's not out of the woods."

Major Wilson frowned. "Do you have the resources in town to care for this man, Doctor?"

"Yes, but—"

"Good, because I do not want him here."

Charles stood up, and opened his mouth to protest, but Hank had had enough. That boy was about to sow himself a heap of trouble. He let the heel of his boot fall hard on the floor as he stepped forward. "You can take better care of him in town anyway. Major, I'll thank you to let me borrow a buckboard for the day. There are three dead men out on the range gathering flies. They need burying."

Major Wilson masticated his cigar for a moment, a fake smile cracking his wet lips. "Fine. You have a buckboard at your disposal for the day, Marshal. Let it never be said that I don't help the civilian law. Doctor, this man will be more comfortable at your office. Sergeant, begin the search for the missing children."

XVI

The fasting had already been accomplished, but quite by accident. Little Elk had not eaten since the previous day, having given her meager ration of corn dodger last night to one of her neighbor's children. No one in the camp had seen any meat besides field mice or rabbit in weeks. Her belly was tight and empty, ready to be filled with the wisdom of the spirit world, her flesh purified of the white man's food.

She stood with the four women she had gathered outside her tent. Chosen because they adhered to the Old Ways, the women regarded her with silent solemnity. They knew their business, but they waited for her to give the word.

They had all done their best to seal the drafty shelter, and the women had all brought blankets to pile over the tent to hold in as much heat as possible, so many that the tent sagged in the middle now, but it would hold. When Little Elk had erected the tent, she had made sure that the entrance faced west. She had prepared a basin of fresh water and dug the sacred pit in the center for the stones. For a moment she fretted again that this was not a proper sweat lodge and hoped that the spirits would not take offense. Must they not acknowledge the earnestness of her actions?

Her chief concern now was whether the size of her fire would gain the unwanted attention of the Bluecoats. Properly heating the stones required a fire of sufficient size.

Others of her people stood around them with mixtures of wonder, disapproval, and fear. They had chosen, or been forced, to follow the Christ of the white man, whose book taught that the Old Ways were evil. Little Elk had further chosen her assistants from those who had not danced the Ghost Dance; because of the speed that the fervor had swept through all the reservation camps, those were but few. While the teachings of this outsider they called "the Father" did not sound inherently evil to her, neither did they ring true to her. His words ran contrary to the stories on which she was raised.

When word had first come of travelers from the west last summer with the Paiute Messiah's disciples, and it spread that he was coming to deliver the world into a peaceful, renewed happiness, Little Elk had felt a deep skepticism. From the time she was a little girl, she had been a Dreamer, and her father, the medicine man, Yellow Hawk, had promised to teach her the mysteries of the universe. At that time, their band had been forced onto the Pine Ridge Reservation, and in the white government's efforts to "civilize" the Lakota, Little Elk had been taken from her family at the age of ten winters, sent to a Catholic boarding school in the east until she was sixteen.

At this boarding school, she had learned English and Christianity. They tried to make her forget the Old Ways, but the Dreams would not let her forget. Even the nuns and rectors with their paddles and accusations of "witch" could not stop the Dreams. In her early life, before reservations and the treaties, her Dreams had become renowned for their truth.

Her chief helper for this ceremony would be Jane Two Hawks, a woman ten years elder to Little Elk, whose husband had once been *akicita*, camp guard and advisor to Crazy Horse. She still carried a pipe that had come down from her ancestors, and it would more than suffice. After her husband had been killed at the Battle of the Greasy Grass, after the subsequent peace treaty of 1876, Jane Two Hawks had taken an English name like many of her people, but her blood and her adherence to the Old Ways still ran true.

Near the entrance, a small hill of fresh earth stood beside the fire in which sixteen stones lay carefully arranged, heating. The earth of the small hill had been taken from the pit Little Elk had dug in the center of her tent. The ground between the two had been properly swept clean, the symbolic path between worlds. The pipe lay across the top of the mound, pointing east. Inside the tent, offerings of tobacco hung from pouches tied to the ceiling.

All was in readiness.

Little Elk took a deep breath and nodded. The four women standing around her raised the blankets in their arms to head height, hiding Little Elk from view. She disrobed quickly and stood nude, gooseflesh rising instantly in the chilly evening air. Taking the spray of sage leaves from Jane Two Hawks and using it to cover herself, she faced in each of the four directions and entreated the spirits to grant her a vision.

Then she ducked inside and seated herself before the pit. The last of her sage leaves lay scattered on the ground around her.

Moments later, the flap parted and a large stone was presented in the crook of a forked stick fashioned for just this purpose, carrying in with it the smells of searing hot stone and blackening wood. Waves of heat emanated from the stone, and she took it in another forked stick before placing it in the pit. Its warmth tingled across her chilled flesh, and three more stones came in solemn succession.

With the first group of four stones in place, Jane now offered the pipe through the tent flap. A thread of pungent smoke followed the pipe bowl toward Little Elk's hands.

She took the pipe, held it before her, and intoned. *"Mitakuye oyas'in." All my relatives, living and dead.*

Raising it to her lips, she drew a deep lungful of smoke and held it for a moment. Three more long draughts of smoke made the sacred count of four and hazed the interior darkness of the tent, thickening the air. She passed the pipe back outside. From the basin of water beside her, she filled a spoon made from the horn of a mountain sheep and poured the water over the stones. A crackling, sizzling blast of steam boiled from the rocks and filled the tent. Three more splashes of water made the sacred count of four, and the interior of the tent grew hot and thick and smothering. The steam burned the inside of her nostrils, made her eyes water, and sweat sprang from her skin. She started breathing through her mouth.

She took up the small skin drum beside her and began to sing the old songs. At this prearranged moment, her assistants and several complicit friends outside began to sing other songs, loud and raucous and unrelated to her efforts. If the white soldiers came to investigate the noise, the women were only singing songs to entertain themselves.

Her words and her mind fell into the old songs, and her wish for a vision swirled with the rhythm of her voice.

XVII

Charles' wagon had been unloaded of its food and medicine shipment from town. Oliver McCoy still lay within the infirmary, sleeping fitfully, his breath coming and going in shallow, ragged starts. The body of Private Garrett had been removed, and poor Spalding lay in shock.

The major had ordered a cleaning detail to scrub Garrett's blood and brains from the floor and wall. With so much carnage within, the place felt more like an abattoir now than a place of healing and rest. Guards were placed at all the doors.

Charles stood outside, watching the rear of his father's buckboard recede on its way off-post.

The way that Wilson had been almost deferential to Charles' father, a civilian, seemed wildly out of character. A civilian who had just shot an unarmed soldier, albeit a murderous one. Charles would have expected Wilson to react with outrage, but he had simply chewed his cigar and accepted yet another death among his ranks, almost as if he had expected it. Wilson was a military man to the core, and the sneer of contempt for everything of the civilian realm dripped from every utterance. Charles' father and Major Wilson had doubtless been acquainted since Wilson's detachment had arrived in January, certainly due to his father's capacity as marshal of White Pine. But for all of Charles' life, his father had worn that old cavalry hat from his Civil War days. Hank had been a quartermaster, so Charles had always been curious about where he had gotten the cavalry hat. Charles had asked on one of the rare occasions where relations between them were less strained, but his father had simply shrugged and grunted and changed the subject.

Wilson barked more orders at his men before disappearing into his office.

Charles released a long, tight breath. His fists ached from being clenched.

How could Wilson expect the Lakota to respect him when he treated them as little more than sub-human? How could Charles not expect to be tarred with the same brush? Wilson was just the latest in a long, erratic succession of incompetent overseers. When Wilson was gone, Charles would still have to work with these people, and they might easily forget all the help he had already given them. His work was already difficult, having to contend with barriers of understanding that went beyond language.

Wilson's earlier treatment of Little Elk had stoked Charles' outrage. He would reassure her before he left that he had the interests of the Lakota at heart. The memory of her warm touch on his hand had nothing to do with it.

He had a vague notion of where her tent lay, out on the fringe of the camp, so he walked through the squalor again and did his best to present the Lakota with a kind face. Nevertheless, the hopelessness of their plight ate at him with every step. Running a railroad track and a train filled with cattle and grain right up to the front gate of the agency would be a worthy beginning for the aid these people needed.

The sound of singing reached him, growing louder as he approached the outside edge of the camp. Two shapes in Army blues, carrying rifles, stalked toward him, muttering between themselves. Their voices sounded tremulous and they gripped their weapons tight.

When they spotted Charles, he said, "What is happening over there? Are you investigating another uprising?"

The corporal answered, "They're having some sort of party, but we can't reckon what they're celebrating."

The private said, "Maybe they're celebrating us shooting each other. You carrying iron, sir?"

Charles shook his head. "I am not."

"Then best not go that way unless you got red skin," the private said.

"I'm not offering violence, so I will expect none."

The corporal shrugged. "It's your scalp." The two of them then moved on.

A twinge of nervousness was not reason enough to hold him back from his intention, so he took a deep breath and continued toward the singing. Little Elk would likely be found there.

However, when he reached the bright circle of singing women around a large fire, Little Elk was not to be seen. Neither were any men in evidence.

He cleared his throat and opened his mouth to speak, but they sang louder, otherwise appearing to ignore him. In the ebb and flow of the song, he heard a drum faintly somewhere nearby, out of rhythm with the music here, but could not pinpoint the source.

The depth of his outsider-ness yawned before him, between him and them, like a bottomless chasm a hundred feet wide.

The women smiled as they sang, with a strange relief on their faces, as if they had not expected what they were experiencing at this moment. How long had it been since they sang together? The tone of the song felt like joyful camaraderie, even though he could fathom none of the words.

For several long moments, he stood and listened, feeling the alien song wash over him, then he hung his head and departed.

XVIII

The darkness and smoke smothered away the earthly world, and the barriers to the spirit world thinned before Little Elk, as if thick knee-deep mud holding back her steps were becoming cool, clear water. Sweat dripped down her back, her cheeks, between her breasts, rivulets following scars on her arms.

A strange keening reached her ears, a plaintive, tenuous sound.

She is Tahca Chistila once again, not the sounds from an alien tongue. Her spirit-self steps outside her sweat lodge into the camp of buffalo-hide dwellings, where slabs of buffalo meat from the recent hunt hang from racks while the camp dogs sit under them, waiting, drooling, tongues lolling, for one of the slabs to shift in the breeze and fall to the dirt. Children scamper and play among the lodges, and everyone is oblivious to the faint cries coming from the direction of the river. Around the camp, stretching to forever, lie seas of swaying grasses.

She follows the sound. The band's herd of horses grazes on a broad sandbar that is straddled by the river.

The tiny wail grows more insistent, building in strength until she can pinpoint the source, a clump of bushes beyond the horses. Through the cold spring river water she wades, past the camp's horses, toward the sound. Reaching the bushes, she parts the branches, and there on the ground lies a child swaddled in a scarlet cotton blanket, a child with curly golden locks, skin as pink and plump as a cherub.

She picks up the child and cradles it. "Strong lungs you have, little one."

It pauses long enough to take a deep breath, and its eyes open, and she sees they are as dark and deep and gray as a storm.

As she returns to the village with the child, its cries wax and wane. At times, the tenor of its voice shifts, sounding at times almost like an old woman, perhaps even an old man. She takes the child to her father, the chief, who smiles and greets the child. Together they open the blanket and see that the child is a girl.

"My daughter," the chief says, "You now have a daughter of your own."

Several men gather at the entrance to the chief's lodge, murmuring amongst themselves.

"What are you talking about?" she says to the men.

Their heads become heads of elk and buffalo, deer and coyote, wolf and bear, eagle and thunder. They say, "Sometimes evil spirits come to camp in the guise of small children."

The chief says, "Let us not be overcautious. This child needs our aid. We cannot leave her for the coyotes. Instead we will have a feast for my new grandchild."

Word spreads like wildfire through the camp, sparking excitement and preparation. The women plait their hair; the men paint their cheeks with bright red paint. Women put on their best dresses, and children frolic in their buckskins. Everyone gathers for the feast, sitting in a great circle, but still the pale-skinned child wails.

When the preparations are made, the feast commences, and the air is filled with the rich scents of many foods, smoke from tobacco and cookfires.

The chief holds up the child and introduces her to his people, and they greet her with cries of *"How!"*

The drummers burst forth into a lively tune, and people jump up to dance and sing. Late into the night they feast, and finally the little girl falls asleep in Little Elk's arms. As the people tire and fall asleep, as the last sounds of revelry diminish, she looks down into her new daughter's face, all pink cheeks and little wet lips slightly parted in slumber. She smiles for a long time, because her own children were shot by white men on the same day her husband was killed.

A deep quiet settles over the village.

In the silence, the web of stars peeps through the smoke hole of the lodge, and she rocks her new daughter in gentle arms. But then she notices the far-off murmur of many voices. The murmur seems to be growing louder, drawing nearer. She stands and listens with increasing alarm. The number of voices is great, as of a whole tribe speaking at once.

Nearby, her father snores quietly. She shakes him and says, "Father! There are people coming. I can hear them!"

And then the child in her arms becomes smoke that chokes her lungs, and she sits in the dark and the steam, drenched in sweat.

Through the veil between worlds she called out to Jane Two Hawks, and four more snapping-hot stones were passed inside. Little Elk arranged them with the others, and then the freshly refilled pipe found its way into her hands again, and she smoked it four times, and she cast four more cupfuls of water onto the stones. Gouts of steam and smoke blinded her and seared her throat, and the sweat poured from her body, and she reached again for the vision.

XIX

The buckboard rattled and heaved under Hank's ass. He would much rather have been in the saddle than out here in a wagon. The wooden wheels cut ruts in the tall grass and sod that hid every goddamn badger hole, which this Army nag found somehow without missing nary a one.

He studied the huge thunderstorm building in the west. A tower of purple-gray clouds reached up to touch the descending sun. The deep gray underbelly of the storm sent thunder rumbling across the endless prairie.

Hank had memorized the landmarks whereabouts he found Oliver, but he still spent over an hour searching the hills and valleys for the cowboys' former campsite, driving the wagon back and forth over an area of several square miles. Oliver had told him of the spot, but Hank was skeptical of the boy's accuracy. Oliver had been so addled this morning, he could have been walking around in Hell and not known the difference.

The cowboys had been tending old Angus McCoy's herd. The Bar-M was a sizable spread stretching toward the edge of Indian lands and then south toward the Nebraska border. The ranches of the Dakota Territory had been skirmish grounds more than once between the ranchers and sheepherders. Fighting between the ranchers and Indians was rare, but not unheard of. Decades of conflict had turned old Angus into a man almost as tough and uncompromising as Hank.

Hank admired that.

A man had to be tough as hell to live here, so far from what the city folks called "civilization." Where hostile savages could be lurking over the next hill, however much the heathens had had the shit kicked out of them. Where the wind never really stopped blowing. Where the nights were filled with the howls of coyotes. Where the seas of prairie grass just went on and on, and the sod was so tough you could make a house of it. Where eking out an existence made men and women as hard and resilient as a boot heel.

So where were the Bar-M cattle? The cattle would matter to McCoy almost as much as his son. Even with his wealth, losing a herd would be felt. Where did it get off to?

Abandoned saddles and a burned-out campfire peeked out of the wind-ripples of grass.

"'Bout damn time!" Hank said and turned the horse that direction.

Reaching the campsite, he reined up, set the wagon brake, and stepped down.

The grass was dense, knee-deep, and just starting to green with spring. Large swatches had been flattened by the presence of the Bar-M herd, but of the cattle there was no sign. All that remained of the campsite was the black splotch of dead fire, with the cowboys' saddles and tack carefully arranged around it. Bloated black flies buzzed, flicking and alighting on the congealed blood, black fluid, and viscera still staining the grass.

The bodies were gone.

Hank scratched his head. "I'll be damned."

Suddenly his short hairs jumped to reveille, and he scanned the grass around him. Maybe coyotes had dragged the bodies away. This morning, he would have said there were no critters in these parts dangerous to man except an occasional rattlesnake, no wolves, or bears, or cougars. But now …

A powerful sensation that something was watching him chilled his blood, and he was sharply glad he had reloaded his pistol.

He threw the saddles and tack into the back of the buckboard. A tether where the cowboys had tied their horses was broken. Hoof tracks reached for the nearest horizon. He picked up a blood-spattered hat, but it clung to the grass for moment, until he tore it free and tossed it in the back of the buckboard. He caught himself searching the grass, with a potent feeling that a snake must be within striking distance, but the grass was an opaque, impenetrable weave.

Something rustled a few steps away.

His eyes flicked toward it, but there was nothing to see. He pulled his six-gun and squinted toward the sound, his jaw and shoulders tightening.

For a long minute he stood there. All he could hear was the wind-driven rustle of the grass, the call of a distant meadowlark, the nervous stomping of the Army nag.

Hank shook his head, holstered his pistol, and climbed into the wagon. Everything he had seen today had knocked his common sense off kilter. He needed to get back to White Pine. There was some digesting to do.

XX

Charles walked back through the Lakota camp toward his wagon. Dozens of women were gathered at the singing circle, but where were all the men? A few scattered old women overseeing the children remained at their tents and canvas tipis. None of the women would look at him. Many of the children ceased their activities when they spotted him, and they froze until he passed. He sensed no disrespect behind his back, just fear and otherness. He was a curiosity, as alien in their world as if an elephant had just trundled through, something to be feared and kept at a distance.

He stopped beside his wagon and noted that the mailbag had been left for him as usual to take back to the Post and Telegraph Office in White Pine. All that remained now was to find someone to help him carry Oliver from the infirmary and put the horses back into harness. It would be dusk now before he reached White Pine.

The sound of a door caught his attention, and he spotted a figure emerging from the commissary. The quartermaster and the line of Lakota women were long since gone with the coming evening. The figure drew out a ring of keys and locked the door behind him, then turned and, seeing Charles, started. Sergeant Weatherly quickly suppressed the look of guilt on his face, but Charles was not interested in that. He needed help with the wounded man.

"Sergeant! A word, please."

Weatherly descended the commissary steps, clutching his woolen coat around him. "What is it, Doctor? I got to get a move on. Just doing rounds."

Charles approached him. "I need a bit of assistance carrying Mr. McCoy to the wagon. Perhaps a couple of men to carry a stretcher."

"Yes, sir, I can do that." He looked to be in a hurry, but would not meet Charles' eye.

"Good, I can—"

Something fell out of the bottom of Weatherly's coat, a heavy lump wrapped in paper and tied with a string. He stooped quickly to snatch it up.

Charles caught the scent of smoked meat. "Is that bacon, Sergeant?"

Weatherly looked abashed and paused as if struggling with how to answer. Finally, he straightened and sighed. "Yeah, it's bacon. You going to tell the Major?"

"Why do you need to steal from your own stores? Are your rations as insufficient as theirs?"

"No, sir, you got it all wrong, sir. We get plenty to eat. It's mostly shitty Army chow, but we ain't hurtin' for vittles. This here." He held the butcher's package before him. "This here is for them." A gesture with it toward the Lakota camp.

Charles crossed his arms. "Two pounds of pork will hardly feed the entire village."

Weatherly shrugged and sighed. "I know that, sir, but it's all I can do right now, today. I'd give 'em a whole beef if I could, but there ain't no way to do it under Wilson's nose."

"A laudable sentiment, sergeant, but why?"

Weatherly sniffed and looked away. "These people don't deserve what they got. We whupped 'em, and after we whupped 'em, we just keep on whupping. I don't truck with no killing of women and babies, doctor."

"Your unit didn't arrive until after Wounded Knee Creek."

"But I heard the stories. I hear a lot, and I see a lot, walking around this camp. Half the time, they have to beg us for food and everything else we promised them. The other half, they want to put a knife in my guts. My men talk, the farmers talk. I picked up a little Sioux here and there. I hear them talk. It's like the sadness and melancholy is just … soaked up into everything." He stretched his arm wide. "You believe in ghosts, sir?"

"I'm a man of science, sergeant."

"Well, I read this book on ghosts and stuff, you see, and it said that places can get … embroiled in bad stuff, kinda like soaked in death or sadness or evil, and that's why some places get haunted. When that happens, sometimes folks just don't feel right when they go into one of those places."

"Interesting theory, sergeant, but what does this have to do with two pounds of bacon?"

Weatherly hefted the package. "This here, this is healing medicine. The Major don't see it, or don't care, but everyone around here needs to heal. Indians and white folks both."

Charles thought about this for a moment. He did not know if he would ever be able to expunge the memory of that snow-blasted, blood-spattered field of death from his memory, or the sound of a heavy lump of hard-frozen meat falling into a mass grave like a chunk of cordwood. What kind of scars did that kind of experience leave on a man's soul? He had gone out there with the newspapermen and the local civilian leaders after the blizzard passed, looking for survivors, anyone needing medical attention, and found himself in the role of gravedigger. Little did he know that three months later he would be digging two more graves.

Too many wounds in succession compromised the body's ability to heal itself.

Charles sighed and said, "I appreciate your candor, Sergeant, and your kindness. I'll not say anything to anyone about this. What if you get caught?"

Weatherly relaxed a little and shrugged. "We should be getting new orders any day now, and Gutterson, the quartermaster, is a lazy bastard content to sit on his ass. I figure we'll be long gone before anyone bothers with an inventory."

Charles nodded.

"I'll just deliver this," Weatherly continued, "and then I'll muster up a couple of men to stretcher that kid over here."

"Thank you. There's just one more thing. Tell me about the man who attacked his fellows last night. Lieutenant Cox was it?"

Weatherly swallowed hard at the surge of visceral memory. "What do you want to know? Green as hell, with a nice, fresh West Point stick up his ass. For all that, still a decent enough young feller, for an officer."

"Had he been acting strangely? Was there any indication of psychological maladies?"

"Psycho-what?"

"Did he ever act crazy?"

"No, sir, just the opposite. If anything, his asshole was tighter than a champagne cork. The only thing I noticed about him yesterday is that he looked awful tired. One of the other officers mentioned this at morning mess yesterday, but the lieutenant said he had been having trouble sleeping. Belly was giving him trouble, he said."

Charles rubbed his chin. "Has anyone else been complaining of that?"

"Not that I've heard."

"How is morale among your men?"

"Today, they are mighty scared. That business last night spooked them something awful, and Sioux in this camp outnumber us five to one."

"But most of those are women."

"You think a Sioux woman can't put a knife in your belly when she's got a mind to? If that was me living over there, I'd be looking for a sight of payback. Wouldn't you?"

Charles was not certain. If he had to change places with them, what would he do? "Keep your ears open, Sergeant, perhaps make some inquiries. I would be most grateful. I'll be back in a couple of days."

"Yes, sir. Thank you, sir."

Another door opened across the yard, and Major Wilson stepped outside, cigar between his fingers. He stood for a moment on the porch, listening. In the distance, the sound of the women singing echoed through the camp.

Weatherly spun his back to Wilson and stuffed the package of bacon back into his coat.

Wilson blew a cloud of smoke. "What is that infernal racket?"

While Weatherly arranged himself, Charles spoke up. "It's singing, Major."

"What in the hell do they have to sing about?"

Charles swallowed the bitterness in his throat. "I cannot imagine. But it's just a group of women."

Wilson spat onto the ground. "We cannot have them building themselves up to a war dance. Sergeant, take a squad of men over there and silence that gibbering nonsense."

Weatherly saluted. "Yes, sir!" Without another word to Charles, he hurried off to gather his men.

XXI

In the village of buffalo-hide lodges, in the depths of the night, Little Elk holds the pink girl-child in her arms.

Her father throws open the flap and searches by starlight for signs of danger. "I see nothing," he says.

"But something is wrong!" Little Elk says. "Where does this sound come from?" The cacophony of voices grows louder, now mixed with the rumble of drums. "It is as if the sound comes from the ground all about me!"

Her father's face darkens. "No." He comes to her and touches the baby's cheek. "Listen."

She bends over and discovers that the sounds emanate from the child's mouth, as if an entire village dwells inside the child.

Her father draws back, fearful, and his voice is grim. "Iya, the Camp Eater, the brother of Iktomi the Spider, has come to our camp in the guise of this child. It is a lucky thing that you did not fall asleep. If you had, he would have cast off this baby's skin and devoured our entire camp. We must leave the child here and flee!"

Suddenly she feels weak and out of breath, stifling hot. The child is slipping from her arms, but if she drops it, it will throw off its disguise and destroy them all. Her fingers clutch at the blanket but can find no purchase. The child becomes immeasurably heavy, and the blanket becomes smoke and steam.

Little Elk walked with her feet in both worlds, and called out for the third round of stones, which were soon passed inside. The already hot air grew even hotter. Fresh sweat burst forth. Four long draughts on a fresh pipe. Four splashes of water on the stones and four more gouts of searing steam. She coughed and gasped and covered her nose to protect it from the heat. Areas of her flesh began to burn, areas where impurities had gathered, so she took sage leaves and chewed them into paste, which she smeared over the burning spots. Her eyes watered and her lungs burned and her limbs felt as if they were turning to water.

She can no longer hold up the baby, so as gently as she can she lays it upon the ground, cooing to it and treating it like a real child.

The baby begins to cry.

The chief runs outside and rouses everyone and tells them that Iya the Destroyer has come to their camp and that they must all flee. The people are afraid, and they pack up their lodges. By midnight, there is nothing left of the camp but small heaps of ashes. They flee across the river and wait for the mother of Iya to catch up with them.

Meanwhile, she sits beside her child and tries to comfort it until her people have reached safety, singing to it, stroking its soft, golden hair. As Little Elk sings, the child's belly begins to swell as if filling with air, and its mouth opens wider and wider until the quivering pink orifice is large enough to swallow a horse.

The sound of the other camp emanating from the child grows louder and louder.

The time to flee has come, so Little Elk dashes away.

Suddenly a great roaring wind bursts forth from the child's mouth and rises into the sky in the shape of a thunderous black cyclone.

Little Elk flees toward her people as fast as she can, but her legs feel like sacks of water. Swirling within the cyclone is not just one camp, but many, thousands of people, horses, dogs, and lodges, a tumult of suffering, trapped forever in Iya's gullet.

Iya's rage booms over the land in the form of thunder in a great voice. "I will devour you all! No one escapes me!"

Her father shouts to her, "Hurry! If day breaks you will be safe! Iya's tricks are powerless in the light of the sun!"

Scalding rain spews from the cyclone, burning her flesh, turning the land around her into a morass of sucking mud. She falls facedown into the mud and tries to breathe but only smoke and steam come from her mouth.

Little Elk sat up in almost utter darkness, gasping, her face feeling tender and scalded from the steam, but there was still one more stage to be accomplished, and it was almost always in the fourth stage that the deepest truths were revealed. Her voice was a mere croak as she called again for Jane Two Hawks.

The final round of stones were passed inside, the final four draughts of smoke, the final four splashes of water. In the stifling, sweltering, smothering thickness, she gasped for purchase until the pungent, crackling sage leaves on the floor came up to meet her cheek.

A young girl's voice says to her in strangely accented English. "Let me help you."

Gentle hands close around her thin arms, her thin arms wrapped in a new gingham dress that the sisters have given her, a dress with long sleeves and a high neck and a lower hem that reaches to her ankles.

The girl's voice says, "You're new here."

"I am ... new."

"You must get up. It is time for morning prayers. If you are slow, the sisters will take away your lunch."

Little Elk sits up, and morning sunlight slants through square windows of glass and wood over the rows of beds lining the walls of the dormitory. The room is empty of other children.

Where is the river? Where have her people gone? Where is the cyclone that had been bearing down on her? She jumps up and looks out the window at the bright sunny sky sweeping over lush trees and soft grass, the open sward where the children play.

The other girl is a little older than her, with a kind face but features that bespeak a different tribe. "My name is ..." Her words were incomprehensible to Little Elk, but somehow she knows them to mean "Laughing Otter."

"We are friends," Little Elk says. She did not know English yet, but somehow the other girl understood her.

The girl giggles. "Perhaps."

"Why are we here?"

"So that we can tell each other stories."

Vague recollections of Iya and Iktomi impinge upon Little Elk's memory, but they do not seem important.

Little Elk says, "All the world is stories."

Laughing Otter nods, "We make our own stories new from the old. But come! We must go."

"What about the stories?" She feels some sort of danger, as if every moment was not to be wasted. "I must know them all right now. It is ... important."

Laughing Otter shakes her head. "Let us live them and touch the face of gods."

And oh, the stories they live.

And then the cyclone descends from the sky and devours the school and the church and everyone in it, an explosion of splinters and dust.

Little Elk feels herself lifted from the ground, rising into the sky, powerless, clutching vainly at anything to halt her ascent, with the thunder of laughter booming in her ears.

With a great thud she landed upon a bed of sage leaves, and her awareness trickled back in. The darkness of the tent pressed her down. Earth and sage leaves clung to her face, to her sweat-soaked flesh, filled her nose with their rich scent, as she righted herself and breathed deeply of the smoke and steam one last time.

With arms that felt like soggy marsh weeds, she crawled toward the opening and called out to her helpers.

Moments later, the flap opened and dresses surrounded the entrance. She wormed out, fought her way to her feet, shivering in the shock of cold, gasping tremendous breaths of cold, clean night air. After a moment to steady herself, she took the heavy leather bladder of water from Jane Two Hawks and emptied the ice-cold water over her head.

A gasp tore from her, and a spasm of pain shot through her skull.

For a moment, an eyeblink, a breath between heartbeats, Laughing Otter stood before her in her Catholic school garb, but her cheeks were drawn and tight, her eyes sunken, her hands skeletal, her shoulder bones protruding from her dress. The girl's face was grim, eyes wide and sharp, lips were wet and red, and they peeled back to reveal broad, bloody teeth, bits of raw flesh clinging to the crevices between them.

Laughing Otter snatched at Little Elk with a skeletal hand, with a hungry gleam in her eyes. Little Elk flinched back, and nails tore across her forearm, startling all the other women who could not see this apparition, and Laughing Otter evaporated into black cloud.

Moments passed, as the water dripped from Little Elk's body, pattering to the earth at her feet. A hush fell over the crowd of women gathered there, singing, and Little Elk's heart thundered.

Three long, red weals burned on her forearm.

A commotion in the distance caught her ear and drew her eye. A group of Lakota men, Red Horse among them, stood between the singing circle and a group of soldiers. Voices raised, harsh words from the soldiers. Stolid, silent refusal in the bodies of the Lakota men. One of the soldiers pointed toward the gathering, shouting something she could not hear. Red Horse shook his head in defiance to prevent the soldiers' passage. Sergeant Weatherly's face was stern but worried. One of the soldiers shoved Red Horse. Red Horse held his ground, but did not shove back.

A coldness shot through Little Elk's heart. She wanted to raise her voice to stop the impending violence, but her lungs were still too full of smoke and steam, her body too unsteady. She could only open her mouth and raise a hand.

Another shove. Red Horse's fist lashed out. A rifle butt rose and smashed across his face, driving him back, but still he did not lose his feet, like a tree that would not be felled.

The singing stopped as the group of women noticed the fight brewing. Their voices rose instead in warning and protest.

Desperation painted broad across his face, Sergeant Weatherly interposed himself between the soldiers and the Lakota as the two knots of fear and anger rushed each other. Weatherly's voice roared. "Stop! Get back!" The soldier who had butt-stroked Red Horse caught Weatherly's fist on his cheek and reeled back. Weatherly roared orders to his men, roared orders to the Lakota, his eyes wide and fearful, but determined. A few more tense moments of scuffling, and they all stepped away from each other, riding the knife-edge of tension.

Little Elk hurriedly dressed herself within her circle of assistants.

The band of women fell into disarray as they rushed toward the men to diffuse the violence.

Red Horse stepped up, holding his head, shaking it. He looked back at the soldiers, then back where the circle had been, and caught Little Elk's eye. His gaze was hard, but he gave her a little nod, then he shouted in Lakota, "Today is not the day!"

The groups parted, and the women dispersed, and the soldiers fingered their weapons but did not fire.

PART 2

"A vision came to me when the sun went into shadow, and I lay dying. And in my death, I saw ... all the Indians that ever roamed this earth, all your beloved ancestors, and mine, and those young ones who were taken by the white man's diseases. Do not grieve for them. They want you to know that they are happy.... And you should not grieve for yourselves, because ... the white man, my children, will soon be no more. Now you must not hate the white man. This will only delay his end. But if you will do the [Ghost Dance] that I will teach you, all the ancestors will return. And the buffalo will be renewed. And you shall all live forever. Forever in the freedom that we as Indian people once knew."

—Wovoka, Paiute messiah, 1889

I

From the top of the one of the endless rolling hills, Hank spotted the Delacroix homestead. The ragged rectangle of a fresh-plowed field, a sod house with the attendant privy, a newly constructed wooden barn with a granary, a chicken coop, a few livestock pens, and brand-shiny-new windmill, spinning its perpetual dance with the wind. Wasn't nothing but guns, grit, and the grace of God keeping the prairie from swallowing it up such that it had never been. Hank had tried to homestead, had a patch of ground outside White Pine for a few years, but too many parched summers and too many hours looking at a mule's ass ahead of a plowshare had broken him of that bad habit.

The two young Delacroix girls spread grain for the chickens and two lean hogs. The elder of them, Emily, soon to be a lovely filly, was likely in a couple more years to get married off. Hank guessed her to be about thirteen now. The other one, perhaps seven or eight, dressed like a boy. He knew little about these girls, since their pa never sent them into White Pine to school. At Sunday dinners in happier days, Amelia often rattled on and on about her students, and she had some harsh words about Cyrus Delacroix refusing to educate his children on arithmetic. Her harsh imitation of Cyrus rang in Hank's memory: *"My youngin' know the Lord's word. Ain't nothing else to teach. Git, woman!"* He smiled for a moment about that.

Cyrus emerged from the house and watched Hank's buckboard approach. The homesteader's lean face was sun-browned below his eyes, with a forehead and balding pate left fishbelly pale by the incessant shade of a straw hat.

The girls stopped their work and watched the buckboard pull to a stop outside the house, coming to the fence nearest the house. The youngest one peered between the pine rails.

Cyrus Delacroix had a face like leather stretched across a fistful of hatchets, with pale, flint-hard eyes, and striped overalls hanging from pale, naked shoulders. His weathered hands shielded his eyes from the sun. "Marshal."

Hank tipped his hat. "Howdy, Mr. Delacroix."

"What brings you out this way?"

Clara Delacroix appeared in the door of the house, wiping her hands on a stained apron. She was as square and stout as her husband was spare and lean. Cyrus edged in front of her.

Hank said, "I'm on my way back to town, and I thought it best to stop and talk to you."

"About what?"

Hank looked past Cyrus to Clara. "Mrs. Delacroix, can I get some of that famous coffee of yours?"

Clara blushed a little. "Of course, Marshal."

She faded into darkness.

Cyrus yelled at the girls. "You two, get back about your chores now!"

The girls picked up their grain buckets again and moved away.

Hank cleared his throat and spoke quietly. "I needed to warn you, Mr. Delacroix, but there was three dead white men over near Sentinel Hill. Could be new Injun trouble. After what happened last winter, they might have mustered up a little more fight. You keep them kids of yours close. No telling what them redskins'll do."

Cyrus's eyes widened momentarily. "The Lord protects his own from Injun heathens. Go with God's blessing, Marshal."

Hank tipped his hat, snapped the reins, and drove the wagon out of the yard toward the faint section-line trail leading toward White Pine.

While Hank was still within earshot, he heard Clara say, "What was that about?"

Cyrus said, "Don't worry yourself about it, woman."

II

Straight as an arrow, White Pine's main street stretched before Charles' wagon. With the onset of evening and incipient dusk, the shadows lay heavy across the fronts of the buildings and the broad dirt thoroughfare.

Oliver lay in the back of the wagon, covered in the same blankets as the earlier medical supplies, a bag of mail for a pillow. He moaned and winced with every lurch and jostle, but he still clung to life. If there was fight left in him, there was hope.

No one was on the street at this hour; all proper folk were at home for family supper.

Charles considered the businesses and tradesmen's shops as he guided the wagon toward his office. Fifteen years ago, there had been nothing on this spot except empty prairie, this emptiness so far from anything. Mining camps like Deadwood up in the Black Hills had brought more and more white men to the Dakota Territory, as hordes of settlers, miners, and immigrants looked to grab land for themselves. The town of White Pine was born of the placement of an early trading post as a midway point between the eastern part of the Dakota Territory and the mining communities of the Black Hills. South Dakota had been admitted to the union less than two years ago, but there was still little civilization east of Yankton and Sioux Falls, especially the further one traveled from the railroad lines. The nearest railroad line passed through Valentine, south across the Nebraska border.

White Pine had not been situated near a railroad line. The telegraph had come through only last year, an arrival that made the town feel less remote, but it was still a far cry from the Pennsylvania of Charles' youth. This was a wild land, so desolate and inhospitable at times, he could not understand how the Plains tribes loved it.

His father had come west after Charles' mother died, and he had sent for Charles and Amelia in Philadelphia when Charles was fresh from medical school, telling them that this newborn village was in desperate need of a physician. Eva was a baby, just like the town. Charles had had his reservations about his ability to get along with his father, but it had been a real opportunity to establish his own practice, to help people.

He drew the wagon to a halt in front of his office, noticing that the large window, painted with "C.F. ZIMMERMAN, M.D.," needed a good cleaning. He set the brake, stepped down, and tied the reins to a post. Stretching his back and sore muscles, he walked around the back of the wagon and unlatched the tailgate.

Oliver's eyelids fluttered.

Charles said, "Are you ready to get up, Oliver?"

"I appreciate the ride, Doc. But I'd rather be on a horse next time." Oliver almost managed a smile.

"I'll be right back." Charles said, then went into his office.

Inside, he plopped his medical bag onto a stool. After a day in the fresh air, he was conscious of the dusty smell of the painted buffalo hide hanging on the wall. Around the hide hung a few other keepsakes—a Cheyenne warclub, a Lakota peace pipe, a buffalo skull—from his meetings with the Sioux several years ago, before all the treaties were broken, before the spread of the Ghost Dance cult that some said reignited the hostilities, before the horrendous slaughter of December. So much needless bloodshed. So much hatred. So much greed. He sighed, crossed the room, poured water into a basin, splashed some on his face, and hung his head.

Something bleak and desolate welled up in his breast, mixing with pain that today's events had briefly allowed him to forget. He opened the medicine cabinet with shaking hands. Inside was the familiar array of jars, powders, and elixirs. To the side was his meager supply of laudanum.

He took down the unsealed bottle in front, uncorked it, the sharp chemical smell wafting into his nose. But this bottle was empty. He did not remember exhausting this one, but sleep had eluded him for over a month. His gaze wandered in familiar patterns to the photograph on a nearby shelf, a photograph of himself, Amelia holding Josephine, Eva in her favorite Sunday dress. Happiness had made Amelia beautiful then—just as its later departure had left her a wretched, ugly shell, with the desiccated heart of a corpse. He could hardly bear to look at her now.

He picked up the picture and touched two faces with two fingers.

Another stab, deep into his belly, like a bullet in the liver, memories flowing like blood from the wound.

The photographer's flash, blinding Charles for a moment, eliciting a wail of protest from Josie. Amelia rocking the infant, cooing and shushing. Eva tugging on his coat sleeve.

"Can I play now, Daddy?"

"Of course, sweetheart."

Eva dashing away from him in a flurry of lace and blonde curls.

Charles reaching for the wailing Josie. "Here, let me." Josie's crimson face relaxing at the sound of his voice. "Daddy's here." Her gaping toothless mouth closing, pursing, plump knuckles against her chin.

Flashes of the girls when they were older, running, frolicking. Amelia calling after them, "Eva! You leave your dress on! It's not proper!"

Charles stopping Amelia with a hand on her arm. "Let her play. She has her whole life to worry about being a proper lady."

He and Amelia smiling at each other, and holding hands while they watched the two girls play.

Amelia reading to them, both girls enraptured by their mother.

Tucking Eva into bed, then the three-year-old Josie. Watching over them as they succumbed to sleep.

Watching over them in their beds, as they succumbed in their final moments.

Charles put the picture down and smashed the laudanum bottle against the wall.

The creak of floorboards startled him into shutting the cabinet door.

Amelia stood in the back doorway, dressed in black, somber. Her head hung low, but he could feel the tautness exuding from her. After a long, tense pause, he got her a chair. She sat and folded her hands in her lap. He sat across from her, his back rigid.

She said, "You left. You just walked out." Something seemed to catch in her throat. "You left without saying good-bye. Again." She tried to clear it. "You left without saying good-bye, and I waited all day for you."

For another of more times than he could count, he did not know what to say. He looked around the room, doing anything to avoid her gaze.

"Say something!"

"Yes."

"That's it? That's all you're going to say?"

"I suppose it is. Amelia, I …" Why must he feel like pleading with her? "Neither of us has slept in days."

"Weeks. And the dreams … so awful. All emptiness and wanting." Her tone shifted as if she were trying to start a conversation between normal people, as if that were possible anymore. "I was talking to Mrs. Johansen yesterday, and she says her dreams are—"

He could not bear another conversation like this now. Lurching upright, he said, "Amelia, I have a patient outside who might be dying. Can this wait?"

She bristled, then restrained her outburst, tried to put her hand on his, summoning uncertain words. "We can try again, if you want. We can try again, Charles."

He pulled away. "I have a patient, Amelia. Can we pl—"

She launched to her feet. "You're a doctor! You think you save people, but you bring home death every day! Why are you blaming me? Why do you think you're the only one grieving? It's *your* fault our family is gone. It's *your* fault that I have to make Sunday meals for two men who sit there like gravestones. Hate your father for all your days, but that's why our children keep dying. That's why everything you touch dies!"

Her words blasted through him like a hail of bullets, and the strength drained from his legs.

A hoarse cough and a clearing throat from the front door snatched their attention. Hank stood in the doorway, his mouth tightened like a line of barbwire, with Oliver's arm draped across his shoulders. Oliver barely managed to remain upright, his face sheet-white.

Hank said, "You got a minute to look at your patient, Doc?"

Charles rushed across the room and took Oliver's other arm. They guided him to a cot to lie down. After easing him back, Charles peeled open Oliver's shirt, relatively clean and on loan from one of soldiers, and examined the fresh blood on the bandages. "His suture came open. Damn it. Dad, get me a needle and thread and some forceps. And wash your hands first."

Amelia stepped around them all, her face hard and cold as stone, and went outside.

Hank scowled after her, then said to Charles, "I'm not your nurse," before following her outside.

Charles sighed, shook his head, and felt happy they were both gone.

III

Hank followed Amelia down the wooden sidewalk for a short stretch, until his longer legs caught up with her. "You hold it right there, little girl."

She spun on him. "I'm not a little girl."

He leaned over her. "Enough. Bullshit."

"I beg your pardon!"

"A gutshot man is dying, and you choose now to have a conniption fit at the only doctor around?"

His words seemed to circle past her, unheard. "Does Charles have a mistress? Is there another woman?"

"Did you hear a word I just said? That's a damn fool question. Charles doesn't have that kinda thing in him, and you should know it."

"How would you know what he's got in him?"

"He's my son!"

"Your son? You don't know him! You don't know anything! The things he's said to me!"

He lowered his voice. "I hear the things you say to *him*!"

"The way he's pulled away. He hasn't slept in our bed since the girls—"

He stuck a finger at her breastbone. "When people lose a child, much less two, they're supposed to stick together, not tear each other apart! For a preacher's daughter, you might show a little more of that forgiveness—"

"You don't get to lecture me, Hank Zimmerman! You haven't a leg to stand on. He grew up watching you walk away from his mother, over and over again. The only father he ever knew was the one who took a switch to him. He's always been a softhearted man, and you've been trying since he was a boy to beat that out of him. To make him a *man*." She sneered the last word.

Rage boiled up in him, and he looked into her frost-blue eyes for several long heartbeats. His voice dropped lower. "You don't know a goddamn thing. Go mind your place and let the doctor do his job."

Hank spun on his boot heel and stalked away from her, wondering what in the hell his boy had ever seen in such a harpy. Talking to Charles and Amelia lately felt like trying to walk through the wreckage of a house fire. He had his own business to attend.

IV

Amelia did not go home. She could not. The Methodist church in White Pine was not the Lutheran church her father had raised her in, but it was the only house of God she could stomach. Reverend

Caldwell was a mild, even-tempered man, if a bit too softhearted. The only other church in down was Catholic, and she could not abide a religion so steeped in idolatry. Perhaps someday, White Pine would grow large enough to draw a good, stolid Lutheran congregation as well.

Hank's harsh words settled in her heart and just sizzled. "'Mind your place,' indeed! You old fool!" She took the handle of the church door and let herself in.

Inside the church, the air was cold and dim. Sunlight filtered through the tall, narrow windows, across dark hardwood pews. The cross hanging above the altar on the whitewashed wall was fashioned of dark-stained knotty pine. It loomed over her as she seated herself in the front pew, clasped her hands in her lap, and let the tears come.

Hank's admonishment lay heavy inside. He was right. She was selfish. Charles' profession required him to rise above petty concerns and work for the greater good of humanity, of his patients. Life and medicine must forever relegate family to second-class concerns. She knew this to be true. She had known this would be the case when she accepted Charles' marriage proposal. He had been so earnest, so idealistic, so kind-hearted, how could she have turned him down?

She hated him for that.

She had thought that being a doctor's wife would be much like being a preacher's wife. Her mother had been a woman of grace and forbearance. But her father was a man of the spirit, and her husband was a man of science, and there was little connection between them. Now, medicine stood between them like a wall a hundred miles high and stretching to both horizons. There was always some sick child to take Charles away just when Amelia needed him the most, some appointment that was more immediate, more pressing. So what could she do but play the role of the doctor's dutiful wife? Forever smiling politely, forever the upstanding matron of the community, forever forced to push her heart aside while he went off to heal others.

She needed healing, too, and where was he?

But Hank was right. She had said so many horrible things to Charles, things born of anger and hurt and fear. All she wanted was for him to acknowledge how she felt—well, that was not all, but it would have been start. She wanted him to tell her everything would be all right again someday, even though it was a lie. The holes inside her shaped like Eva and Josephine would never be filled. She wanted him to *listen*.

She also felt hypocritical for her angry words at the Heavenly Father earlier, like an ill-behaved child now about to beseech her father for candy.

She clasped her hands on the rest before her. The air hung still and expectant with the scent of wood and old hymnals. Shadows from the vaulted ceiling draped the cross.

"Dear Lord, what should I do?"

For a long time, she sat silently, listening, squeezing her fingers until they went red, then white.

And then, she knew.

V

Charles stood for a moment overlooking Oliver McCoy, at the sutures torn by a wagon ride that had been a little too rough in spite of Charles' best efforts. Damn Wilson, but Oliver needed a night in a soft bed, and the infirmary would have improved his chances. Then again, what if he had been infected by the same mysterious disease that had taken hold of Ferrell, Lieutenant Cox, and Private Garrett? Rabies? Some sort of communicable madness? An even worse thought sent a chill down his spine: had Charles brought a new deadly epidemic to town in the body of this poor wounded man? Isolation was definitely in order to prevent any possible spread of infection.

Oliver wandered in and out of consciousness. Fresh, dark blood trickled from the corner of the wound. Something about the coagulated blood looked wrong. It was too dark, brown verging on black, like a crust of soot. Charles had never seen anything like it.

Anger held him in place, seethed in him, thumbs clenched in trembling fists.

How dare she talk to him that way! She knew precisely how to hurt him in the worst possible way, and she had just done it—

84

when he was in the midst of trying to save a man's life. Every word she spoke had been carefully chosen to pierce him like a dagger slipping between his ribs, and then twisting, twisting, *twisting*. He deserved none of it. He was a good man.

But was he a good doctor?

He wondered how the Lakota cast out an irreconcilable spouse. Divorcing Amelia was out of the question; they had made their vows before God and their families and everyone they knew. The thought of breaking those vows felt like some sort of monumental failure, filled him with such shame that he immediately cast the thought away. He knew she was grieving still, and people said terrible things when they were in pain. If he were a better husband, more attentive, she would come around. It was his fault, after all, that things between them had gone so far astray, with his being gone so often and working such long hours. He had not paid enough attention to her, lost in his own grief—and lost in guilt at their daughters' deaths. He must do what was right, and never mind the cost to himself. That's what his father had taught him.

Oliver stirred again, and the trickle of blood freshened. Charles retrieved a needle and thread to re-suture the corner that had torn open. He moistened a cloth and sponged at the strange crust around the edges of the wound.

A sudden stench jumped up and pummeled his nostrils. He jerked back, hand against his nose. It was a smell that he had encountered once before, when he was removing the bullet in Oliver's belly. The stench was almost like decomposition, but more intense, sharper, and it was far too soon for the wound to be gangrenous.

He had thought himself hardened to the stench of decomposition, but this was worse somehow, as of a slaughterhouse in high summer. What would the massacre site have smelled like after three days in the blistering prairie summer, rather than winter?

He shook such thoughts away.

Oliver moaned as Charles swabbed the wound with alcohol. How much pain must the young man be experiencing now in his half-conscious state?

Charles prepared a potent injection of morphine and administered it to help Oliver sleep. With the next few passing moments, Oliver relaxed onto the bed, and his breathing deepened.

As Charles watched Oliver succumb to the morphine, a strange soporific sensation washed through him, as if he had just drunk a healthy dose of laudanum himself. He wove on his feet for a moment, legs and shoulders tingling.

He sank onto a stool—it was that, or he would fall—and sat there for several minutes, putting his face in his hands, trying to swallow the lump in his throat, squeezing his eyes shut against tears he could not explain. For a few moments, he let the tears come and his nose run, like a locomotive releasing just a touch of steam before sealing back up and charging down the tracks.

He needed some air, or perhaps something to eat. He had not eaten anything since a stale lump of bread and a jolt of coffee before leaving town this morning. Strangely, he had not been hungry all day, and his belly still felt like an echoing chasm.

VI

The jailhouse was one of two brick buildings in White Pine, the other being the bank. Hank had left his Army buckboard sitting out front. The jailhouse was situated across the street from the saloon, a placement he had lobbied for as the town was being built, a bit of a deterrent to the buffalo hunters, itinerant prospectors, wild cowboys coming in from cattle drives, and others of the unsavory element that found haven in the wide open spaces of the West.

He opened the jailhouse door and stepped up beside his desk. Where the hell was that whiskey? In the drawer, right where he left it. He poured himself a slug in his cup, sat, and put his feet up on the desk with a groan. His back and shoulders were a knotted net of burning aches from carrying Oliver so far this morning. They would be giving him flaming hell tomorrow.

A stirring in the jail cell caught his attention. The figure stretched out on the cot lay with a hat over his face.

Hank said, "So. You're gonna tell me something now, Jimmy."

The figure spoke from under his hat. "I am the fount of all wisdom, Marshal."

"Tell me how do some people have great brains but lack the sense God gave a goat?"

"Are you meaning someone in particular?"

"Never mind."

Jimmy sat up on the cot, re-situating his hat. "Now you tell me something. Does this hotel have a bath and whores?"

"Fresh out of whores, but I can piss on you if you like. I checked the town charter."

"How about a line of credit for the faro table?"

Hank could not hold back a grim smile at Jimmy's audacity. "You got caught robbing a stage filled with marshals two days after you steal $15,000 from a bank in Omaha. Is 'idiot' too big a word for you to understand the shit you're in?"

Jimmy stood and thrust his arms through the bars, clasping his hands, as relaxed as if he were leaning on a poker table. His eyes glinted with youthful mischief. "First off, they wasn't marshals. They was Pinkertons. Second, they was on *top* of the stage."

What was a fresh-faced kid like this doing robbing stages anyhow? Jimmy looked like he should be escorting a new bride to Sunday service. Hank shook his head and said, "That doesn't change your living arrangements, does it, Jimmy?"

"Fucking Wade told me that stage would be filled with old ladies and their quilting sticks. If I had a dollar for every time that asshole steered me wrong ... I wouldn't'a stopped that stage and asked for a ride in the first place."

Hank shook his head and drew a slow, incandescent sip of whiskey. "'Hanging Judge' McHenry gets here this week. Right now, I intend to recommend you as an insubordinate and uncooperative prisoner. Tell me where the money is, I might change my mind."

Jimmy turned his palms up and clunked his forehead against the bars with a sigh. "I told you I don't remember where the money is. I was drunk when I hid it."

"Admirable convenience."

Jimmy's unwashed brow wrinkled a bit, and he paused. "But what if I can tell you something you do want to know?"

Hank shot him a skeptical glare.

"I saw some bodies two days ago."

"Bodies?"

"Two days ago, I was camped along the river about ten miles from here. I went and took a piss and I saw this hole dug in the ground. And this hole was full of bones. Fresh, human bones. Not dry. Some of the meat on 'em was still fresh."

Hank put his feet on the floor and held his cup in both hands. "You sure they weren't critters?"

"I know what a goddamn human skull looks like. I tell you, put me right off my feed. And it weren't no proper burial."

"Injuns, most like."

Jimmy shook his head. "It weren't no Injun burial. A couple of them skulls had long blonde hair."

Hank gave him a long, searching look. Jimmy was a bank robber, most certainly a liar, but was he a storyteller? Was he clever to enough to just make up some wild tale and expect Hank to believe it? "If you are filling me full of shit, so help me I'll feed you to my hogs."

Jimmy raised his right hand with an expression of profound earnestness. "I swear on my momma's snatch. I can take you there."

Hank shook away an unpleasant vision of this kid's momma's nethers. "I'm whupped. We'll talk about this more in the morning."

"So, uh, how about some of that whiskey in the meantime?"

Hank shrugged and grabbed a coffee cup. He wiped out the dust and cobwebs and poured a dab for Jimmy.

Jimmy accepted it and saluted Hank, drank it, and sighed, smacking his lips with appreciation. "Much obliged, Marshal." He handed back the cup. "What about them whores?"

VII

All that was left was the potatoes.

Amelia drained the boiling water from the pot, careful not to damage their soft bodies. Charles did not like when the potatoes fell apart. He liked them firm, still within their reddish skins.

Reddish skins. Why was Charles so friendly to the Sioux? To be sure, they were a beaten, downtrodden people, deserving of a modicum of mercy, but they were heathens after all, each of them destined for damnation, unless they converted to the Word of God. Charles spent too much time among them. He should be here, among his own people. Too much contact with the heathens could put Charles' immortal soul in peril.

Unless there were other reasons for his absence—

After almost an hour of quiet reflection, a tiny voice in her mind told her that it fell to her to remind Charles that they were a family, that she was his wife, so she should start with being kind to him and doing what a wife should do. Her efforts at housekeeping and cooking had been sporadic at best in recent weeks. Both of them had been relying on gifts of food from their neighbors as comfort in their bereavement, or, more in her case, eating practically nothing at all. She had learned to accept the constant ache of hunger in her belly.

Nevertheless, her sharp words earlier with Hank lingered in her memory. She should have kept her fears to herself. A man like Hank would not understand. He was as hard and unyielding as a pebble in one's shoe, an irritant that could only be cast aside, never changed.

She wiped her hands on her apron and surveyed her handiwork.

Charles would enjoy this. She had not made him a full supper for … a while. Fresh bread, potatoes, green beans canned from last year, and the entire house was redolent with the succulent aroma of roasted chicken. Fresh-churned butter, picked up from the creamery on her way home, and even a small jar of honey.

Yes, they would sit down together and enjoy a meal, and she imagined a conversation where Charles would apologize for being gone so much, and she would forgive him. And then she would tell him about the new life growing within her—had she been eating regularly, she would likely be showing a bulge already—their chance to start a new family, to fix things. She guessed it now at about two-and-a-half or three months, conceived on a rare night when all was well between them, before the girls fell sick, before the entire world fell into bleak, dismal wreckage.

But perhaps there was hope for them now.

And maybe, just maybe, they would smile again. She remembered what it was like to be happy, but she could not find the path toward it these days.

She heard a footstep on the porch, and the door creaked open.

Charles stood in the doorway, his face blank, unreadable as he regarded her. She had somehow lost her ability to read him.

She sat down across from Charles' empty chair, trying to muster a smile, almost succeeding.

Charles took off his hat, placed it carefully on its hook, set down his medical bag. His eyes scanned the table, and she searched them for signs of pleasure, appreciation, or appetite. When there were no such signs, her stomach turned cold. Conscious of her scrutiny, he approached the table, and rested his hands on the back of his chair.

His eyes went to each of the other two chairs, the empty chairs.

She spooned some green beans onto his plate, then some onto hers. Charles loved green beans.

He pulled his chair out slowly, taking his time to sit. He rested his hands on the table.

Amelia took a slice of fresh bread, still warm, from the bowl, and extended the bowl to Charles. He looked at his plate, and the bowl hung there in his hand. She placed the bowl down on Charles' half of the table and then reached for the potatoes. They were cooked to perfection.

He took a small piece of bread, with a languor that seemed every movement was a step toward a gallows. He dropped it on his plate and stared at it.

Her face became a stiff, porcelain mask of control. She would *not* admonish him tonight. She wanted to be able to forgive him.

Charles exhaled, a long shuddering sound, folded his hands, and covered his face as though to pray.

Amelia folded her hands. "Dear Lord, thank you for this—"

Charles pushed his chair away from the table, got up, red-eyed, his gaze floundering about the room as if he wanted her to have no place in his field of vision. His mouth worked as if he were trying to speak, but no sound came out.

Then he left the house.

For a long time, Amelia sat, while the potatoes cooled, and the chicken turned chewy, and the green beans lay limply in puddles of half-congealed butter.

She refused to cry anymore.

VIII

Katie Delacroix turned the knife over in her hands, admiring the scrimshawed bone handle again, then went back to absently whittling the dry stick she had found. She was still amazed that her father had given it to her.

After they had finished gutting and skinning the jackrabbit, Pa had looked at the bloody knife for a long moment, then wiped it clean with his handkerchief, and handed it to her. "Don't tell your ma." His eyes held hers until she sensed a meaning deeper than the idea that her mother would not approve of giving Katie such thing as an Indian knife, but she could not fathom that meaning. Nevertheless, whatever it was felt like something she should go nowhere near.

Evening had settled over the land. She gave those clouds on the horizon a wary look, too, happy for the moment that it had stopped coming closer. The storm just hung out there and built itself, higher and higher, with towering clouds obscuring the sunset.

The cry of a mourning dove echoed over the grass, punctuated by the crow of a cock pheasant. The only other sounds were the wind and the scruff of the currycomb as Emily raked it through the Porky's coat. The draft horse shivered with pleasure after a long day in the yoke. Pa had just plowed another plot of what would be a cornfield this summer. He had said earlier, "Maybe this year, Lord willing, we'll have four kernels to rub together instead of just two."

Then their mother's voice echoed from the door of the house. "Katie and Emily! For the last time, come to supper!"

Katie called back, "Coming, Ma! We're finishing up with Porky!"

Emily looked at Katie with a sour face. "You're supposed to be helping me."

Katie ignored her and admired her knife.

Emily said, "Where'd you get that knife anyway?"

"Pa traded it from the Injuns up at the agency."

"What did he trade?"

"Two chickens."

Emily put down the currycomb and unbuckled the bridle from Porky's head. "That knife is worth a sight more than two chickens."

Katie shrugged. She was tickled to her toenails to have it, even though the idea of Pa cheating some starving Injuns did not sit quite right with her.

Again from the house, more shrill this time. "Girls!"

Katie called back. "Yes, Ma!"

Porky tossed his head and whinnied.

Emily stroked his face. "Easy, Porky. You're so skittish. You ought to be tuckered out."

Katie smirked at her. "Maybe 'cause you stink."

"Shut your mouth! I don't neither. Ain't nobody breaks wind like you."

Katie leaned over and cracked off a loud fart, then giggled.

Emily gave her the usual withering glare. "Oh, that's so ladylike!" Emily giggled more.

The horse jerked its head and shuffled. Since when did a horse mind people farts? Katie approached Porky, stroking his warm shoulder.

Ma's voice came again, "This instant!"

Emily glanced nervously toward the house, then said to Porky, "I'll bring you a sugar cube after supper."

Katie slid the knife back into its fringed leather sheath and stuck it in the back of her britches. "Let's go before Pa gets mad." She climbed over the fence. From the other side, she looked back and saw that her sister had not moved. Emily stood staring off toward the storm, with a strange, frightened expression on her face.

IX

The wind blew swirls of dust across Charles' feet as he walked the dark streets of White Pine, hands thrust deep into his trouser pockets. The air cut through his vest, tightening the flesh on his arms, but he hardly noticed it, too caught up in thoughts of despair and empty wishing. The thought of another single word of conflict with Amelia filled his gut with a sour gobbet of dread. He was sick of it. The look on her face when he had walked out was one that he knew too well. There would be hell to pay for walking out on her supper.

The town had shut down for the day, except for the saloon. Most of the respectable folk were home at the supper table, or so he thought, until he spotted lights burning in the Methodist church at the end of the block. By the time he reached the corner where the church lay, the front doors had opened, and a handful of dark silhouettes were filtering into the night.

He paused near the gravel path leading toward the church entrance and greeted the members of the congregation as they dispersed. Reverend Caldwell had apparently been successful in his drive to inaugurate a new weeknight Bible study group. Charles had known most of the congregation members since he arrived in White Pine; they were fine, upstanding people. He had never been a devoutly religious man himself—his training as a doctor and a man of science had proven an untenable mix with whatever religious instruction he might have had as a younger man—but Amelia had insisted.

The congregation had been terribly kind to him and Amelia in all their recent tragedy. Amelia had not had to cook for a solid two weeks after the funeral, with people bringing more food than a family of ten could have eaten. Since neither of them could eat, most of it had gone bad on the kitchen table. Reverend Caldwell still called on them occasionally, if less frequently now, and while Charles had always found him a kind, personable sort, Caldwell's incessant proselytism often wore thin.

After the attendees dispersed, a familiar silhouette stood in the yellow square of church door. Reverend Caldwell waved to Charles.

Charles found his feet turning up the path and approached.

The reverend smiled. "Good evening, Doctor Zimmerman. A pleasant night, isn't it?"

Charles looked toward the west. "There's a storm coming. A big one."

"Well, perhaps the Lord will send it off in another direction before it reaches us."

Charles nodded noncommittally.

"What is it, Charles? You look like a world of troubles rests on your brow."

Charles almost laughed. Where could he even begin? He took a deep breath, let it out. "A day or two of relentless tribulation I can bear. But it has been weeks, months, since I slept the night through."

"Since the girls—"

"No, before that. Since the troubles with the Sioux."

"It's admirable that you care so much for their welfare. They are God's children—"

"It was the massacre, and what I saw up there by Wounded Knee Creek, I can't get those things out of my head."

"The Lord works in mysterious ways. There must have been a reason—"

"A reason for soldiers to shoot pregnant women in cold blood?" Charles snarled.

The reverend held up his hands. "The Lord does not control the actions of men. He gave us free will, and the world is full of the Devil's influence. There can be no question that Satan had a hand in that day, seizing upon the minds of those soldiers."

"I apologize for my vehemence, Reverend. It has been a long day of murder and prejudice."

Caldwell stood aside and gestured toward the door. "Would you like to come in and discuss things further? I still have some tea and biscuits left from the Bible study meeting."

Charles thought for a moment.

Caldwell said, "Sometimes, the time is for comfort. Sometimes, the time is for anger and outrage at the evils of world, so we must fight against them. Injustice must be stamped out by courageous men wherever it is found—"

"Injustice is taking two innocent girls from a world that needed them!" Charles snapped. "Am I to stamp out God, Reverend?"

"There is no need to be sacrilegious, Charles. Eva and little Josephine are at Jesus' bosom now. I know you miss them."

"I miss them terribly." The words felt like shreds of flesh in his throat.

"Fear not, they are not suffering anymore and never will again. In the end of days, the Son of God will come down again from heaven, and we will be reunited with all our lost loved ones, and after the great upheaval, we will come together, forever young, blessed with an earth that has been renewed, and sing the praises of the Father to the music of the heavenly host."

Charles sneered. "When will that be, Reverend? How long must we wait?" He recognized his behavior as unacceptable, but he did not care. He would apologize to the reverend someday, but not today.

"The Bible tells us it will be any day now," the reverend said patiently. "Perhaps tomorrow. Perhaps next year. But the End Days are coming. Ah, forgive me. I see your skepticism. This is not the right time to wax apocalyptic. We were reading Revelations tonight." The reverend scratched his thin gray hair. "For everything there is a season. This is a season for forgiveness. Amelia was here earlier tonight, sitting alone and praying. I saw her but didn't wish to disturb her. Forgive me if I'm intruding, but is everything well between you and your wife?"

"No."

The reverend nodded. "Perhaps the two of you could come and talk to me. You both have much healing to accomplish, but with the Lord's aid, everything could be fine very soon. Love and forgiveness, Charles."

Healing indeed. Charles shoved his hands deeper into his pockets. "Thank you, Reverend. We'll see."

"Good night, Reverend." Charles shuffled away.

The reverend called after him, "Good night, Charles."

Physician, heal thyself, Charles thought as he wandered back toward home. Alas, he hadn't the slightest inkling how to begin.

X

Amelia's face was wet with tears. Night blackened the parlor windows. She sat at the writing desk her parents had given her as a wedding gift, which had come with her and Charles all the way from Philadelphia. It was lovely; polished cherry wood fashioned in elegant lines and curves with brass knobs and hinges.

What would it look like smashed into kindling?

The house was empty. Yawning, silent, vacant.

She opened one of the desk's many nooks, withdrew a fountain pen and a slip of stationery.

Almost of its own accord, the pen's nib began to slide across the paper. She wondered what the note would say.

When it was finished, she looked at it as if someone else had just written it, read it over and over, as if to assure herself that it was true.

> *"Dearest Mother, I have earnestly tried. I have prayed and prayed on this, but I can stand it no longer. I am taking the next stage out of White Pine on Saturday to the train station in Valentine. I will see you soon. My love to you and Papa."*

She folded the letter and placed it in an envelope. Tomorrow, if her courage held, she would take it to the telegraph office.

XI

Red Horse sat before his fire, its warmth on his face, the chill of night descending on his back. He savored the pain in his face, the taste of blood in his mouth, the swelling in his cheek. A strange part of his heart thrilled again that he had stood his ground against the soldiers. His warrior spirit stirred in its slumber, like an old man in sleep.

His belly had stopped growling long ago, soon after he had given his portion of stale bread to a child who had gotten nothing tonight.

Women kneaded meager balls of breadroot flour in portions too small to feed a single person, much less a family. Thin soup bubbled in a few pots around the camp, but instead of buffalo meat in the pots, there were a few slivers of bacon. They would not have to sup on the few scrawny field mice and rabbits that had been scrounged from the area that day. Those could be saved until tomorrow.

The Bluecoat known as Weatherly was an enemy, but he was a man of honor, a man of courage. The same could not be said of the other Bluecoats.

Red Horse thought of the days of his youth, when food had been sacred, and every meal had been filled with reverence and ceremony. He thought of feasts of buffalo meat and venison, summer berries, wild onions, when the land had given them everything they needed. Now, the white men had outlawed the Old Ways, taken their children away to teach them how to be white, slaughtered all the buffalo, driven out or destroyed the rest of the game, given them maize and wheat to plant, shoved Bibles into their hands, and demanded that they learn to read such things.

Behind him, a bout of coughing erupted from his tent, the harsh, racking sounds of a breast being torn apart from the inside, and then a quiet groan.

Other coughing echoed around the camp.

He thought of the surge of hope that had washed through the tribes a year and a half ago as the Ghost Dancers had told tales of miracles, and the Messiah coming in the body of Paiute medicine man to teach the Ghost Dance to all the tribes. And the dance would bring back the spirits of all the dead, and restore unity and harmony to all the tribes, and the earth would be renewed, giving rise to a time of plenty, and the white man would be wiped clean from the earth. It had been such a beautiful dream. Such a beautiful dream that his people had embraced it with both arms and held it close, and for a year they danced. Spotted Elk had danced with them. Sitting Bull had danced with them. Their dance had terrified the white man, and the Bluecoats had come again.

Now, all gone. Dust and bones. The spirits of the dead had not returned; there was no harmony among the tribes; there was no time of plenty; and the white man still stood tyrant over them.

He could not look around him at the sullen faces, the hollow cheeks, the shadowed eyes, the sunken bellies.

A carefully tended coal of rage and bitterness flared in his chest, and his teeth clenched. All would be made right when the Father returned. The day would come soon. He only had to survive until then. Born-with-a-Smile would be made well again, and young, and they would live with Quick Strike and their ancestors and relatives in a great buffalo-hide lodges in a land verdant and rich with game and free of the white man.

Thunder rumbled from the throat of the *Wakinyan tanka*, the snow-white bird flying behind the distant clouds, having ventured out from its home in the *He Sapa*, what the white man called the Black Hills. Lightning speared from its eyes. It sounded angry. Perhaps it was angry that his people had forsaken it for the Christian god.

Born-with-a-Smile's soft, ragged sigh escaped from the tent, a sound so different from the many nights of love they had shared. In those days, contentment. Now, despair and pain.

He stood, fists clenched. He must act.

XII

Little Elk spotted Red Horse striding purposefully through the camp, so she ran to catch him. Catching his arm, she said, "I want to thank you for stopping the soldiers. That was a brave thing."

"We saved you from much trouble. If the soldiers had seen your ceremony, they would have taken you away. You were foolish."

"I had a vision. The spirits spoke to me."

His eyes brightened. "What did they say? Did they say when the Father is coming?"

In the hours since the ceremony, her vision had consumed her thoughts. However, the meanings of her visions seldom came clear immediately. Often, subsequent dreams built clarity like a sand painting trickling into place. But, more than any dream she had ever experienced, this one sent cold rushes through her blood.

She said, "I am still listening to their whispers for the wisdom of the vision. But they said nothing of your Messiah."

"He will be the savior of all!" Red Horse pointed at the storm in the west. "He could be riding that storm to come here even now!"

Distant thunder rumbled across the countryside. The storm hung there on the horizon, masking the stars in a towering column of cloud.

"Brother, I Dreamed of a storm, but the storm was not the Son of the Great Spirit. It was Iya, the brother of Iktomi the Trickster. Iya is the Camp-Eater, the Destroyer." The terror of her dream washed through her afresh. She had *been there* in that lodge, watching the child's skin—a white child with golden hair—slough away to release the cyclone.

Red Horse's face darkened. "The Evil One."

"Iya comes in cyclones and eats entire villages. Sometimes he is evil, capricious, but what he destroys makes room for renewal." At that moment, she had been simply speaking, letting her thoughts fall from her mouth, but she realized she had said the wrong thing when she saw Red Horse's face.

Red Horse raised his arms to the sky. "Then let him come! Let him be the Father's harbinger!"

"No! You don't understand! What if we are to be destroyed?"

"Then we will all be reunited that much sooner. If we are all that stands in the way of the Father's coming, if we must be eaten by Iya to bring the Father here, let Iya come."

"Those Iya eats do not join our ancestors in the Happy Hunting Grounds! They are trapped in his black gullet forever!"

Red Horse took a deep breath and rubbed his swollen cheek. "The Son of the Great Spirit will entreat the gods on our behalf. He will not let those who dance the Ghost Dance be lost. Even Iya and Iktomi must bow to the power of the Son of the Great Spirit." A faint smile of satisfaction spread across Red Horse's scabbed lips.

Little Elk snatched Red Horse's wrist. "There is great evil coming, Brother. Please, listen to me!"

"I have listened to you. You have told me happy things. Now let me go. There are things I must do."

Her heart sank, and she released his wrist.

XIII

Charles made his way toward home, having completed a couple of circuits of White Pine's streets. Lights burned still within homes, but shadows on upper story windows bespoke many people readying for bed. He could not purge the cauldron of emotions from his mind, from his heart. Endless circles of despair, self-recrimination, doubt, guilt, anger, frustration, grief, all that on top of the gruesome mystery of the soldiers' deaths and fear that some heretofore unknown disease had come to town in the body of a gutshot young man.

Half of the sky had been swallowed by clouds, with silvery fringes glowing with moonlight at the edges of cloud. Such a massive storm, but slow moving. Lightning flickered at the horizon. The wind tugged at his hat, at his clothing, peppered him with grit from the street.

Even in the dark, every street and house in White Pine was as familiar to him as his own yard. He could have found his way home in his sleep, and, with his face downcast, was only vaguely aware that he was passing beside the house of Robert and Olga Teague and into the shadow beneath the boxelder tree, its branches still bare from winter.

Something soft squished under his foot.

He stopped and lifted his shoe with a moist squelch.

In the filtered starlight, a smudge of black glistened. Kneeling, he saw that it was part of a squirrel. The wind ruffled tufts of fluffy tail, but the legs and part of the pelt were gone; the head, spine, and part of the ribcage remained. The moment lingered as he considered this small animal's tragedy. How much death and violence had he seen today? What confluence of fortune had consigned this animal, with its small life, to the jaws of a larger creature that could only sustain itself by the squirrel's destruction? To the predator, it was simply food. Humans were the world's supreme predator, with their weapons and their machines and their brains and their boundless, relentless appetites. But what were they without those things? What were they, fleeing before the charging lion or surrounded by the pack of wolves? Meat, just like the squirrel. Perhaps its flesh had fed a hungry dog or perhaps a tomcat. In the jaws of a lion, all of a human being's hopes and dreams and inspirations and loves and family became as nothing; everything he had ever been, ever would be, a masticated gobbet of meat in the lion's belly.

Such morbid thoughts.

A small shifting sound in the branches above drew his gaze upward. A black mass sat on a bough, leaning against the main trunk. Two thin legs dangled.

"Hello?" Charles said.

A small, shadowed head turned toward him. "Hello," said a child's voice.

"Is that you, Jacob?"

"Yes, sir. Hello, Mr. Zimmerman."

"What are you doing out here in the tree?"

A moment of hesitation. "I don't know. I just like it out here I guess."

There was a strange timbre in the boy's voice. Charles stood up to get a closer look. Jacob sat with practiced ease on a bough perhaps ten feet up. "Is everything all right?" Charles said.

The boy did not answer. Jacob and Eva had been schoolmates, and occasionally playmates when their families met for social occasions. All Charles could see of him now was the crisscross of suspenders over the white shirt back, a pale neck and shock of pale hair.

"Perhaps you should come down and go inside," Charles said.

Robert Teague's voice came from inside, harsh and angry. "Where is that little rapscallion?"

Jacob sidled closer to the tree trunk, head bowed.

Olga's voice said, "Calm yourself, Robert, you'll frighten him."

"He ought to be frightened! If he doesn't turn up this instant, he is in for a thrashing!"

The boy's head hung lower.

Charles said, "Jacob, are you in trouble?"

Jacob shrugged.

Something crashed inside the house.

"Robert!" Olga gasped.

Robert Teague had always been a civilized man, a fine, upstanding man. Charles sensed the boy's fear. "Jacob, what do you say I go and speak to your father, and you go inside and speak to your mother? How would that be?"

The boy's head cocked as if considering this.

"Come on down, and just wait here for a moment," Charles said.

Charles circled to the front veranda and stepped onto the porch. The Teagues' house was one of the finest in town, two stories with stained glass in the front door, a broad veranda with a porch swing, beveled glass in the parlor windows, fine lace curtains, and fresh whitewash.

The shouting from somewhere inside continued until Charles took the knocker and rapped three times.

After several moments, Robert grumbled within, "What the devil? At this hour?"

Robert peeked through the curtains. A strange expression tightened his face when he saw Charles. The door opened.

Robert cleared his throat. "Good evening, Charles. This is a late hour for calling."

Charles realized that he had no idea what he should say, and the words stumbled over themselves in his mouth. An unfathomable weariness stole over him. "My apologies, Robert. It's just ... I was just passing by and ..."

"Well? Spit it out man." Robert's mustache was usually waxed and teased, but now hung limp over his mouth, stealing his habitual cultured appearance, his hair also tousled as if he had either just aroused or been pulling at it. The anger simmering in his eyes set Charles back a step.

"I ... saw something near your house. A raccoon perhaps, or a 'possum."

"You don't expect me to *shoot* it do you?"

"I just wanted to warn you. I'm still looking into it, but there might be an instance of rabies in the area. Perhaps warn your children to stay away from animals, dogs and cats and such."

Robert chewed on his upper lip and looked away, eyes narrowing, considering.

Charles cleared his throat and continued, "You know, better to be safe than sorry. I thought I would warn you." He glanced toward the tree; Jacob had let himself down. The boy stood looking down at the squirrel and wiping his hands on his pants. Then he glanced at Charles and ran around the back of the house.

Robert took a deep breath and let it out. "I appreciate the warning, Charles. It has been a difficult year." His voice almost resumed its cultured tenor. He glanced over his shoulder at something inside. "All this trouble has everyone on edge."

"Yes, difficult."

"You visited the agency today, didn't you? How are the Indians?" Robert's tone did not indicate worry about their welfare, but their disposition, their level of discontent.

Charles said, "They are not well. There is insufficient food. They are sick from winter and tragedy."

By the end of Charles' utterance, Robert had already lost interest. "Quite a shame, that. Quite a shame."

Olga's voice filtered through the house. "Jacob, what is on your hands? Blood?"

A small, unintelligible reply.

"Well, go wash them this instant! Then get your bedclothes on!"

Robert glanced over his shoulder with a flash of anger.

Charles said, "Perhaps you and Olga would like to come by for whist, Saturday after next?" The thought of such a pastime felt meaningless at this point, but perhaps by then, he would be up for it. "Amelia would love to have you."

"I shall discuss it with Olga."

Quick little footsteps thumped up stairs.

Charles sighed. "Well then, I'll bid you good night, Robert. Sorry again for calling so late."

"Good night, Charles." Robert shut the door with a bang, driving Charles back another step.

Robert's voice came from inside quieter now, "Where is he?"

Olga said, "He's upstairs in bed, Robert!"

Heavy footsteps.

"Robert!"

Charles walked away. He could do nothing for Jacob now. What could the boy have done to evoke such ire? How often had he ran in terror from own father?

XIV

Amelia lay in bed, staring at the ceiling, her nightgown buttoned tight around her throat. The tears had dried for now, but they would be back. Charles would bring them with him. The bedcovers lay in disarray from the hour she had tossed and turned, her insides a sick wash of anger and sadness. Her life as a respectable woman would be over if she divorced Charles. She might as well be dead. But perhaps then her entire life would not be a lie. Endless spirals of suffering, with a decision nowhere to be found.

She heard Charles' footsteps downstairs, moving softly through the house, as if afraid to wake her.

As if there were any chance of sleep tonight. She remembered her dream of two nights past, so steeped in fear and violence and bizarre depravities that she could recall few details, except blood, and the taste of raw meat.

The stairs creaked under Charles' feet.

What had shocked her the following morning was that, as horrific as the dreams had been, they had not awakened her. She would never admit this to anyone, but she had reveled in them, awakening afterward with the vague yearning to go back; at least in the dreams, the vast emptiness of her heart had been filled, as it had not been in a very long time.

The bedroom door opened, and Charles came in. He glanced at her, surprised to see her wide awake. Their eyes met for a moment, and she thought for a moment that he must be able to see past the porcelain mask she had assumed. How could he not see the roiling storm of emotions just behind her face?

He undressed and put on his nightclothes, then slid into bed beside her, on his back, staring at the ceiling.

For a long time, they both stared at the ceiling.

He reached out and took her hand, gently, tentatively.

She considered how she felt about this. After a moment, she pulled hers away, and rolled onto her side away from him.

He lay still, his breathing so, so slow, so shallow, so tentative. Then he slid out of bed again, put his clothes back on, and did not once look at her before he departed.

XV

Red Horse knelt beside the track of flattened grass leading away from the tent village. Lakota cookfires and Army lanterns glimmered in the distance.

As night had fallen and no one had returned with any knowledge of the missing children, Red Horse had taken it upon himself to continue the search. Tonight he needed to feel the wind on his face and hear the rustle of the grass. It had not taken long for him to discover a track.

To his knowledge, this track was fresh, and not made by any of his people. There was no sign that the track had been made by game. The impressions were too heavy to be smaller than man-sized, too broad to be hooves, too light be horses. They were puma tracks perhaps, or bear, but he had never heard of them so far to the east. Pumas and bears held to the mountains.

He had crossed the outer perimeter of the Army patrols. If he wanted to, he could run for the horizon now, and the white men would never catch him. His wife was still in the camp, his family, everyone he had ever known—those that remained. He felt naked out here in the open without his horse. Without a horse, without his weapons, without his tribe at his back, what was he?

The track led him perhaps a mile from the camp, and he followed it, tense with alertness and silence.

Then he spotted a patch of grass that lay dark with wetness. He touched the stickiness, rubbed his fingers together, smelled it. Fresh blood.

XVI

Katie slid onto the chair at the supper table, wiggling until the knife handle stopped digging into her ribs. The table was situated in the center of the two-room sod house. After supper, the table would be pushed aside to make more room for Katie's cot and Emily's bed, with its mattress stuffed with cornhusks. Katie did not know why Emily got the nice bed, but Pa had insisted that it was proper for Emily, now that she was growing into a woman, to have a proper bed. Only a blanket separated the low-ceilinged main room, where Katie and Emily slept, from their parents' bedroom.

A lantern burned in the center of the rough-cut tabletop, illuminating the food that her ma plunked down on the table. Katie sighed. The rabbit stew of yesterday was so good that they had gobbled it up like coyotes, and now they were back to the same meal of recent weeks—a few chunks of cornbread that would not feed a good-size field mouse, potatoes with most of the mold trimmed off, and a few morsels of pickled pig's feet. One of the pieces of hock still had a tuft of hair on it. Her appetite skedaddled.

Pa sat there reading the Bible before supper, as always, and Katie fidgeted while they all waited for him to finish, as always. Then he snapped the Good Book shut, set it aside, and took his daughters' hands, and the girls took their mother's hands. He lowered his head and prayed. "Dear Lord, thank you for the food and family, and we pray for a dash of rain to get the corn started. Amen."

They all chorused, "Amen."

Clara turned away from the table and reached for the enameled pitcher of water near the stove. Katie pulled her hand away from the hard calluses of her father's fingers and noticed that he still had hold of Emily's hand, his thumb stroking the back of it. Emily's face turned the milky white of unripened sweetcorn. She pulled her hand away with a little too much effort. A wash of frost-cold queasiness splashed around in Katie's belly, and she suddenly had the urge to run for the outhouse.

Ma sat back down, and Pa's hand was back in his lap. Why did Katie feel so queer about this? It was just Pa's way; he was always telling Emily how pretty she was. Was it because of the powerful scared look on Emily's face?

Dinner passed in silence, as it always did. Pa would not countenance any idle chatter at the supper table; it was supposed to be for quiet reflection, not silly female prattling.

Later, when the supper dishes were cleared and the lantern put out for the night, Katie lay on her cot listening to the crickets chirping outside. It was the first night she had noticed them since the coming of spring. Her stomach was still queasy on account of the pig's feet hadn't tasted quite right. Beams from the full moon spilled through the lone window in the front of the house.

Emily lay in her own bed, a pale smear amid sheets and nightclothes and moonlight. Katie could tell from her sister's breathing that she was still awake. The sound of Ma's snoring snuck through the blanket covering the bedroom door.

Katie turned and tossed, unable to understand why the sickness in her belly would not go away. Then she heard a shuffling step, quiet, like a coyote sneaking. She opened her eyes and looked toward the sound. Her father's hand pulled aside the blanket curtain.

Katie tried to close her eyes, but could not help looking through slits. Emily gasped.

Her father crossed the small room, lifted Emily's bedcovers and slid into bed with her.

Katie squeezed her eyes shut then.

Emily whispered, "Papa, please—"

Pa's voice, quiet and persuasive, "It's all right, sweetheart. You know I love you very much."

The bedcovers ruffled.

Katie clutched her blankets over her ears, but sounds still found their way through.

Pa's breathing quickened. Emily whimpered and gasped. The bedcovers continued to rustle, settling into a kind of rhythm. Pa's breathing grew stronger, more ragged.

Then Emily's plaintive whimper. "Papa."

Hoping not to be noticed amid the activity, Katie slid against the wall and silently lowered herself to the floor behind the cot, covering herself with a dark blanket, squeezing her eyes closed.

Then she heard the quiet, distinctive squeak of the front door. The rough-plank door eased inward. Filthy fingers with long, sharpened nails snaked around the edge of the wood.

Katie's throat seized. The squeak of fear halted there, held there, and neither would her breath pass inward.

Enormous, hulking figures made of prairie grass whispered into the room. Their heads almost touched the ceiling. Moonlight limned them with silver and shadows.

Pa sat up. "What the—?"

Katie glimpsed a filthy arm, a hand gnarled like a boxelder branch, a strange club-like weapon as it rose and fell with a heavy thud against her father's skull.

Emily screamed.

A clawed hand snatched a handful of Emily's hair, jerking her with shocking speed off the bed and onto the floor.

Katie cowered behind the cot and hid within her blanket.

Her mother's voice came from the bedroom, groggy, "Who are y—"

Another blow cut her short.

Emily cried out, *"No!"*

Rough hands dragged Emily out into the night, her legs flailing in her nightgown.

Her mother's face hung bloody and slack as she was dragged outside by the hair, leaving a swath of blood behind her on the dirt floor.

Katie's scream stuck in her throat like it was glue.

Then her father's limp feet disappeared through the door, too.

And Katie was alone. The scream never came out.

XVII

Gray light turned the front windows of Charles' office into pale swatches in his blurred vision. He rubbed his eyes and leaned forward in this chair. The hard wood had turned his back and neck into knotted rawhide. Nearby, Oliver's ragged breathing proclaimed the spark of life still within. It had been a long night, fraught with howling winds, evil dreams, and Oliver's cries of pain. How much morphine had Charles given him before he finally slept?

Charles stood before the mirror, splashed water on his face from the basin in an attempt to clear the grogginess and erase the dark circles under his eyes. He gave a start. When had he started looking fifty? Perhaps it was just the patchwork look of a tortured soul.

His stomach rumbled with hunger. After the squalor and starvation he had witnessed on the reservation yesterday, the sight of so much food on the supper table for only two people had driven a spike of guilt into him so deep that he could hardly look at the food, much less eat it. He sighed at the thought of Amelia going to so much work, especially after it had been so long since she had made an effort to please him. Her timing could not have been worse. She could not have known the real reason he left the meal untouched, but he had no strength left to try to explain. He was always *explaining*, always *wrong*, always *cold*. Often these days, when he could muster an appetite, he just ate his meals from cold cans of vegetables and fruit. He did not know what Amelia ate lately.

In the mirror, a shadow appeared on the front door, a shadow that coalesced into Little Elk as she opened the door and came inside.

"Little Elk! What are you doing here?"

"I have a problem, Doctor, an ache." She stood by the door, tentative, hands folded.

He wiped his hands on a towel. "Well, what is it?"

She approached him. "I came all this way."

"What's wrong? Let me help you." Some part of him thrilled that he might be able to help her in some way.

Her eyes would not look at him, but she stood before him. If Amelia came in and saw Little Elk here, no amount of protest would save him. Did he even want to be saved?

Little Elk took a step closer, and he could feel the warmth of her. She took his hand in gentle, callused, truncated fingers and raised it to her face to touch her soft cheek. "It hurts here."

Something inside him leaped like an antelope shot with an arrow.

She moved his hand down the side of her throat, brushing through her hacked, ragged hair, across her collarbone, down her breastbone, to her heart. "And here."

He tried to work his mouth, to protest, to stop her. This was wrong, unseemly, forbidden. But his protests died in his throat.

She moved his hand down her belly, and her navel passed by under his fingers, and she squeezed them up against her groin. "And here."

He jerked his hand away. "I can't! We can't—! Not here."

Her eyes bored into his, and she guided him back into his chair. "We must."

She sat him down in the chair, straddled him, and hiked up her dress.

His feeble noises of protest waxed and waned, but formed no words.

She took his face and kissed him, her lips tasting of berries and … something else, something bitter and deep, like the breath of a Badlands wind. For a moment, he let his lips seek hers, locking onto them. Something howled within him with echoes of Amelia's voice, something with eyes as cold and flinty as his father's.

He pushed her off and stood. "I can't! I'm married!"

Vicious black claws sprang from Little Elk's fingertips; fangs sprang out from between her lips, her eyes empty and coal black. With a gurgling hiss, she swiped at his face with her claws, slashing open his shirt and laying bloody furrows in his chest. He caught her wrists, but they felt as rigid and inexorable as a wind-driven bough. Her fangs snapped at his face; spittle spattered him. She threw him against the wall, and the mirror shattered against his back. His breath exploded out of him, robbing him of pleas for her to stop. The washstand and basin raked across his ribs, and he fell on shards of mirror, a bouquet of pain exploding up his rib cage.

She lunged at him again. He threw up an arm in defense. His other hand fell across a long shard of mirror, closed around it.

A claw raked across his eyes. He brought up the shard and stabbed her in the belly. Blood like tar poured over his hand, but she did not react to the wound, raking his scalp with her claws, digging furrows in his skull.

He stabbed her again, his own crimson blood smearing the glass, and fought his way to his feet. The stench of the black ichor was the concentrated stench of a thousand charnel houses, a thousand morgues, a thousand crypts. He retched.

Her claws clamped onto his skull, his shoulder, and he found himself launched into the air toward the gray windows, crashing through into …

⊕   ⊕   ⊕

Gray light turned the front windows of Charles' office into pale swatches in his blurred vision. He rubbed his eyes and leaned forward in this chair, groaning, his heart hammering. The hard wood had turned his back and neck into knotted rawhide, and he still felt the lacerations on his hands, on his face, on his chest, but he was whole, uninjured. His neck was sheened in cold sweat. Nearby, Oliver's ragged breathing proclaimed the spark of life still within, but his endless cries of fear and pain had only fallen silent perhaps a couple of hours ago. Charles sat for a time, watching the door, expecting a shadow to fall across it. The street outside still lay in the shroud of sunrise.

He stood and moved to the mirror and washbasin, splashed water on his face to clear the grogginess and erase the dark circles under his eyes. The memory of the savage dream hollowed his eyes, made them look sunken and haunted. He thought he remembered a succession of such dreams going back into the night, but they were disappearing into fog.

A shadow appeared on the front door, and his breath caught. Heavy boots thumped on the sidewalk outside. The door opened, and Hank stepped through.

Hank said, "I got a problem needs tending to."

Charles stammered and froze.

"You got a problem, boy?"

Charles could not reply.

"Jesus, you look like someone just walked over your grave."

Finally, Charles found his voice. "What is it, Dad?"

Oliver stirred on the bed behind Charles, a ruffle of twisted bedclothes and the tang of cold sweat and blood. Oliver's voice sounded like a rasp dragged over dry wood. "Some water, Doc. Please."

Charles poured a cup of water for him and carried it to the bed. "You had a rough night."

Oliver slurped the water and let the empty cup fall. "I'd rather you put a nip of that laudanum in it, Doc."

"That might be two of us, but you've had enough for now. How are you feeling?"

"You tell me, Doc. I can't feel much of anything, but I reckon the pain is still there. Am I gonna die?"

"Of course not. You'll be fine in no time." Rarely in his life had Charles felt more like a liar. If Oliver had contracted some form of rabies from the coyote bites, he may as well start making arrangements for burial. Rabies was a horrible, horrible death. Better to die gutshot.

"I reckon I know a line of shit when I hear it. I heard you all talking about rabies yesterday."

"That was just speculation, Oliver."

"What about the others? They'll need buryin'."

Hank's books thumped closer, heel-toe, heel-toe. "I went out yesterday to bring their bodies back, but—"

Oliver clutched Charles' arm. "You'll see to me, too, won't you, Doc?"

"Don't talk like that. I've seen men recover from worse."

Oliver sagged back onto the pillow, squeezing his eyes shut. "What about the herd? I bet Pa is fit to be tied."

Charles said, "We'll send someone out there to get the herd."

Oliver turned his jaundiced gaze onto Hank. "Marshal, did you bring 'em back?"

Hank's face hardened. "As I was saying, I went out there, but ... Charles, did you send somebody out to pick up them bodies? Tell their kin?"

"Not yet. Why?"

Hank motioned Charles closer, and they walked away from Oliver. Hank whispered, "'Cause they was gone last night. The herd was scattered all over hell and gone. I found them boys' saddles. But no bodies."

"The bodies are gone, but not the tack? Who would take just the bodies?" Charles looked over his shoulder and saw that Oliver had fallen senseless once again.

"Goddamned Sioux, that's who! The boys were grazing the herd near the reservation."

"What are you saying?"

"Maybe we oughta string a few redskins up and see if they'll talk."

"Blaming the Sioux is patently ridiculous!"

"Ridiculous? What's ridiculous for a bunch of starving heathens? You got no idea what desperate people will do! You think they won't steal a heifer or two? Maybe them cowboys caught 'em up to no good." Hank snorted and shook his head, flickers of unpleasant memory behind his eyes. "I'll be gone a piece. Back this afternoon." With that, he spun on his heel and left.

Oliver stirred again. "Is it true what he said, Doc? About Injuns? About the other bodies? Dawson and Reese ought to have a Christian burial. My Pa oughta know about all this."

Charles went to his cabinet and opened it. "First, I'm going to check your sutures, then the whole county is going to know."

"It was Ferrell. There ain't no question. I just want you to know that. And none of us had been bit by any animal. You got to believe me, Doc."

"I believe you." Charles scratched his chin. Rabies seemed to be a likely culprit, but some of the pieces of the puzzle did not fit. The feeling of malaise settled deep, deep into his belly.

XVIII

Little Elk and Laughing Otter hide behind the hedge at the border of the school, listening to the bell toll for morning services. It is a bright spring day, with the grass coming green and the trees budding.

The Dream is more vivid than any day since her children were slaughtered.

Laughing Otter giggles. "We're going to get in trouble again."

"I know, but I would rather go without supper than sit through another sermon. You don't have to come with me."

"We have become sisters. Where you go, I go. I love listening to your stories."

"I love yours, too."

"Have you thought about how strange it is our peoples' stories are different and alike at the same time?" Laughing Otter says. "Until the white man came, our people had been enemies for a long time. Do you suppose they decided to fight over whose stories were right?"

The bell tolls again, harsher this time, demanding, discordant. If the nuns come looking, the two errant girls would get more than a scolding.

Laughing Otter continued, "The spirits and gods of your stories are different from mine. The stories are different. If the stories are really true, shouldn't they be the same? Maybe none of them are true."

"But they *feel* true!" Little Elk said. "Their words are like the blood of my people. My father told me there are many worlds, many truths. The voices of the spirits never talk a straight line. Truths are curved, my father says, like the hoop of my people."

The sky darkens. The bell peals again, but with such a deep underlying rumble that it hardly sounds like a bell at all. Little Elk feels it in her bones.

Laughing Otter nods and hugs her knees, tucked as they were within her dress. "Who was your father?"

"A very wise medicine man. He told me many of the old stories."

"Really? My grandfather was a medicine man, too! He was older than the rivers."

The sky falls so dark it is black as soot, as if a blanket just fell over the heavens. The hedge is gone, and they are sitting beside a wigwam near a vast lake, and the water is peppered with the hooting cries of birds resembling ducks but with pointed bills.

The thunder comes again in the soot-black sky.

Laughing Otter's face is fearful now. "This is a night when *they* come."

"Who?"

An old man stands over them, his lined, leathered face glowering, reproachful. "If little girls don't behave, *they* will come for you."

"Who?" Little Elk said again.

The old man said something unintelligible.

"I do not understand!" she said.

He shook his head. "Best not to speak their name again."

The snow falls around them in great, muffling blankets of white, thick and wet and clinging, covering the shore, gathering upon their heads and shoulders, and she finds herself terribly,

terribly hungry. The winter stores are gone. Inexplicable dread tightens her shoulders because she knows there are bodies under the snow.

There is meat under the snow.

"It comes often in winter," Laughing Otter says with her grandfather's voice. "But not always." She grins, and her teeth are sharp, her eyes black and empty.

Emerging from the darkness behind her, distant figures shamble through the knee-deep snow, gaunt figures with war paint on their faces. Members of the band who have gone missing in recent days, disappearing from their wigwams into the snowy forest. A bitter chill washes over her.

Little Elk gasps and scrambles away, piling into the canvas wall of her tent.

It is not war paint on their faces and hands.

She was alone now. The air of the tent was still tinged with the smoke of tobacco and sage. Her flesh tingled with the lingering touch of the Dream. Danger and a lurking fear quickened her heart, the near touch of something vastly awful.

It had been fifteen winters since she last saw her old friend Laughing Otter, the Ojibwe girl from a land of vast lakes. So many stories had they shared. On the day that Little Elk had been sent away from the school for refusing to pray before the crucifix, they had wept together in the dormitory until the nuns came for her.

A pang of yearning shot through her. Many times, Little Elk had written to the school to ask for a way to contact Laughing Otter, but her letters had received no response. She had no idea if her friend still lived. If only Little Elk could speak to her, she might be able to close the loop of truth.

Outside, she heard the camp stirring with another coming day of hunger and melancholy. The answers to her questions most often came when she occupied herself with other tasks. It was time to do so.

She would start by mending her clothes.

XIX

Jimmy tried to roll over onto the ache in his trousers, but the ratty jailhouse cot was too narrow. He pushed away Redfield Sue, felt her scarlet hair under his fingers, but she came again and told him how she really wanted to suck his cock but somehow could not cipher how to get it out of his pants, and his pants had no buttons and were somehow attached to him at the waist like they were glued on, so it was just stuck down there aching and bone hard, and she had such nice, meaty shoulders and thighs, and her wanton, whimpering voice, moist and luscious, started to turn hard and angry, and her claws grabbed the crotch of his trousers and ripped, and a cry tore out of him as his boner jumped to attention through the gash of fabric, and she grinned with sharp teeth and a vicious, hungry glint in her eye, and she snatched his cock with her fist, jerking the rest of him with it like it was a mop handle toward her gaping mouth, and he yelled and tried to kick her away from him, but she just used his pecker as a pivot and suddenly she was straddling his head, thighs clamping against his cheeks, and her ass looked like two succulent roast hams and he couldn't help himself, he—

"*Fuck!*"

He rolled face-first onto a hard wooden floor. A spasm of pain shot through his groin and tore a groan from him. He rolled onto his back, half gasping, half laughing.

Jesus Christ. That should go on his grave marker. *Here lies Jimmy Wright. Fell on his hard-on.*

His laughter was hoarse as a crow's on account of his mouth and throat felt like they were packed with dry cotton. He lay still for a few moments, tried to rub the sand out of his eyes, but they felt like he had just pulled an all-nighter in Omaha, except without the fun parts.

Redfield Sue was so named on account of the color and expanse of the thick patch between her legs, and when he last saw her at the brothel in Omaha, she was as sweet and soft as could be, not that snaggle-toothed witch who had just tried to bite the head off his pecker. The weight of an entire night of dreams lingered on his chest.

Hams.

"What the fuck was all that?" he whispered, and the sound of his voice echoed in the rafters of the jailhouse and gave him comfort that he was somehow back in real life.

Somehow his little feller was still standing at attention, straining against the inside of his trousers, throbbing like he was sitting in a roomful of naked titties, rather than alone in a jail cell in the ass end of the Dakota Territory—pardon, they called it South Dakota now. He struggled to his feet, trying to muster up even a drop of spit to wet his tongue, worked out his boner and stuck it through the bars toward the brass thunder mug in the corner. The morning piss usually took care of the morning boner, but somehow not today. He tucked it back in as best he could and sat on the edge of the cot.

God Almighty he had never had such a string of nightmares before. They were fading now into the black mist of forgetfulness, but the unease remained, like he knew a whole posse of angry Pinkertons was right over the next hill. For the last few nights, his dreams had been troubled in ways he could not remember, but he guessed that was because he would be lucky to be sent to prison, rather than simply hanged.

Unless he could escape, of course.

And he was hungry. His guts were an empty hole big enough to drop a whole steer into.

And his mouth was still so, so dry, dry enough to drink a gallon of horse piss.

A pitcher of water on the marshal's desk lay out of reach.

The old town marshal had not been here yet this morning, at least as far as Jimmy knew. Calling for someone to come would do no good. The people in this one-horse town wouldn't give him the time of day. All he could do was lie here and lament his sorry state.

Then, like a prayer answered, the jailhouse door swung open, and a woman in a frock so stained and threadbare it was practically gray came inside carrying a tray. She was maybe thirty, uglier than original sin, with mousy brown hair and huge titties out of proportion to the rest of her. She stopped just inside the door, wary as a rabbit.

Jimmy liked being a "dangerous fugitive."

Ravenous hunger roaring in his empty belly, he leaped to the bars.

She edged back. "The Marshal told me to bring you breakfast."

"Well, bless his Christian heart. Why don't you just tuck that tray in this gap here under the bars?"

"You ain't going to give me no trouble, are you?"

"Why would I do that? I am a perfect gentleman." And he was so goddamned hungry he would do anything to get his hands on that tray, even apply his little feller to a gargoyle like this one.

Something in his voice must have made her hang back.

"Look," he said, "I ain't gonna do nothing. I just want some breakfast and drink of water. Please, ma'am. You look like a good Christian woman, and you have my word as a gentleman." *Just gimme that goddamn tray!*

After another few seconds of consideration, she came forward, set the tray on the floor, keeping her eyes on Jimmy while she slid it through the gap under the cell door with her toe. He knelt and drew the tray in.

Now he got a good look at his breakfast. A chunk of bread the size of his fist, a hunk of fatty bacon and two pickled crab apples. Most other days he'd have thought this meager but acceptable. Today, though, he could have eaten five such helpings. He snatched up the tin cup of water and downed it one gulp.

"Please, ma'am, another. I'm powerful dry." He held his cup through the bars. "There's a pitcher there yonder."

She picked up the pitcher, extended her arms as far as they would reach, and poured him a new cup, which disappeared in another huge gulping draught.

"One more, please, ma'am."

She obliged, and he withdrew further inside the cell to pick up the food.

Gnawing on the chunk of bacon, feeling the grease moisten his lips and coat the parched soreness of his throat, he said, "Much obliged, ma'am, but tell me, what would I have to do to get another helping?"

"Of what?"

"Of everything."

"I'm sorry, sir, but that's all we can spare."

"Begging your pardon, ma'am, but what do you mean, all you can spare?"

"Well, the hotel is running low in the larder, and the grocer, too."

"Why's that?"

"I couldn't say." She shrugged. "Long winter maybe. People eating up all their stores maybe. Too long between grocery shipments maybe, but the last week it's been getting worse."

"What could I do for a slice of cherry pie?" He gave her the grin he'd used on Redfield Sue.

She blushed a little and smiled, revealing a barnside of brown teeth. "Nothing, except maybe go to Rapid City for it."

His heart sank more than he expected it to. "Well, I'm much obliged, ma'am. A feller gets powerful lonely and hungry sitting here by himself."

She sniffed at last. "Then perhaps you might shouldn'ta robbed that stage."

"A man's gotta eat, ma'am. My family was starving." Of course, he didn't have a family, but he always liked telling that story.

"Then they must be awful proud of you!" She *hmphed*, turned and departed without another word.

He watched her through the grimy window as she hurried away to whatever ugly-tree she dropped out of. Before she had crossed the street, his breakfast was gone.

Maybe he could talk the marshal into a nice leg of mutton.

XX

"Get out here, boy!"

The harsh voice dragged Red Horse from sleep. Born-with-a-Smile stirred, but did not awaken.

He shook his head to drive back exhausted sleep. Through the narrow gap under the tent flap, he saw Bluecoat shoes.

Maybe today would be a good day to die. They had come to take him away for leaving camp last night. Most of the night he had been gone, not returning from his searches until the quietest hours before dawn. But who could have seen him? Who would have turned him in to the Bluecoats?

His cheek and mouth still pained him from the blow of the rifle butt yesterday. One of his teeth felt loose. But it was just pain. He had learned to accept pain from boyhood.

He crawled out of the tent and found himself surrounded by three Bluecoats with carbines. "What you want?" he said.

One of them said, "Major Wilson wants to see you."

"Why?"

"Ask him yourself, boy." The corporal fixed Red Horse with a contemptuous glare. The other two shuffled their feet uneasily, their eyes flicking about as if the tents were a dense forest filled with enemies. All of them looked pale even for white men, with eyes shadowed as if they had not slept.

Red Horse gestured for them to lead him. Two fell in behind as they crossed the camp to the Major's office.

A porcelain cup of coffee sat in a porcelain saucer on Major Wilson's desk. The Bluecoat leader gave Red Horse a brief look of stern appraisal, then picked up the palm-sized silver pitcher of cream and poured it into the coffee. Red Horse did not understand the white man's love of such a distasteful drink.

Wilson took a sip, smacked his lips, and leaned back in his chair. For a long moment, he looked Red Horse up and down.

Red Horse could not see but felt the presences of the steel muzzles of the carbines behind him.

The oak-leaf Bluecoat said, "Do you know why you are here?"

Red Horse fixed his gaze on the wall above Wilson's head.

"I know you speak English." Wilson then spat a word that Red Horse did not know, but the contempt in it was plain. "You can either answer my questions or else this will be much more difficult and painful for you."

Red Horse did not move or look at Wilson.

Wilson stood up and unsnapped the flap on his holster, pulled the pistol and checked the cylinder. "There is no one here to see," he said. "Of course, if a wild, savage Indian attacked me for no reason, I would be forced to defend myself. Do you understand?"

Red Horse's gaze remained fixed. Today would be a good day to die. Born-with-a-Smile would be joining him soon.

"Perhaps if I brought your wife in here and shot her instead."

"What you want?" Red Horse said, bitterness coating his tongue.

"That fight yesterday. You need to control your men."

Red Horse's gaze almost wavered. "I am not chief."

"Perhaps not, but I am told the people here respect you. The other men listen to you. You must control them. I am asking you to control them. No one wants more needless bloodshed. That fight yesterday could have turned ugly very quickly. What was it about?"

"Women sing. They not sing for long time."

"Why were they singing?"

"We try be happy. We have no food. We must do something for spirit."

"So they were trying to lift their spirits."

"Yes. This is not crime."

"As long as that is all they were doing. Red Horse, this is your only warning. My men are already on edge. If there is any more trouble, you'll be the first in the stockade."

"But I am not chief."

"Perhaps it's time you were. Perhaps you should join the Indian Police. Be an example to your brothers."

Red Horse suppressed a snarl. "My brother is dead."

"You know what I mean, damn your heathen eyes."

Among the Lakota who resisted the white man's ways, the men who worked as police for the Bureau of Indian Affairs were often reviled as traitors, selling out their people for a place in the white man's world.

Wilson's eyes drilled into him, demanding an answer.

Red Horse spoke slowly, as if in deep thought. "I will think on this."

"You do that. You're dismissed."

As Red Horse stepped outside, his hands and arms tensed to fight, an urge more powerful than he had experienced since he was a young man.

The entirety of the western sky was an ominous black mass. The storm would come today. He paused to peer as hard as he could up into those caverns for any sign of the Father's presence. Perhaps the Father would come today, and he would never have to bear the contempt of a dog like Wilson ever again.

Nevertheless, he had to consider Wilson's words. Had he become the leader of the men in this camp? Did he want to claim that honor, that power, however meager it might be under the white man's yoke? He had never been a leader. He had always been happy to lend his strong arms to strong men like Sitting Bull. He had always considered himself the warclub, not the hand that wielded it.

Perhaps it was time to change that thinking.

XXI

Amelia stood outside the door of the schoolhouse. Little Coralee Dvorak, the last of her charges, scampered inside, a flurry of blonde pigtails and gingham, swinging her knotted kerchief full of lunch. The kerchief left the scent of bacon and spiced apples in the little girl's wake.

Could Amelia go through with what she intended? Spasms of contradictory emotions clutched her chest so tight it was like she was drowning in a well. She clutched her hands in her armpits, hugging herself tight. Was she willing to destroy her life, burn it to the ground, in the hope that it might be made anew?

In those quiet moments in the church yesterday afternoon, God had spoken to her, told her to make that sumptuous meal, and throughout her efforts she could think of little else except wishing that her daughters were there to share it all. And Charles had treated it, and her, like so much rubbish, as if he could not bear the sight of her. Even worse, he had had the nerve to try to touch her afterward. When she thought about that, her hands turned to fists.

And now, it was her duty to administer lessons to White Pine's children. The children who had not died.

Many times since she pried her gritty, swollen eyelids open this morning, she had had the thought simply to call off school for reason of "illness."

Today she would make preparations for her journey back east. Charles would never see her again. He would never know the child growing in her belly. She would take the Tuesday stage to Valentine, where she would board the train for Pennsylvania. Looking around at the town, she wondered if she would miss White Pine. She wondered what people would say about her, bearing a child with no husband in sight. Should she tell them that her husband was dead? She would have to be careful to bring no shame upon her parents.

She and Charles had been cornerstones of this town, Charles being the first and only doctor, and she being one of the few educated people in the area, and thus the natural choice for the town's schoolteacher. She herself had organized the fund drive to build the schoolhouse. Her blood was here, her reputation was here, her heart had been here for a long time.

Part of her was being ripped away.

She was the one doing the ripping.

But much of what she was ripping away had become a gangrenous, black cancer on her spirit. Like amputating a dead limb, it had to be excised for healing to begin. The Almighty would have to forgive her. Her parents would have to forgive her.

She did not care if Charles ever did. More likely, she expected him to rejoice and run to whatever whore was holding his attention. If he could not muster the courage, she certainly would.

The finality of it all shuddered through her.

She would never see White Pine again, or this schoolhouse, or any of these children. One of her great joys had been watching them grow into the people they would become, seeing them marry and swell with their own children. After she left, these children would forever remain in her mind the children she knew.

Just like Eva and Josephine.

The anger boiled fresh, and then the sadness, in their endless familiar dance.

She closed her eyes and took a deep breath to compose herself before she entered the classroom. The wind tugged at her hair, at her clothes, the endless, relentless prairie wind. During the night, the storm had advanced to cover most of the sky, and the sun still hung just beneath the front edge of immense gray shroud.

Within an hour, the sun would pass out of sight behind it.

A high-pitched cry of outrage erupted from inside.

She wiped her eyes dry and hurried through the door. There was Coralee, a louder wail of protest rising from her gaping mouth, tears beginning to glisten in her saucer-sized blue eyes, as she strained to reach around Alphonse Tucker for something he was keeping away from her. He was ten, three years older than Coralee.

"Give it back!" Coralee wailed.

Alphonse hunched over something. "Shut up!" His mouth sounded packed with something, chewing.

"Give it back! Give it back!" Coralee scratched at his shoulder. Alphonse tried to shrug her away.

Amelia hurried toward them. "Children!"

Coralee flinched back at Amelia's sharp tone, and at that moment, Alphonse spun on Coralee and punched her in the eye. Coralee tumbled backward over a bench with an expression of frozen shock on her face. Her head struck the floor with a sickening thud.

For two heartbeats, the schoolroom stood as a silent as a grave, with all eyes transfixed on little Coralee, all mouths agape, except for Alphonse's, which was packed tight like a squirrel's as he chewed, juice trickling down his chin. Coralee's empty kerchief hung from his other hand.

Then Coralee found her breath, and her wail tore through the schoolhouse to the rafters.

Amelia rushed to Coralee's side, and with the aid of Hilda Frankel, one of the older girls, helped Coralee to her feet. Coralee buried her face in Amelia's skirts and wailed and wailed, tears streaming down her face. Her eye and cheek were already beginning to swell.

Amelia began trembling and her knees turned to water. She clutched the edge of a desk for a moment to keep herself from wringing Alphonse's neck like a chicken's. When she could move again, she knelt beside Coralee, hugged her close, and stroked her hair.

Ten little voices peppered Amelia with fragments of the chain of events. Coralee had taken her seat as usual, and then Alphonse said he was hungry, had not eaten enough breakfast, and he just came over took her lunch and started eating it himself right then and there. Two preserved apples and a bacon sandwich.

The children all glared at Alphonse.

Alphonse swallowed the mass of food in his mouth. No trace of remorse burdened his face.

Virgil Smith said, "That bacon sure smelled good."

With Coralee sniffling into Amelia's sleeve, Amelia fixed her gaze upon the perpetrator. "Well, *Mister* Tucker, what do you have to say?"

Several children flinched away from Amelia.

Alphonse Tucker's mouth worked, but no sound came out.

Amelia gave the still-whimpering Coralee over to Hilda and stood before the boy. The kerchief fell from his fingers.

"I'm waiting, Mister Tucker," Amelia said.

"I ... I ... I'm s—"

Amelia rushed toward him and slapped him across the cheek, so hard that her hand stung.

He howled in pain.

As one, the students gasped.

Her belly became a sick ball of swirling black. She snatched his ear, pulling, twisting hard between her nails. He howled louder and dropped to his knees. She dragged him toward the front of the schoolhouse, where his howls mixed with screams. She flung him hands-first across her desk, scattering papers and chalk and lesson boards.

Her voice was low and cold. "Don't. You. Move."

He blinked through a fountain of tears, his face milk-white, eyes like eggs as he bent over the front of the desk.

From the desk drawer, she withdrew the smooth, polished slab of knotty pine as wide as her hand.

Alphonse sobbed. "Please, please, no, I'm sorry I'm sorry I'm sorry, please no!"

Girls in the room began to cry.

Amelia's hand clenched the handle of the paddle with all the fury in her being, and then she circled the desk, raised the paddle high, and started beating.

XXII

The horses shied away from Hank, even the one with Jimmy on its back. Daisy had run off yesterday with Hank's best saddle, and she had not turned up. It was possible she would still find her way back to town, but in the meanwhile, he had to use the old saddle that had made his ass hurt even when he was a young man and ride a jittery young gelding he had borrowed from Johansen the stable master.

Hank took the reins of Jimmy's horse and tied it to his own saddle.

Jimmy held up his handcuffed wrists. "Come on, Marshal. These things chafe something fierce."

Hank ignored him, went inside, and hung a sign in the window of the jailhouse: "BACK IN THE PM."

Stepping back outside, he said, "Maybe you'd prefer a hanging rope. I hear they chafe worse." He climbed into the saddle. "And by the way, just so you know, I'm a damn good shot." He pulled his shotgun from its saddle holster, a Winchester model 1887 12-gauge lever-action. There were not many of these around.

Jimmy hawked and spat. "I'm a perfect law-abiding citizen. Anything I can do to help balance the scales of justice. How's that gutshot feller? I heard him hollering last night."

"I guess that means he's still alive. Ten miles, you said?"

"Give or take."

Hank glared at him.

"Swear on Grandma's titties! Did you pack us a big lunch? I'm fit to drop dead from famishment."

Hank grunted, gave the gelding a nudge with his knee, and then a wary look to the storm. He sure as hell did not want to get wet.

XXIII

Charles finished tying the bandage over Oliver's sutures. The sharp scent of alcohol from his cleaning helped mask the sickly sweet smell of the wound. "There, Oliver. All set. Just rest now, and I'll bring you some breakfast when I come back."

Oliver gave him a wan smile. "As long as you're sure it won't leak back out."

Charles managed a wan smile, then went outside.

White Pine's main street stretched away from him, four blocks in one direction and three in the other. A normal day for all these people, a town of roughly forty total blocks, laid out neatly east to west and north to south, an imposition of geometric order on the chaos of undulating prairie, meandering creek beds, and endless grass. Many houses in town were still under construction, as land speculators built for the steady influx of people coming west, all of them oblivious to or callous of the plight of the Sioux on the nearby reservation, oblivious or callous to the dying man in Charles' office, a man with parents, with hopes and dreams, with a past, but little chance of future.

White civilization had an insatiable hunger for land. Homesteaders were chewing it up in 160-acre chunks, fencing it off, building houses from the land itself, with wood such a scarce, expensive commodity. The government annexed bigger and bigger chunks of land that had once belonged to the Indian tribes. Even on Lakota land, white men had carved gold rush towns like Deadwood and Lead in the Black Hills, a hundred miles or so to the west.

Charles had put on a good façade for Oliver's benefit, but the scarlet glow of infection had set into the wound. By the end of the day, the young man would be ravaged by fever, if he lasted that long. Another sunrise would bring untold agony.

Charles sighed and crossed the street to the Post and Telegraph Office. The doorbell tinkled as he stepped inside. Ernest stood and gave Charles a genial smile, crossing his fingers over a portly belly, porkchop sideburns making his round face look even rounder. "Good morning, Doctor Zimmerman. A pleasure as always."

"Good morning, Ernest. I wish it were under better circumstances. Are there any telegraph stations closer than this to the Bar-M Ranch?"

Ernest's face darkened at Charles' grim tone. "This is it, I'm afraid. Nothing between here and Rapid City."

"That's what I was afraid of. Is Sean free today? I need to send a rider out there with a message."

"He is."

"Get him, please."

With growing alarm on his face, Ernest left through the back door, leaving Charles with the scent of dust, paper, and copper wire. Approaching footsteps outside caught his attention, sharp heels on the sidewalk, a gait he recognized instantly. Unbidden, annoyance flared in him.

Amelia entered with a letter in her hand, her eyes snapping to Charles, widening, narrowing, hesitating, so many emotions cascading behind her mask, like looking at the outside of an iron-plate boiler.

She looked at the floor. "Oh. I ... I didn't know you were here."

Charles shuffled his feet and scratched his right sideburn. "Well, I have to send a telegram to the county sheriff. There is some serious trouble brewing."

"Can your father handle it?"

"He's off somewhere now, and I need to spread the word."

She crossed the room as if her legs were made of wood and placed the letter in the box on the counter labeled "OUTGOING." Her fingers lingered on the letter for several long moments, as if reluctant to release it. "I have to get back to the school house."

Then she spun and hurried out. Charles' gaze turned to the letter.

XXIV

Katie Delacroix's mind was full of screams.

Emily's voice. Her mother's voice. And all her own screams that she could not get out the night before. Porky's naked back was warm and moist against her legs, and a lot of miles of grass and wagon rut had passed behind her. She did not know how many. The tighter she wrapped her fingers into Porky's mane, until her fingers turned red, then white, the more she could deaden the screams. And the horrid sound of a club against her mother's head. And the way her mother's face had been misshapen, the blood running from nose and ear, so quickly, like the way it happened when Pa shot a hog for butchering. Right between the eyes. The bullet. The bright red screams and dark brown thuds. The taste of blood in the air, and guts, like when he skinned the hog and dumped the guts out. The sound of terror and her heart pounding.

She wiped at the blood on her hands. What would the folks in White Pine say if she came to town with blood on her hands? It was sticky between her fingers. She had it on her clothes. She had it in her hair, somehow. Or was it just dirt in her hair? She had it in her mouth, somehow. Had she put her fingers in her mouth? Was it just the smell from the house still there? Her nightclothes had almost come to town with her, until she realized dimly that she could ride better in her boy trousers.

Porky stopped to drink some water from a street-side trough. She looked around at the main street of White Pine. She had made it to town? It was so different this time, by herself. Bigger, without Pa to hide behind. She had never ridden so far by herself before. Suddenly her arms and hands went slack, and dizziness washed through her. After a moment to steady herself, she eased her leg from Porky's back.

A few townspeople watched her from across the street. She was too short to put the bridle on Porky by herself, and hoped vaguely that he would not run away. He was all she had left.

She shambled toward the jailhouse. Ma had taught her enough letters to read the sign in the window: "BACK IN THE PM."

She sat on the stoop and sighed. She must not cry. She had to be tough until the marshal came. Porky's soft nose brushed her hair, and his warm breath burst down her neck. He had followed her from the trough. Good Porky.

Footsteps approached on the sidewalk. She looked up at the couple, dressed awful nice they were. The man even had a shave and some sort of round city-hat.

She said, "Where's the PM?"

The woman said, "Beg your pardon, where is the what?" Her words sounded strange, flat.

"The PM."

They looked at Katie the way Pa looked at Ma sometimes, as if she were the dumbest wretch ever born.

She spat and wiped her nose. "Never mind."

They crossed the street. They were not out of earshot, when the woman covered her nose with a lace handkerchief and said, "Robert, was that smell her or the horse?"

The man said, "Are you certain that's a 'her'?"

"I'm happy that our children will never smell that way."

Katie wanted to shout after them that their children might not smell anything ever again if the grass monsters came for them, but she could not. She would just have to wait for the marshal to get back from the PM.

XXV

A few minutes after Ernest departed, he returned to the Post and Telegraph Office with a youth of about sixteen, skinny, fair complected and orange of hair. Sean looked nervous, a demeanor heightened when he looked at Charles.

Ernest said, "What's this about, Doctor?"

Charles said, "Oliver McCoy was shot yesterday, along with several other men out near the reservation. His family runs the Bar-M. They should be notified." He handed his letter to the boy.

Sean paled and swallowed hard before he took it. "Is it the Injuns?"

"I don't think so." Charles slipped a silver dollar into the boy's hand. "But ride hard, and be careful."

Sean pocketed the coin, puffed up, straightened his back. "Yes, sir." Then he hurried out the back.

Charles turned to the telegraph operator and postmaster. "Now, Ernest, has the marshal been here today?"

"No, Doctor, I have not seen him."

"We must send a message to the county sheriff, as well. There might be another outbreak of disease, this one more dangerous even than measles."

Ernest's face turned white, and he swallowed hard.

✦   ✦   ✦

The thought of Amelia's letter there in the telegraph box lay heavy upon Charles' mind as he stepped out of the Post and Telegraph Office. Her nervous behavior was uncharacteristic, in fact, the only sign of emotion besides bursts of anger that he had seen in weeks. She would not be sending a telegram unless she had an urgent message; she was too parsimonious for a casual expense. He would have to speak to her. To whom would she be sending an urgent message? Her parents? And what might she have to tell them that was too urgent for the overland mail?

The sight of a dismal, exhausted figure, sitting on the stoop outside the jailhouse, drove out such vexing distractions. A little girl in boyish clothes, disheveled, her face and hands filthy, hunched over her knees whittling a twig with a large knife, with an air of expectancy about her. A horse lacking a saddle seemed to stand guard over her.

He approached, and she looked up at him with wary, bloodshot eyes. Eyes fringed with tear-dust, as if she would not let the tears grow large enough to fall.

In that moment, another little girl's face rushed over him, slammed into him. He staggered and gasped as Eva looked up at him with teary eyes, her knee skinned and bleeding, pleading with Daddy to make it better.

Eva said, "You all right, mister?"

But it was not Eva.

Charles rubbed his face, collected himself, and swallowed the lump in his throat. "I'm fine. The question is: are *you* all right?" He knelt before her. There was blood on her hands. "Let me see your hands. Are you hurt?"

She put the knife down, an impressive blade with a scrimshawed bone handle, too big for such a little girl, and showed him her hands. "I need the marshal, sir."

"He'll be back this afternoon."

"I'll wait." She picked up the knife again and returned to whittling.

"Do you want some water? Have you eaten anything today?"

"No, sir. Water would be real nice, sir. But I ain't hungry."

Charles stood and offered his hand to help her up. "Come on. We'll see to your horse and then—"

"I need the marshal, sir."

"Why?"

"My family's all gone. Someone came last night and took them."

Her words took a moment for Charles to absorb, and then a chill ran down his spine. "Took them? Took them where?"

"They busted in and whacked Ma and Pa on the head. Drug 'em outside and took my sister, too." The desolate depths of her eyes could brook not the slightest exaggeration.

"Indians?" The moment he said it, the moment that reflexive assumption struck him, a gobbet of guilt congealed in his belly. He was no better than his father.

"No, sir, weren't no Injuns. They was something else."

"White men? Robbers?"

"Something else."

"Where did they take them?"

"Can't rightly say, sir."

"What's your name?"

"Katie."

"Who's your father? I've never seen you in town before."

A hood fell over her eyes, and the corners of her mouth turned down. "Cyrus Delacroix. I ain't never seen you either, but I seen the marshal yesterday. He came to talk to Pa."

A commotion behind him caught Charles' attention. Heavy footsteps clumped toward them. Ernest's breath huffed in and out of him. "Doctor Zimmerman! Doctor Zimmerman! I can't send the message. The line must be down. All it takes is a good wind to knock over a pole, and it was a-howling last night."

Charles' shoulders tightened, and rubbed his face. Could be a coincidence, just bad luck. But what if it was not?

Ernest waited expectantly, as if for Charles to have an answer.

Finally Charles said, "Then when Sean comes back from the Bar-M, send him out again. We must get the word out. There's trouble coming."

XXVI

Sean found his mind wandering to the fullness of Sarah Johansen's bosoms. And her lips. And those huge blue eyes that made him get all squirmy whenever they fixed on him. He had taken the job as stable hand because her pa ran the place, just so he could be around her, and damned if she hadn't given him a smile yesterday.

His horse ran at an easy gallop, southwest toward the Bar-M, and also toward the huge thunderstorm that darkened the entire western horizon. He felt like a rich man with a whole dollar in his pocket. Thoughts of how he would gain Sarah's favor circled the silver disc. Flowers? A peppermint stick? Some piece of jewelry maybe? Maybe he should just save up for a wedding ring and ask her pa if he could court her.

Sean felt bad for that McCoy fella. Word was all over town that the fella had been shot by one of his friends who had gone crazy. When Doctor Zimmerman had told the story to him, it was not the first time he had heard. Rumors were all over town that it was the redskins had shot poor Oliver, scalped the other cowboys, and stolen the herd. The McCoys were a fine upstanding family with a big spread that bordered on the reservation.

Sarah sure had nice titties.

No one could hardly blame the cowboys for letting their stock wander into the reservation. Weren't no fences out there anyway, anywhere between here and the Black Hills. Just endless waves of green-brown grass, a few stands of scraggly cottonwoods and plum thicket.

There was one wagon trail leading generally west toward the McCoy spread, two dirt ruts cutting through the grass, a trail that wandered back and forth past a few homesteads. The only real landmark was Sentinel Hill. The butte could be seen for miles in every direction, and it rose over the undulating landscape like a pile of mashed potatoes with dark, greenish gravy on top.

God, what would it be like to touch Sarah's—?

His horse lurched under him, shying away from something in the grass. Only the experience of being ahorseback since he was six years old kept him in the saddle. His horse neighed and snorted and skidded, tearing furrows in the sod.

Sean drew back on the reins, using his knees to try to control its sudden spinning and thrashing. "What the hell?"

He caught a glimpse of something heavy and dark spinning toward him from behind, wooden and curved and glistening with black shards, the instant before it slammed into the side of his head, exploding stars and pain through his awareness. The ground slammed into him, driving out his breath in a painful whoosh.

On his back, gagging for breath, blinded by tears, his cry of pain frozen in his pummeled lungs, he saw several mounds rise from the grass around him. The mounds rushed toward him, descended upon him, and he raised his arms weakly in defense, until the claws tore into him.

XXVII

Approaching the schoolhouse, Charles heard Amelia's voice in the midst of an arithmetic lesson. The pounding of little feet had beaten the grass flat around the building. An errant baseball awaited the next recess. He opened the door and stepped half inside. Amelia stood at the blackboard, chalk in hand. Her eyes were red as if she had been crying, but her face was stern and focused on the lesson. A roomful of little eyes fixed upon him with curiosity. Her gaze turned toward him, and he met it for a long moment.

"I am sorry to interrupt, children," he said. "Amelia, may I see you outside?"

She stiffened and hesitated, but put down the chalk.

Outside, he led her away from the door so the children could not hear. "I need you to watch over the wounded man in my office for a while. He's dying, and shouldn't be alone."

She looked at him for a long time, long enough that he opened his mouth to repeat himself, but she said, "What's going on?"

Katie's words shot through him again. How could he lay these horrors upon Amelia? She looked as if she was on the verge of a sobbing collapse. He didn't want to have to pick up the pieces in that event, not today. "I'll be back by nightfall." He turned to leave and took three steps, but she stopped him.

"And what of the girls?"

"Huh?"

"What of the children? I am a teacher, Charles. What do I do with these children? Can't you find someone else?"

"I don't have anyone else!" The desperation in his voice surprised him, hung between them.

"Is it another woman, Charles?"

He spun on her. "What?"

"I said, is there another woman?"

"Of course not! Now, please! Come to my office! I need your help! A child needs my help, a little girl in dire straits!" His voice cracked. "A little girl."

The heat in her eyes guttered and dimmed. "Just give me a moment." She clasped her hands tightly before her belly, then went back inside the school. Her voice reached through the open door, "Hilda and Jake, please finish the arithmetic lesson for the little ones. After that, you are dismissed for the day."

She came back outside and stood stiffly before him. After a moment, she gestured impatiently for him to lead the way.

◇   ◇   ◇

Charles opened the door of his office for her. Katie sat on the floor across the room from the bed where Oliver slept. When she saw them, she stood and smoothed her filthy clothes.

He gestured to both of them. "Katie, this is my wife, Amelia. Amelia this is Katie Delacroix."

Amelia immediately crossed the room and knelt before Katie. "Oh my gracious, child, how you've grown! Are you all right?"

"Yes, ma'am. Nothing hurt."

"Is that blood on your clothes?"

Katie had washed the blood from her hands. "Yes'm, I suppose it is."

Charles said, "She just wandered into town, said her family has been taken somehow. Something terrible is happening, and we must get to the bottom of it."

Amelia rubbed at the grime on Katie's face. "And what do you intend to do, Charles?"

"I'm going to take her back there and look around, try to find her family."

"You're taking this little girl into danger?"

Charles picked up his medicine bag and tucked it under his arm. "I don't see any other choice. The marshal is gone—"

"Then find someone else! She needs to stay here where it's safe!"

"Who? Ernest? Robert? Whip up a posse in the next five minutes? I don't know when Dad is coming back. She needs help, and I don't know where she lives. She tells me she can ride—"

Amelia turned on him. "This poor girl looks like she's seen the Devil himself, and you—"

Katie stood straighter and thrust out her chin. "Begging your pardon, ma'am, but I can ride. Pa lets me ride the plow horse all day sometimes. And I got to find my sister."

Amelia said, "And I suppose that's why I never have seen you in school."

Katie stuck out her bottom lip. "Don't need no school. Daddy says the only book worth a goddamn is the Bible."

"Nevertheless, you should stay here with me, where it's safe."

Katie said, "I was safe in my house, ma'am. When the grass monsters come, ain't no place safe. I got to find my sister."

The determination in her face told Charles that this little girl was quite capable of getting on his horse and following him, with or without his consent.

He moved to lay a hand on Amelia's arm, but stopped as if some invisible force held him at bay. "Amelia, we'll be back by nightfall. I'm just going to look around their farm. Maybe I'll find something." Something related to four dead soldiers and a gutshot cowboy. "When Dad comes back, let him know what's going on. Maybe he can meet us there." Then he reached past her, took Katie's hand, and led her out.

XXVIII

Yellow Horse Creek meandered across the prairie in a narrow gully, flanked by cottonwoods and cedars and thickets on both sides.

Hank let Jimmy lead the way along the edge of the tree line. The creek was swollen with snowmelt, and now ran perhaps twenty feet across, perhaps thigh deep in places. The hoofprints of deer and pronghorn antelope pocked the bare patches of earth near the edge of the gully. But there were no buffalo. Not anymore. It was a crying shame what all them hunters had done. He still remembered the hills of buffalo hides as big as a house, stinking to high heaven. But room had to be made for the white folks.

Jimmy pointed to a cottonwood, one with a distinctive gnarl to its boughs, almost like the shape of a three-fingered hand. "Head for that tree."

Hank took a moment to marvel as they approached. He had never seen a tree of its like, like some huge arm reaching up out of the ground, clawing at the sky. The last snow had been too recent yet for new leaf buds to appear.

Jimmy reined up next to the tree. The remnants of a long-dead campfire lay in a little pit, bits of gray and black charcoal sifted with dust. "Good to my word, Marshal. That's my campfire."

Something about the tree gave Hank's short hairs a call to attention, and he found it difficult to peel his gaze away. Then he snorted and slid off his horse, flexing his legs. "Get your ass down and show me what we came to see."

Jimmy climbed down and led him about twenty paces toward the creek bed, where the edge had collapsed, eaten from below by the flow of the water, forming a cleft in the earth. He could see that the edges of the pit had also been enlarged by human efforts. Hank heard the buzzing of flies as they approached, constant as a beehive.

"Sweet Jesus."

Before them, the yawning pit was filled with human bones, skulls, ribs, and scattered piles of ragged offal. Movement caught his eye, a fat bull snake slithering through a shattered ribcage. Clouds of shiny black flies darted from putrescence to putrescence.

Jimmy gagged and covered his nose. "Fuck. They're a tad riper than when I seen 'em last."

"Christ Almighty."

"See? Like I told you. That one has blonde hair." Jimmy pointed to flensed skull fringed by wisps of straw-colored hair that clung to tatters of a scalp around a jagged hole.

A gingham dress, torn and crusted with dried blood, a pair of overalls, boots, strips of ragged leather, cloth and lace, more bones, few of them attached to anything, even the heads, as if they all had been dissected. A child's skull.

Rage and revulsion boiled up in Hank. He pulled out his handkerchief, clamped it over his face, and slid down into the pit, careful not to lost balance and tumble into the pile of corpses. He waved the flies away, his jaw so tight he could have bitten through a horseshoe. "Goddammit." He picked up a stick and prodded through the bones, trying to see how deep the mound went. Were there other layers beneath? The bones were not bleached; they were still fresh, some with morsels of flesh still attached.

All these people—he counted at least fifteen skulls—reduced to so much wreckage, like a deadfall. These bones were too fresh to have the flesh rotted and gone. A mound like this could have been a tremendous feast for a pack of coyotes like those yesterday. A pack of coyotes would not drag a bunch of human corpses here into a pile, however; they would eat the meat where it lay.

As Hank prodded through the charnel mound, something small and dark and spindly rolled out and lay against the dirt. He picked it up.

Roughly the size of his hand, it looked of vaguely human shape, an elongated torso, headless, with two lithe arms and three asymmetrical legs. It was fashioned of black glass or flint, rough-hewn, with some edges as sharp as a knifepoint. Each leg was tipped with a cloven hoof. An image, a miniature idol, from some heathen tribe?

Something about it twisted his gut a little tighter.

He put the idol in his pocket.

Behind him, Jimmy knelt at the edge of the pit, clutching his mouth. "Fuck me."

Hank climbed out of the pit. "What is it?"

Jimmy's gaze was fixed on something in the pit, and his face was white. "Shit. Shit. That is ... oh shit. Who would do that?"

Hank followed his gaze, but he could not grasp what had Jimmy in such a state.

Jimmy pointed. "That bone looks like something my old hound just got done with."

Hank leaned closer and looked at it. A human thighbone, the end broken, with the marrow sucked out. The sides of the bone were scored and gouged with teeth marks. "Holy Jesus."

XXIX

Katie rode her weary-looking horse beside Charles, using a saddle and bridle borrowed from the livery stable. She said, "That storm sure has been hanging around, almost like it's waiting for something."

Charles had never seen a thunderstorm persist for so long. It filled the western horizon like a roiling, cyclopean edifice, fraught underneath with deep dark caves where lightning flickered. Usually they built, unleashed their rain, wind, and thunder, and disappeared within the matter of several hours. They did not linger on the horizon for days at a time, drawing ever nearer. There was no question, however; it was drawing nearer. He and Katie had to get back to town by dark, or the storm would be upon them.

He had tried to draw her into conversation on a couple of occasions, but her responses had been terse and unenthusiastic. Understandable, considering what had happened to her. Thus far, the picture of events he had constructed was that monsters made of grass had come into their house, at least three of them, and they had claws like a bear, and club-like weapons. Katie was afraid that they had killed her mother, but her sister and father might still be alive.

After her observation, they rode in silence. Such taciturnity from a child made him uncomfortable, but she was clearly unschooled in social graces. Eva had been a gregarious child, a girl who loved the outdoors, where every day brought fresh wonders of discovery for her, from roly-poly insects to wounded earthworms, from sprigs of wildflowers left on his dresser or

Amelia's writing desk to the wonder of an onion emerging from the earth. He sensed similar enthusiasms lurking beneath Katie's fog of tragedy, but whereas Eva had been like a rose, Katie was more a prairie wildflower, born and bred to the harsh climate, to the loneliness, to the toughness this land required.

Maybe he was on a fool's errand. Maybe it was wrong of him to bring her back to this place, but it was her home. She needed help, needed to know that someone would help her right now, not when the marshal returned to town. Charles stopped himself from thinking about what he needed. He did not even know where Hank had gone, and the Delacroix family was so reclusive that he could not find the homestead without her help.

Wind rustled the sea of grass around him, and his horse followed the wagon track toward the Delacroix homestead.

The fear was clear on her face, but she bit it back. The knife lay sheathed in her lap, one hand on the handle, the other on the reins.

They rode up to the meager sod house. A bony sow regarded them from a dusty pen. The front door hung ajar, creaking gently in the wind. A lone chicken pecked at the bare dirt between the house and the livestock pen. The barn door gaped like an empty cave. The windmill spun in the ceaseless wind.

Dark spatters in the dirt, a little trail.

"Stay back while I have a look around," he said. "Don't worry that whoever did this might come back. They are long gone."

She reined up well clear of the house.

He slid off his horse and approached the house.

Remaining mounted, she clutched the bone handle of her knife.

"It's all right. I'll just do some looking around. Don't worry." For a moment, he wished he was more like his father. He had not even brought a gun, not that he would have much skill with it if he had. His poor marksmanship as a lad had been a long-running source of chagrin with his father. When his father had tried to take him hunting, when he had seen what a shotgun blast could do to something as fragile as a quail, when he saw the suffering of a deer when the shot was not an instant kill, when he saw the fear in the bleating rabbit's eyes as it gasped out its last breaths, he had known he could never be the man his father wanted.

He stopped in the doorway and surveyed the interior of the two-room house. Dust motes swirled in the light from the door. He paused to let his eyes adjust to the gloom.

Blankets from what must be her sister's bed were strewn and dragged across the earthen floor toward the door. The crude woolen blanket separating the elder Delacroixs' bedroom from the rest of the house hung by one nail, half-torn from the ceiling.

He knelt for a better view of the floor. In the dirt on the girls' side of the room were spatters of blood. From the bedroom came a trail of blood, with a small handprint in it that could only belong to Katie, along with drag marks that bespoke flailing legs.

He stood and called outside, "Did they have horses, Katie?"

Her voice quavered. "Can't say for sure, sir, but I didn't hear none."

Thunder rumbled over the prairie, coming toward them like a wave.

"Did they steal anything?" Charles rubbed his chin. The hard-packed earth bore no footprints, only scuffs and drag marks.

"Just my family, sir."

He stepped back outside and followed the drag marks. The marks led toward the prairie grass at the edge of the homestead, then turned into a swath of flattened grass leading away.

Toward the storm. The thought came to him but he dismissed it just as quickly. How could it be significant that these attackers went toward the storm? All it meant was that they were going northwest, toward the Black Hills, toward Indian land.

Grass monsters? Men concealing themselves with coats of grass? That was a cunning detail. Could the attackers be Lakota? Some other tribe? What were they going to do with captured white homesteaders?

The longer he waited, the colder the trail would become. What would he do if he came upon the attackers? Talk to them? He could speak practically nothing of the Lakota tongue, or any other of the prairie tribes' for that matter. If the perpetrators were Lakota from the reservation, they might know him, trust him. Perhaps he could convince them to release the Delacroix family. Perhaps he could reduce the severity of their punishment when

Major Wilson got the Army involved. Kidnapping a homesteader family was not something even a pompous ass like Wilson could shrug off so easily. They must know that kidnapping a white family likely meant a death sentence for their entire band.

But what if the perpetrators were not Lakota? Charles could not hope to face three outlaws hardened enough to bludgeon a helpless woman to death. And if they were Indians bent on exacting revenge for Wounded Knee, it would not matter that Charles was a benefactor. They might just as easily scalp him. No, this was the threshold of his father's world, that of justice and retribution. He could not cross it alone, much less with a traumatized little girl. Let his father come back here with a proper posse.

"We're going back for the marshal, Katie."

"Is that the way they took my sister?" She pointed down the path of flattened grass.

He nodded.

"We're not going after them?" She pulled out her knife and held it for stabbing.

Charles could not peel his eyes away from the knife. "Not yet."

"We have to get her back."

"I know. We'll bring her back alive."

He mounted his horse and pointed it back toward town. He hated himself for lying to her, but she needed hope right now, not truth. Those kinds of lies were second nature to him now.

Beyond the beaten-down earth of the farmstead's central yard, where the dirt became the wagon ruts of the path back toward town, clumps of grass began to move. His horse screamed and reared.

XXX

Red Horse looked around the circle of men and women standing and sitting in the center of the camp. Many of them cast nervous eyes away from the circle toward the Army barracks. They had been specifically warned not to form groups of more than three or else risk punishment, so Red Horse had posted a few trusted men away from the gathering to watch for soldiers. Nevertheless, this was too important, and if the prophecies were true, they would all be free of the white men soon. The Ghost Dance had brought them hope—that hope had turned to ashes at the slaughter of Spotted Elk's band. But it was spring again, and the grass was thigh high in places.

The people gathered here were those who had danced the Ghost Dance, who believed the words of the Father and his disciples. Many of them had fallen dead during the dance, seen the world on the other side, seen the gatherings of their departed relatives, tasted the buffalo meat, and returned to life.

"I have heard many of you talking," Red Horse said to the assembled group. "I have seen you looking with hope toward the coming storm. We danced for the Father's coming. We danced to remake the world, and to see our sons and fathers and mothers and daughters again, our ancestors all the way to the beginning. Have you all felt the power in the air? Have you felt the tension like a bowstring?"

Many nods of agreement spread around the circle.

"Not all of our people believe what we have seen. So we danced for them, too, hoping that they would come to see the beauty of the coming world."

Long gray hair hanging over his shoulders, Two Knives raised his scratchy old voice and tottered forward on thin, bowed legs. "I am old, and I dream of being young again. I dream of hunting in lands replenished with their game. I dream of my wife, and my father and mother. For a week, I have dreamed of food every night, but the dreams have been of darkness and death, too. We were told how beautiful everything would be when the world was remade, and when we danced, we were happy. We looked forward to it all with great anticipation. This feeling—" He spread is hands to the sky. "—is not happiness and anticipation. It is fear and hunger."

This got a few nods from the throng.

Red Horse nodded. "I cannot deny that we are hungry, that we are afraid. I do not need to tell you who is to blame for that."

"We cannot fight them anymore," someone said, a woman's voice. Her name was Sings-by-the-River. "There is no one left.

Spotted Elk and his band were not even going to fight. They were just running away from the soldiers. The Bluecoats have more guns. They have more and better horses. More of us will die if we fight them anymore. All I dream of these days is food." There was a darkness in her face as well, as if she held something back.

"I did not call you here to speak of fighting." Red Horse took a deep breath and let it out. "We must dance again. If this storm is the Father coming to save us, then we must show him our faith. If we dance the Ghost Dance, we will hasten the coming of the new world."

"The soldiers will not allow this," said Spotted Bull. "If we try to dance, they will stop us."

"If this storm is the Father, it will not matter what the soldiers do," Red Horse said.

"If this storm is the Father," Two Knives said, "then he is already here, and it does not matter what we do. Why should we endanger ourselves if the Father is already coming?"

Black Arrow stepped forward. "Revenge."

A murmur passed around the circle.

Black Arrow slammed his fist into his palm. "Our friends and relatives were butchered with Spotted Elk at Wounded Knee Creek. If we die to bring the new world, does that not reunite us with our ancestors that much sooner?"

"And some of us fought afterward because of it," Two Knives said. "It was all for nothing. More people died, and things are still the same."

Black Arrow scowled, "Some of us have become weak and beholden to the *washichu*. Some of us are still warriors."

"Revenge!" said a couple more, quietly so that their voices would not carry.

"But they have taken our weapons!" said Sings-by-the-River.

"No," said Black Arrow, "not all of them." His eyes burned into Red Horse's, and he gave a little nod. Black Arrow was still a young man, not yet thirty, too young at the time to fight General Longhair at the Battle of the Greasy Grass. He was old enough to fight now.

Red Horse said, "They will never take all of them. There is something great coming. We must be prepared."

Nods went around the circle, and he could see hope flickering in their eyes.

Then a new voice rose from the rear of the circle. "Something *terrible* is coming." Little Elk stepped into the circle and approached Red Horse. "You already know that I sought visions yesterday. I must tell you what I know."

The circle stirred and hushed again.

Red Horse scowled.

"People," she said, "listen to me. My visions were not of Wovoka or his disciples, nor were they of the Ghost Dance, nor of a world remade without white men. I dreamed of Iya, the Camp Eater. You know the story of Iya. We have seen this storm coming for two days, and it is not the season for such a storm. Many of us feel something coming, something great and terrible. We have frightening, awful dreams. We yearn for change, for freedom, for food, but none of those things are to be found in the belly of Iya."

"Are you saying that Iya is coming, that he is that storm?"

"I do not know that this storm is Iya coming to destroy us. When Iya destroys, he sometimes comes like a wolf in the underbrush, sometimes in disguise, and sometimes in the shape of a cyclone. I have seen the Ghost Dance, and I have seen the happiness and hope that fills those who believe, but this!" She pointed at the black, looming clouds. "This does not feel happy or hopeful. It is destruction!" She paused to let her words hover in the air.

Red Horse took a deep breath and considered them. Her words were diminishing the hope that had started to rekindle. "We have been sad and hungry too long. Sometimes I cannot remember how it feels to be happy."

Many in the circle nodded even as their chins drooped to their chests.

"What would you have us do, Little Elk?" said Sings-by-the-River.

"Do no violence," Little Elk said. "Leave the soldiers alone. Let there be no more death. Tonight, let us protect one another. Something is coming, and it does not mean us well. This is the same feeling I had as I camped with Running Wolf and Spotted

Elk, before the soldiers caught us, the feeling that something awful was coming, but I could not see it. Two days later ..." Her children were dead. Her husband was dead. Her people were dead. "Many have called me lucky to have escaped alive, but like you now, I must suffer the loss of all my family every day." Tears burst from her eyes and down her cheeks. "Red Horse last night went out searching for the lost children. Tell them what you told me."

Red Horse had not made public the blood trail he had followed, but he had confided in Little Elk earlier that day, after his meeting with Wilson. "I found a trail of blood, leading away from camp. The trail disappeared in the grass, as if whatever left the blood was lifted into the sky."

"Listen to me," Little Elk said. "Those children were taken from the fringe of the camp. Tonight, we must gather in the center of camp and burn our fires high. We must protect each other from an enemy that can come in any form."

Black Arrow frowned, "And if this 'enemy' does not come?"

Little Elk answered him, "Then tomorrow we will rejoice to have come unscathed through a night when evil spirits stalk the land."

Red Horse said, "And if the Father comes tonight, we will be ready to welcome him as one people."

XXXI

Amelia sat in Charles' wooden chair, utterly unable to comprehend the paragraph that she had read four times. How many times had she lost herself in the complexities of *Pride and Prejudice*? It was her favorite book, and she had often turned to it for enjoyment, for contemplation, for escape from the loneliness of this prairie life. Today, however, whenever scenes of flirtation or romance arose, she found herself getting inexplicably angry. Jane Austen had never before made her angry, but today, as she read of flirtations and dalliances and desire ... How had love come to betray her so? She snapped the book shut.

Oliver stirred on the bed nearby, his face covered in sweat. Outside, the wind had strengthened. It never really went away, even at night, but this afternoon it had whipped up to howl down the main street of town, driving swirls of dust before it. On the sidewalk, Robert Teague, White Pine's only attorney, passed by, clamping his bowler onto his head with one hand, squinting against airborne grit. For a moment, Amelia missed her occasional teas with Robert's wife, Olga. Olga and Robert had come from Boston society, and still carried that peculiar Boston accent, similar perhaps to the way Austen's characters spoke. Olga would speak only in vagaries about why they had come to the West, but she was determined to maintain some semblance of society, even in a place as empty and wild as the Dakota Territory.

Alas, those gentle, genteel meetings had ceased when the girls fell ill. It was just as well; Amelia feared she was terribly poor company lately.

Of all the people in town, she would probably miss Olga. Perhaps she would post a letter to Olga from somewhere along her train trip back east.

She crossed to the window. On the opposite walk, Toby, the hardware man's little brown dog, yipped and spun and chased its tail. Many a dog had chased its tail, but something in Toby's movement held her attention, a desperation, a yearning, a hunger that was building in frustration toward savagery. Mr. Whitney came out of his store at the dog's commotion, initially amused, but when he tried to get the dog to stop the dizzying spin, Toby snapped at him. Whitney snarled and spurned the dog with his foot. Toby flopped and rolled, and lay for a moment, wobbly, disoriented, shaking his head. He hunched low, ears back, tail tucked tight against his lean rump. Whitney stepped forward threateningly, and the dog fled.

A confrontation with an unruly dog was hardly a matter to concern her, but something about Toby's behavior unsettled her, built tension in her shoulders. He had always been a friendly little mongrel who claimed the whole town as his playground.

Oliver groaned. His hands were tight fists at his sides, knuckles white.

Amelia walked over and dipped a clean cloth into some water, wrung it out and dabbed his face, moistened his crusty lips. His eyes flickered with awareness. "Easy, Mr. McCoy. Easy. You need to rest."

She eyed the bottle of laudanum on the table. Oliver's hands clawed gently at hers.

"Shhh. Lie still." Best to ease his pain. She reached for the bottle, but Oliver's hand snatched her wrist. She tried to extricate herself, but his grip tightened like a vise, tighter, until she felt the bones of her wrist grinding. "Ow! Mr. McCoy! Ow! Please. Lie still. Please. Charles will be here soon."

He lurched half-upright, moaning, his body quaking, eyes wide.

"Mr. McCoy! Stop! Please!"

Oliver pulled himself upright on her arm, then turned his head and spasmed. Black vomit spewed from his mouth, a noxious deluge that splattered over the floor, onto her dress, the consistency of hot tar, and it just kept coming, from his mouth, from his nose, an amount more copious than any human stomach could contain.

Amelia stepped back, clutching her arms to her chest, covering her nose and mouth at the stench, like a slaughterhouse in high summer mixed with the stench of burnt hair and flesh like a crematorium.

As quickly as it began, he fell back onto the bed, limp as a rag, strange unintelligible mewling, gurgling sounds emanating from him. His eyes slid closed.

For perhaps a minute, Amelia could only stand frozen in shock, clutching her hands to stop them from shaking. But the slow rise and fall of his chest told her that he clung stubbornly to life.

XXXII

Charles's horse lurched at movement in the grass perhaps twenty paces away.

"Easy!" Charles hauled on the reins, and the animal fought the bit with a scream of fear. It jumped to the side, flopping him against the saddle horn. A desperate handful of mane kept him in the saddle.

Katie gasped and grabbed the side of her neck. Something thin and dark, like a scorched needle, stuck between her fingers.

Porky jerked, snorted, and almost reared. She leaned unsteadily in the saddle. Charles grabbed the draft horse's reins.

Katie's voice slurred, "What's happening? What is that?" She pulled the thing out of her neck. A thin dark needle with a tuft of wadding on the blunt end. Some kind of dart.

"Come on!" he cried, silently cursing himself for a fool.

She leaned further in the saddle.

"Go!" He slapped Porky hard on the rump. Porky jerked, spun, and charged away from the lumps that had spooked him, toward the open prairie. Somehow, Katie managed to stay ahorse, but her eyes were losing focus.

Charles kicked his horse's flanks, and it leaped after her. He laid the reins like a whip against the animal's flank. They pelted into the empty sea of grass. An empty sea infested with sharks and krakens.

Something stung his back.

Again he cursed himself for a fool. All he could now was run. Numbness spread from the sting. He tried to reach behind his back to pluck out the dart, but he could not reach it. Another sting. His vision slid out of focus. The tearing of horses' hooves over the sod took on a strange, muffled character. His horse overtook Porky, an older, slower animal more built for long hours of slow work. Katie leaned against Porky's neck, clutching his mane, her small body flopping loose in the saddle. He lashed Porky's haunches with his reins, lashed his own mount. The horses screamed and stretched their bodies into a terrified gallop, until all Charles could do was hold on, until his fingers grew numb.

Somewhere, he lost his hat.

Katie sagged sideways in the saddle.

Charles tried to cry out to her, "C'mon, Katie, faster, honey!" But his voice was slurred, unintelligible.

Porky suddenly balked, drawing up hard, and Katie tumbled off, crashing onto the ground.

He hauled on the reins and almost followed her to the earth, but managed to slow and turn his mount, sloppy in the saddle.

His voice was thick, "Katie! Katie, get up!" The world swam. "Eva. C'mon. C'mon, get up."

Then the ground rushed up to meet him.

Something warm and velvety rubbed against Charles' forehead. Hot breath washed over his face, driving back the chill that suffused his bones. One of his eyes opened and gazed up into the wrinkled cavern of Porky's nostril. The other was pasted shut by blood. He raised a weak hand to fend of Porky's muzzle, then used it to pry apart his fused eyelids. A sticky crust of blood had run from a scratch on his scalp, into his eye.

The sun had disappeared, left the heavens as a deep black-and-gray cloak.

Porky poked him with his nose again, and Charles tried to speak, but his tongue felt like a dry, swollen sock; his words came out as gibberish.

Around the edges of his vision, the grass encroached. Something in its susurration comforted him, made him feel invisible, safe.

Until he heard footsteps, heavier than Katie's could be, rustling nearer. A spike of fear drove out a gasp, until he clamped both hands over his mouth.

He could see only Porky's silhouette against the night sky. Porky turned his head toward the sound and nickered.

Heavy feet hit the ground.

Then a human silhouette emerged from the surrounding grass. "You all right, Son?"

XXXIII

The lights of the tent village were dim in the distance. Surrounded by the vastness of wind-whipped grass, with the shroud of thunderstorm soaring overhead to obscure the moon and stars like the wings of the Thunderbird itself, Red Horse crouched beside the lone thicket of brush. He knew this spot well, found it easily even in the dark.

The Bluecoats were stupid. Did they think a warrior people would so easily give up all their weapons?

He leaned under the branches, brushed aside a covering of grass from an earth-colored buffalo hide, and lifted the hide from the cache beneath. The dull gleam of steel shone even in the darkness, and the odors of gun oil and powder rose, wafted by the blanket.

These weapons were indeed all his people had left. Warclubs, bows, arrows, and a meager handful of rifles and pistols. He pulled a large knife from the cache, slipped it from its sheath, and tested its edge. The white men called it a Bowie knife, after one of their great warriors. It would do.

He gathered up the weapons and wrapped them in the buffalo hide, then set about stuffing handfuls of grass among them to prevent them from clattering against one another. Silence would make or break his task.

XXXIV

Charles huddled closer to the fire. His breakneck flight with Katie had ended near a creek bank. Hank had scavenged a few chunks of driftwood to make a fire, but the wind-driven chill still ate into their bones. The flames danced and crackled in the gusts. Hank passed Charles a flask of Tennessee bourbon, which he refused. His head was still swimming, his vision blurred from the poison on the darts.

Jimmy wrapped himself in a horse blanket, rubbing his cuffed wrists. Katie sat looking into the fire, her eyes glassy, mesmerized by the flames. A flash strobed through the sky and the crack of thunder rolled by a few seconds later.

Charles tried to rub sense and reason back into his face and put his face in his hands. The world had lost all measure of both. "They chewed on the bones?" His voice was still groggy. "The bones? The actual dead—"

Hank said, "Look, it could have been coyotes chewed on the bones."

Katie's face was pale, terrified. She choked back tears. "Oh god. Oh god. Those monsters took my sister. And my ma." She stood and looked around helpless, as if stuck in place. "We have to follow them!"

Hank put a hand on Katie's shoulder and sat her gently back down. "First of all, the good doctor is a fool for bringing you along, little missy. We need to get you back to town. You're lucky as hell I found you, and luckier still *they* didn't." His voice went from kindly to stern. "You awake, Son?"

Charles snapped upright, unaware that he had been listing. "A little groggy. But I'll be fine. Give me a moment. I'll take her back to town."

Katie's lips began to move with a whisper only she could hear. Charles thought she said, "They had claws."

Jimmy stood up and began to pace. "Who knows what that poison is actually meant to do? Do you, Doc?"

Hank growled at him. "Will you ease up on that poison talk in front of the girl?" He took the flask from Charles and drew a sip. "But Jimmy's right, she'll be safer with all of us than just you."

Charles motioned to Jimmy and said to Hank, "What about him?"

Jimmy straightened and put a hand on his chest. "Sir. I rob stages and banks. I ain't never hurt no little girl! Hell, I even check dogs for nuts before I kick 'em."

Hank held the strange dart between his fingers, examining it in the firelight. "Never seen Sioux use anything like this before."

Charles jumped up. "Because it's not the Sioux, you mule-headed bigot! They don't use darts!"

Hank's eyes narrowed, his lips in a thin line. "And they didn't use rifles until not so long ago."

Dizziness washed through Charles, forcing him to sit down again. "It doesn't make any sense! Using darts and eating the dead. The plains tribes don't do that. Who eats the dead?"

Katie's voice was the hushed whisper of a ghost. "What if they ain't dead when they're eatin' 'em?"

Hank's voice fell uncharacteristically quiet, and flames danced in his eyes. "Boy, you don't want to know what people will do when they're hungry."

Charles snorted. "So you admit the Sioux are people. You rarely make that allowance. I care for the sick and hungry up there all the time. Those people are in danger, too. I think Little Elk can help us make sense of this."

"What does an Injun witch know about anything? If the culprits are the Sioux, do you think she would tell you? And it's an hour ride. Three in your condition. In the dark. What possible good—?"

"What makes you think you know about anything? You didn't get past the sixth grade!"

Hank's eyes flared, and he bared the star on his chest. "This means I know quite a little. When I came here, White Pine was nothing but two patches of scrub brush and a prairie dog town. I've had my fair share of run-ins with the Sioux."

"And never once bothered to talk to them. That star doesn't make you any less an ignorant fool."

"But it does make what comes out of my mouth carry a sight more authority. You know what separates us from them? The law. Civilization. This here star is all that stands between civilization and destruction of everything we know, the world that made *you* into a doctor, the world where your kids can go to school, and you can sit down to supper in a proper house."

"You don't think the Indians have laws? Or homes where they gather to eat? Do you think that they teach their children nothing?"

"They were savages until we came along."

Charles snorted and shook his head. He stood, and his legs went wobbly again. "I have to talk to Little Elk." He sank back down.

Hank gave him a long, searching stare, then said, "No, you're resting. If you fall off your horse, I'm liable to leave you lay. I'm not chasing this darkness into its own fucking den, Son—" He turned to Katie. "Pardon my language. Cover your ears, little girl."

Katie pretended to cover her ears.

Hank turned Charles, "—And *not* into some goddamn Injun tipi."

"You sound like that slack-jawed half-wit Wilson. Those 'Injuns' survived in this godforsaken land alongside these cannibals for who knows how long."

"Maybe it's the Sioux we're after. If you weren't such an Injun-lover, that might cross your mind."

Katie's voice rose quietly, "My Pa trades with them all the time."

Hank sniffed and kept his gaze in the fire.

The wind kicked up a sprinkling of loose grass and dust. Jimmy pulled his blanket tighter, in spite of the glistening sweat beading his forehead.

Charles stood. "If the Lakota were cannibals, don't you think they'd have eaten Custer?" His gaze locked with his father's. "Starving people don't have the strength to lift a weapon, much less overpower a homesteader and carry away three people. I know these people! I am going to find out just what is going on here, with or without you!"

Hank said, "You're gonna take this little girl amongst a bunch of heathens? Maybe you oughta wait till your head clears."

Charles was again overtaken by dizziness. This time he almost collapsed but managed to sit.

Jimmy looked Charles up and down, then said, "He's getting away, Marshal. Want me to track him?"

XXXV

The light of a meager few street lamps filtered in through the office window. The sky had clouded over with the approaching storm, and the wind had not relented. It simply surged with breathy, moaning gusts down Main Street. Somewhere, shutters slammed open and closed.

The chair creaked as Amelia lowered herself wearily into it. Mopping up the deluge of Oliver's black vomit had been the most distasteful task she had ever undertaken. Its stench was so overpowering she could not bear it. The mop and the bucket sat out, and the floor looked clean, but the putrescence lingered like an outhouse in high summer.

Amelia rocked. Fatigue had long since filled her eyes with grit that tears could not wash away. Part of her just wanted to sleep, to succumb to the profound exhaustion that sucked at her soul, to go away and let the world pass her by, and she would awaken a decade from now, long after the world had forgotten about her and her pain. After tomorrow, it would not matter. The stage would bear her away from White Pine, and the train would bear her away from South Dakota, away from her guilt and failure, away from any semblance of respectability. What stories must she concoct to spare her parents sharing her humiliation?

Oliver stirred on the bed. Sweat soaked his clothes, sheened his face that was boiling with fever. A half-empty bowl of chicken broth rested on a table near him.

Yet again she got up to stretch and to pace. She had been sitting too long. Where on earth was Charles? He had been gone for hours, and furthermore, Katie had been exhausted when they left. The thought of him keeping that little girl out there, putting her in danger, lent a sizzle to her growing anger. Taking that little girl with him had been a damn fool thing to do. She should not have allowed it. What had happened to them? They should have been back by dark.

She walked to the basin and splashed water on her face, toweled herself dry. Perhaps there was a bit of coffee left to help her stay awake. She did not want to fall asleep in case Oliver needed her. A person should not die alone, so she would sit beside Oliver until Charles returned, and then she would kill Charles or make him wish he were dead. The stove had gone a little cold as she picked up the coffee pot and shook it. A bit of liquid sloshed inside. It was time to replenish the fire.

Just outside the back door, she took up a few logs from the stack. The wind sliced effortlessly through the fabric and seams of her dress, chilling her flesh. Signs and shutters creaked, and fingers of lightning stroked the underside of the clouds.

A shadow fell across her from behind.

She spun, and found Oliver standing face to face with her, his expression slack and devoid of emotion. The logs clattered around her feet. "Mr. McCoy, you startled me. How are you feeling?"

His head snapped forward, slamming into her eye. Blinding pain shattered her awareness and stole the breath from any possible scream. She staggered back, eyes bursting with tears. A hand snatched her throat, squeezing off her breath and scream, and jerked her inside. The back door slammed shut. Something hard, metallic, smashed across her face, and blackness claimed her.

XXXVI

Jimmy pointed to the roundish silhouette, highlighted by a tremulous weave of lightning through the clouds, the high butte of Sentinel Hill. "What is that?"

Hank clamped his cavalry hat tight against the wind. "Sentinel Hill. Used to be an army lookout."

"I know that," Jimmy said. "I mean *that.*"

Charles peered closer. A dim orange glow shone from the copse of trees at the summit.

Jimmy said, "Who do you suppose is up there now?"

Hank said, "Can't rightly say. Army quit using it after the last treaty. Used to be some old heathen junk up there, though. Circle of stones and such." He stood. "I'll ride up and check it out. If they're white folk, we should warn them about what's happening."

Charles said, "I'm feeling better now, but I'm not about to stay here with your prisoner."

Jimmy smirked. "Scared of little ol' me, Doc?"

Hank glanced pointedly at Katie, then Charles. "I can't take a prisoner into what could be a dangerous situation."

Jimmy raised his wrists. "Then get these manacles off me. I'll lend a hand. I'd rather be out front anyhow, where I can see things coming."

"You expect me to trust you?"

Jimmy put a hand over his heart. "I give you my word, Marshal. Swear on my momma's cooch."

Charles snapped, "Watch your language in front of the child."

Jimmy leaned toward Katie. "You know what a cooch is, kid?"

"No, sir," she said.

"You'll find out soon enough. They pretty much always get you in trouble anyhow."

Hank squared on him. "Jimmy, shut the hell up."

"What do you say, Marshal? Have someone watch your back or go it alone?"

Hank considered for a moment.

Jimmy held out his wrists with an exaggerated Cheshire grin.

"Damnit." Hank pulled out his keys. "Remember what I said about being a good shot."

"Wouldn't forget it, Marshal."

Hank unlocked Jimmy's manacles and said, "I'll tell you one thing, if we can see their fire, they can see ours."

High on the hill, flames danced with shadows.

XXXVII

The dim fires of the tent village guided Red Horse back. He crept low through the tall grass, the cumbersome mass of steel and wood bundled across his back, keeping vigilant for Bluecoat sentries patrolling the camp's perimeter, stopping every twenty steps to listen.

The rustle of movement in the grass gave him warning, feet shifting their weight.

Red Horse crouched low, peering through the grass tops. The sentry clutched his rifle like a medicine bag, his eyes pale pools of unease in the shadows of the fast-approaching storm.

"Halt! Who's there?" the sentry called. Then came the metallic click of a hammer being cocked.

Red Horse lunged toward the sentry, throwing his Bowie knife, a droplet of silver flickering across the distance. The point sank to the hilt in the sentry's throat, driving him back, gurgling, clutching at the blade.

Red Horse stole to the Bluecoat's side, pulled out the knife and cut his throat deep across. Dark blood spurted, and final gasps through the slice sprayed warm droplets over the grass. Red Horse stripped the man's gun belt and ammunition, searched through pockets, added rifle and ammunition to his bundle, then grabbed the man's collar and dragged him away from camp to hide the body where it would never be found.

XXXVIII

The silence stretched between Katie and Charles, with only the sounds of wind and flames and distant thunder to keep them company. Charles watched her, trying to figure out where her thoughts might be. Her gaze fixed on the hypnotic flames, the glowing coals. The shocks she had endured in the last twenty-four hours Charles could barely imagine. She kept her hands tightly clasped inside her blanket, as if clutching something.

Finally he said, "I am sorry about bringing you into danger."

Flames danced in her eyes, set her cheeks aglow, even grimed as they were. "It ain't no trouble, sir. I figure I've been in danger since yesterday. If you didn't take me, I'd've found it myself. I gotta get my sister back."

"And your parents, we'll find them, too."

She shrugged. "I think Ma is dead. Her head looked like a jackrabbit I shot with my slingshot."

"And your father?"

She shrugged again. "Emily can't take care of herself like I can. She's gotta be scared out of her mind if them grass monsters ain't killed her yet. You got anything to eat? I'm powerful hungry."

"I'm sorry, I don't." He handed her a canteen. "Drink some water. That will help the hunger pangs."

She took it, tipped it up for a long drink, and handed it back to Charles empty, wiping her mouth. "Thanks. Just now, I'd about eat that poor jackrabbit raw."

"I know what you mean. These last two days have been extraordinary."

"We ain't had much to eat for a long time. Ma tries to make things last, but you can only make soup from the same ham bone so many times. Pa says we just need to have faith in the Lord and that He'll provide. I suppose he must be right. He brung us that jackrabbit, I s'pose, let my rock hit it square in the head."

Something hovered behind her words, unspoken, unguessable truths. Charles could tell by the way she looked into the fire, cocked her head. "Tell me about your sister."

A great sadness swept over Katie's face. "She's mad at me a lot, but you know that's my job. But she's real sweet, and a lot prettier than me. I like boy stuff. She likes girl stuff. Always says she wants to be a proper lady, so I …" Tears burst out of Katie's eyes. "So I …" A racking sob. "So I teased her about breaking wind!" She collapsed into weeping.

Charles moved beside her and put his arm around her, the barely scabbed chasms of his own broken heart threatening to break afresh.

She jerked away from him. *"No!"* Jumping to the opposite side of the fire, she stood wary, poised to run.

He reached out to her then stopped himself. In that instant before she slipped his embrace, she had felt hard, writhing in his grip like a desperate wild animal. Now her hand clutched the bone handle of the Indian knife thrust into her belt.

"It's all right, Katie, no one is going to hurt you! We'll find Emily. And your parents."

"Ma's dead." Her voice was cold, almost lost in the wind. "I hope they kill Pa, too."

Charles stood speechless.

Katie sat down again, clutching her belly, her eyes returning to the fire.

He stood there for a long time, the murderous vehemence of her words sending cold worms up his backbone.

XXXIX

Hank's belly tightened into knots the closer he and Jimmy rode to Sentinel Hill. The vague orange glow became a large bonfire turning the shadows under the trees to dancing ghosts. The silhouettes of people jumped into the trees—many people, moving around the fire.

The incessant wind made it difficult for Hank to hear his own thoughts, much less Jimmy speaking to him.

"Hey, Marshal. You wouldn't lend me that scatter gun would you?" Jimmy pointed to the shotgun hanging from Hank's saddle.

"I don't recollect giving you any opium today."

"Come on, Marshal! That looks like some kind of pow-wow up there!"

Hank shushed him.

"How about we circle around the other side and come at 'em from behind the trees? Might get a bit of a look that way."

Hank was tired of folks offering ideas that had long been obvious to him. "How about you keep quiet for two seconds and follow my lead?"

They skirted the fringes of the hill to the opposite side and left their horses tied to a thicket. They would climb Sentinel Hill on foot. No sign of any mounts belonging to those on top the butte. The ground was a mix of gravel and pale, jagged rocks, interspersed with tufts of grass, yucca, and dense clusters of cactus bulbs the size of a quail's egg. The slope was steep, and boots found little purchase. More than once, they sent a cascade of earth and pebbles sliding down the hill, and Hank thanked the good Lord that the wind would likely mask the noise they made. The two of them sounded like a couple of buffalo bulls fighting in a gravel pit.

As they crossed the lip of the flattened summit between two sandstone boulders, they found a veil of trees and brush between them and the bonfire. A cacophony of unintelligible voices filtered through the trees, just audible now over the howl of the wind.

"Sounds like a pow-wow," Jimmy whispered.

Hank led the way, crouching low and darting for cover, shotgun in his hands.

Strange, guttural voices chanted to the discordant piping of a flute's bizarre, breathy melody. He had heard Indians play their flutes before, and it sounded something like that, but this sound was dark and bitter, corrupt.

He and Jimmy wended their way through the trees, until firelight filtered through the black branches. Shadows danced in and out of sight.

Every scrape of brush against his skin and clothing sounded like an enemy call to arms. It had been thirty years since a reconnoiter represented so much danger. The shotgun felt slick in his grip, and his heart beat a cadence for the rhythm of the flute, aching in a way that made him wonder if he was fit to just keel over and expire on the spot. But those were not rebs over there.

Lord knew what the hell they were. And there were a damn sight more of them than he had ammunition.

He and Jimmy reached the bushes that bordered the fire-lit clearing. In the seconds while he gathered his courage to peer into the light, he thought his hairy old ears caught the soft weeping of a girl, strained through the mad melody of the flute.

He peered through the bushes.

Fifty-odd ruddy-skinned savages whirled and thrashed around the central fire. Men and women and a dozen half-naked whelps, their only clothes were leather loincloths. They writhed bestially, their bodies tall, lanky, and gaunt. But their nudity was eclipsed by the horrors that were their faces and flesh. Grotesque, distorted features, some with strange pointed skulls, or ears clipped into points like they were Satan's elves, wide, flabby lips, deep-set beady eyes. Spears of bone pierced and protruded from their cheeks, brows, ears. Splinters of bone through their flesh crossed their breasts and arms in rows and patterns. Whorls and jags of scars decorated their cheeks, their arms, their torsos. Each individual was a unique nightmare of savaged flesh.

Filthy naked children and hideous women chewed slabs of semi-seared flesh as they squatted in small groups. Then he saw their teeth, all filed to points. Even the fingernails of the adults were sharpened into claws.

Then he saw some of the men, taller than him, and lithe, wearing cloaks made from what looked to be prairie grass. From behind they looked like tall walking haystacks. Some of them carried war clubs encrusted with shards of black glass or flint. He also saw long thin tubes that looked the right gauge to blow those little darts that had taken down Charles and Katie.

A crude ring of boulders encircled the clearing. At the center, on a flat altar-stone rested a larger version of the idol that Hank found earlier that day, a black, twisted, wispy shape. The awkward shape in his pocket suddenly felt sharper, pressing through his clothes.

This one stood about four feet high, its flickering shadow falling upon the trembling, squirming shape of Cyrus Delacroix. Black, sinewy straps bound Cyrus to the altar. His eyes were half-lidded, bleary. Drugged perhaps.

Squatting before the fire was a shape wearing a more elaborate costume. Taut muscular arms, a loincloth of black-dyed leather, painted with jagged, arcane scrawls. A tall wooden mask was carved in a style that seemed vaguely familiar to him, like he had seen something like it once in a museum back east, but this wooden face was the embodiment of corruption, madness, a semi-human screaming face, or the Devil himself. On a woman. Small breasts dipped below her arms, dark nipples pierced by bone rings.

An animal, about the size of a large squirrel, jumped onto her shoulder with incredible dexterity, scraggly black fur and tail, little hands, casting furtive beady eyes about the proceedings. Some kind of goddamned little monkey. But it was the face of the monkey that sent a tingle through Hank's small hairs. He had seen monkeys before in zoos and traveling circuses, and they all had strange human-like qualities, human-like faces. But this one possessed a little face, no bigger than a silver dollar, that could have been plucked directly from a madhouse, frightfully human, with eyes more intelligent than any beast's had a right to be. It was not only watching; it was calculating.

The woman stood and approached a nearby fire, where roasting on a spit was a human leg. A few stripped, blackened bones lay nearby. She had a knife in her hand that glinted like black glass, and she sliced a strip of flesh from the thigh. From the look of the foot, a woman's leg.

Beyond the fire, Clara Delacroix's eviscerated torso, limbless, distorted face bloody and staring, hung from a crude wooden rack. And beside her hung a young man's body. Hank's face went tight when he saw it was Sean Ritterbush, a boy of sixteen who helped out at the stable and telegraph office. Sour bile filled the back of Hank's throat, and a wrath such as he had not felt in decades surged like black fire right under his heart.

"What the fuck?" Jimmy whispered. Jimmy's quavering voice reminded Hank to put a bridle on that wrath, but like a mean stud, it would not be restrained for long. Hank shushed him, but he would not keep silent. "What the fuck? What the fuck? What the fuck?"

Hank grabbed him by the back of the neck and yanked him nose to nose. "If you give us away, I'll shoot you first and leave you for them."

Jimmy swallowed, lip quivering, and clamped a hand over his mouth. Hank scanned the campsite, looking for the source of the weeping.

On the opposite side of the throng, Emily Delacroix sat bound with tight leather thongs to a gnarled tree. Tears streaked her face, and bloodshot eyes stared straight forward. How in the hell was he going to get over there, much less set her free? He was no Indian scout.

Perhaps twenty paces away, a savage warrior sharpened the point of a blow dart on a whetstone, tested it, seemed satisfied, and dipped the point into a bowl full of black paste, a bowl made from a human skull. Around the camp, a few women who did not have young ones attached to them also prepared darts. Another one squatted before a small, square stone, chipping a fresh edge into a dagger of black glass. The pommel of the dagger was the bulb of a human thighbone, scrimshawed with arcane scrawls and incomprehensible images.

With solemn reverence, the witch in the awful mask hung strips of Clara Delacroix's flesh from the gnarled hands of the idol.

Cyrus' head lolled, mouth slack, eyes half-open and unseeing as the witch stood over him with her jagged blade. Her voice rose in harsh dissonance with the music of the flute, a singsong rhythm with the dagger dancing as if striking an invisible drum.

Ia-hey! Ia-hey!
Ph'nglui mglw'nafh Cthulhu R'lyeh wgah'nagl fhtagn!
Ph'ngha Wiindigu nogshogg.
Ia-hey! Ia-hey!

Cyrus' eyes fluttered open. "What—?" Seeing the witch looming over him with the dagger, he began to struggle, feebly as a child, against his bonds.

The tiny monkey leaped down onto his chest, stalked on all fours toward Cyrus's face, tail flicking with malevolence. Hank could not see for certain from this distance, but he would have sworn in court on a roomful of Bibles that the monkey grinned at Cyrus with pure, intelligent menace.

The witch's chant continued:

Ia-hey! Ia-hey!
Ph'nglui mglw'nafh Cthulhu R'lyeh wgah'nagl fhtagn!
Ph'ngha Wiindigu nogshogg.
Ia-hey! Ia-hey!

Jimmy's voice noosed tight, strangled. "Aw, no fucking way. No fucking way!"

Hank clapped a hand over his mouth.

The witch stepped closer to Cyrus, and the monkey danced on his narrow chest with maniacal glee. Cyrus cried out in unintelligible protest, his voice growing ever more shrill.

The revulsion in Hank's belly swirled fresh, and he expected at any moment the dagger would drive down into Cyrus' heart. But what actually happened was worse.

The witch seized Cyrus' private parts with one hand, dagger rising in the other.

Cyrus screamed.

She brought down the dagger and began to saw.

Jimmy spewed vomit, but a sudden rising wind howled over them, drowning all over sound. Thunder and lightning pounded the sky with fury. Dark clouds roiled and bulged, pulsing in time, rising and falling like breath. The throng of cannibals howled with joy, some with fists upthrust, others falling in prostrate supplication.

The witch placed the dripping mass of tissue into a coarse wooden bowl, then raised the bowl to the idol, chanting.

Across the clearing, Emily stared into nothingness, the intellect draining from her eyes.

The witch sliced the contents of the bowl into smaller pieces with the point of her knife. Gaunt, towering warriors approached, knelt before the witch, and accepted bloody morsels of flesh from the bowl. The witch took a tiny piece and offered it to the monkey. The monkey leaped and scampered onto her shoulder, nibbled the flesh from her fingers and licked them clean.

Jimmy's face was the color of curdled milk, and he collapsed onto one elbow.

Hank shook his shoulder. "Brace up, Goddammit! Jimmy!"

Jimmy nodded and steadied himself upright. "What are we gonna do?"

Hank took a deep breath. These devils—he could hardly call them men—looked mighty occupied at the moment. "Stay here." He sneaked away in a crouch, around the perimeter of the firelight toward Emily.

No one seemed to notice his shadow among the bushes, and he made his way quickly, trusting the wind to mask the sound of his passage. The cannibal warriors all knelt before the witch now, and she continued the unintelligible syllables that somehow made Hank's stomach queasier with every passing sound.

Finally he reached the tree where Emily was tied.

The warriors stood all at once and then moved to form a circle around the central bonfire. A great arrhythmic booming, like a massive drum, seemed to come from the sky itself, and the men began to dance around the fire. The women joined the witch's chant, and the children fought over scraps of flesh.

The monkey took another morsel of flesh from the witch, leaped back onto Cyrus's chest, and Cyrus's eyes, streaming tears, popped back open. Before he could scream again, the monkey leaped forward the stuffed the flesh into his mouth. Cyrus's eyes bulged with madness, and something broke in his sudden shriek.

Hank eased up behind Emily's tree, keeping to the pillar of shadow.

Her mouth hung slack-jawed, eyes as empty as a used dinner plate.

He hissed at her and said, "I'll get you out of here."

XXXX

Jimmy could not pry his gaze away from Hank's efforts to untie the teenage girl. Every goddamn second was an eternity, a hell of thundering heart and shaking hands. He had not been this scared in his whole life, ever. Well, except maybe when he was ten, when Pa caught him with his hand in the register at the general store. He had been afraid his Pa would skin the hide from his bones. It had been the whipping of his life and his ass still bore scars to prove it. He wasn't too scared of dying—a good shoot-out with the friendly neighborhood law was a passable good way to get the blood flowing in the morning—but being eaten alive, having your pecker hacked off and fed to you, that wasn't no way for a man to go.

He could barely hear anything over the wind's moaning like a whore, driving the branches and grass to rustling. A tingle on the back of his neck, maybe his own little guardian devil, made him glance over his shoulder.

A stack of grass was reaching for him.

He flung himself back, and the cannibal warrior lunged at him. Eyes blazed, pointed teeth gleamed behind lips that looked like they had just sucked a dead horse's ass.

The warrior fell upon him, snarling, pinning him to the ground. Claws dug into his shoulder, snatched for his throat. Jimmy grabbed an iron wrist and struggled to keep the clawed grip at bay. Goddamn this feller was strong! A claw tore a furrow through his cheek. They strained at one another, ragged gasps merging with the wind. Those razor teeth, dripping, bore inexorably toward his face. Jimmy's hand closed around the cannibal's throat and he squeezed with every spark of strength in him. The savage's windpipe flexed in his grip, started to close, but the savage's other hand sought Jimmy's throat.

XXXXI

Hank had to put down the shotgun to work at Emily's bindings. The leather thong was so tight against the bark of the tree that her wrists must have been half-severed. Untying the knot was hopeless, so he fished out his pocket knife, opened it, and began to saw. Finally the thongs snapped free, and Emily's hands fell to her sides, limp as a doll's. "Come on, little girl. Snap out of it!" he whispered.

One glance at the throng told him that something else had their attention. The eyes of the witch and several other cannibals turned toward a thrashing in the bushes where Jimmy had been waiting.

"Damn it! Stupid. Stupid," Hank muttered as he pulled his pistol. "This is stupid."

He sighted on the nearest warrior standing with back turned, and shot him through the head.

The entire throng, all fifty-odd of them, turned toward him.

XXXXII

Jimmy realized it was only a matter of heartbeats before the cannibal overpowered him. To die at the hands of this mule-fucker. Maybe it was better than waiting two weeks for a hanging rope.

Then the gunshot startled both of them. The cannibal's grip slackened for an instant, an instant that Jimmy seized to shove him off. The old marshal had not thought to check Jimmy's boots. He snatched out his boot knife and struck quick as a rattler, stabbing his assailant right under the misshapen ribs. "Cocksucker!" He stabbed the cannibal a few more times for good measure, like the needle in a sewing machine.

Something black poured down onto him from those neat little wounds, but it wasn't blood, and when the stench hit him, his gorge exploded out of him, geysering as he rolled onto his side.

The camp exploded into uproar.

Tarry, black stuff that was not blood soaked his shirt, clung to him, smelling like a shit-house pit with a corpse floating in it. He kicked the cannibal's corpse away from him and struggled to his feet, still gagging.

A world of peril was twenty paces away from him, all of it looking in the other direction, toward where Hank stood, smoking Colt in his hand. "Sorry, Hank."

Then he turned and fled into the safety of night.

XXXXIII

Hank leveled his pistol and blasted a hole through another warrior. Women snatched up filthy children and scattered into the night. Warriors snatched up their weapons. He fanned his six-shooter at the closest group and three of them spun with roses of blood and flesh exploding on their bodies.

The warriors unleashed bloodcurdling screams of war against the hail of lead, and then scrambled for cover.

Hank's pistol clicked empty. He shoved it back into its holster and snatched up the shotgun. "Damnit. This was not a plan."

The clearing stood empty of all but corpses and fire, but movement in the shadows seethed with imminent threat.

He reached for Emily's arm. "Come on! Can you run?"

Her arm felt like a bundle of sodden noodles, her head lolled to the side as if she were already dead, even though her chest still rose and fell.

"Goddammit!"

Twigs and branches rustled and snapped, growing nearer.

XXXXIV

Strange chanting filtered down the slope toward where Charles and Katie stood watching the light on Sentinel Hill. Lightning blazed across the sky, freezing images of the tree-lined silhouette in their eyes. Thunder blasted over them like cannon fire. A sharp orange flash erupted up there under the coarse tree branches. A heartbeat later, the sound of a shot rippled down the slope. The fire-born shadows danced like a cloud of startled bats. A barrage of gunshots followed.

The clouds roiled, directly above the hill, languorous as they began to swirl and rotate, picking up speed with a strange crimson light burning behind the fringes of cloud.

"Dear God, a twister." Charles' mouth went dry. "Damnit, Dad!"

Katie tugged at Charles' shirt. "Sir? We have to get down, get low."

The cloud above Sentinel Hill reached down like a wispy, expanding funnel, like a finger coming down.

Katie tugged harder. "There's a gully over there!"

Charles cast a last worried glance toward Sentinel Hill, then toward the storm, then toward the gully. "Damnit, Dad."

XXXXV

Hank took cover behind Emily's tree, leveled his shotgun, and fired a blind shot in the direction of the approaching noises. "Come on, you sons-a-bitches!" He levered another shell into the chamber and blasted again. A grunt of pain rewarded him.

By the third shot, he could see that whatever flowed in the veins of these bastards was not blood. It was black as tar, as coal, as the night of an evil soul, and when his smoking lead opened them up, the stench roiled like an infernal cesspit, like a pile of maggot-infested body parts outside a battlefield hospital in Georgia summer.

Then, over the ragged treetops, he saw something that turned his legs into pillars of frozen wood.

Above him, the clouds were swirling like water going down a drain, and a long slender finger of wispy gray reached down from the lightning dappled sky. A roar smote his ears like a hundred oncoming locomotives at full steam. Scarlet lightning crackled down the sides of the funnel, and the funnel expanded, pulsed like a heartbeat. The tip of the funnel came down on the plain below and swept toward Sentinel Hill, driving up enormous clouds of dust and debris.

A tiny puff of wind like a bug passing by his ear, then a small impact of a dart piercing the bark of the tree, both brought his attention back to immediate peril. He ducked to the other side of the tree. Goddammit, they were going to flank him, and if they did, he was a dead man.

And there was no way he was getting out of here with Emily. The emptiness in her eyes told him all he needed to know.

The roar of the oncoming tornado built like an avalanche of deep, booming noise. There was no time to run. But he hoped the cannibals would not be fool enough to attack in the midst of a twister. If they had any sense, they would be hoofing it for shelter already.

Nearby stood a pair of chest-high boulders, wedged against each other. In an instant he realized the boulders would offer a bit of shelter, let him put his back to a wall, in case the cannibals came for him. He dashed for the boulders and threw himself into their crook, cradling his shotgun.

Wind slashed across the hilltop, scattering the logs of the bonfire with clouds of orange sparks. Coarse debris tore through the air.

Hank could just see Cyrus' body, lashed still to the altar stone, wood splinters embedded across his body. The black idol loomed over Cyrus, and he squirmed.

"Holy Jesus, he's alive!"

The strips of Clara's flesh in the idol's hands waved like little pennons in the wind.

Cyrus wept and gagged and struggled, jets of blood spurting from his horrific wound.

The wind lifted him from the altar stone, pulling his limbs into excruciating contortions. He screamed.

Even from this distance, Hank could hear bones cracking, joints popping as Cyrus was drawn into the air, toward the hovering maw of the storm, until he was jerked suddenly free and swept up into the funnel, out of sight.

As quick as an eyeblink, Emily was snatched into the air and disappeared into the black vortex like a spinning ragdoll without so much as a whimper.

Hank wedged himself as tight as he could into the stone cleft, clamping his hat tight over his head and face.

XXXXVI

Charles and Katie tied their horses to a boulder in the bottom of the rocky gully while they themselves took shelter against the embankment of rocky earth, hugging close as dust and debris hissed overhead.

He marveled that Katie did not look frightened. Her demeanor was calm, almost business like. "Are you frightened, Katie?"

"No, sir. I ain't done nothing wrong, at least that Pa ain't already switched me for."

"What do you mean?"

"Ma always tells me that God don't never hurt nobody that don't deserve it. That twister up there, that's the finger of God. No, He ain't gonna hurt us, as long as we don't bait him. We just got to wait for Him to quit punishing whoever is up there."

Charles did not know whether to laugh or cry at her words. He had no doubt that his father had a few things to answer for.

The cyclone pummeled Sentinel Hill, and a cloud of flying debris coalesced around the base of the funnel like a halo.

The roar intensified like some hellish thundering beast drawing nearer. They clutched their hands over their ears against the screeching, maddening roar.

Scarlet fingers of lightning crackled across the landscape, rippling in waves down the slopes from the summit, rippling in waves across the grass and scrub, brushing over everything.

Katie jerked away from Charles, her gaze casting about, eyes wide with surprise and something else ... perhaps recognition, as if seeing a long-estranged friend—or someone from a dream. The Lakota knife appeared in her hand, and for a moment he thought she might attack him with it. A cold, murderous spark flashed in her eyes and disappeared.

For long moments, she sat stock still, barely breathing, her whole body trembling. Then she relaxed, and her face became a little girl's again.

When Charles took his eyes off her, the finger of tornado was withdrawing into the roiling clouds. The power and frequency of the lightning diminished. He had the vague sense of something receding, almost a living presence returning to the heavens for now.

The silence of the thunder's absence felt like the same sort of roar. The light atop Sentinel Hill had been obliterated.

They waited perhaps ten more minutes to be sure the tornado would not return before they coaxed their skittish horses out of the gully.

"What do we do now, sir?" Katie asked.

"The reservation is the closest shelter. We have to get to there and warn the Army."

"What about the Marshal?"

A stab of worry fought with a sick sense of finality, inevitability. "He can take care of himself. Or he's already gone."

"I never seen red lightning before, sir."

Charles cast a worried glance at the sky. "Neither have I."

Her voice filled with awe. "I never seen that kinda power before. That had to be God himself."

His first reaction was to tell her she was wrong. But how could he in good conscience attack her faith? She was so innocent, so earnest; he kept silent.

With one last look at toward Sentinel Hill, he lent Katie a hand to help her onto her horse.

XXXXVII

Jimmy's chest burned with exertion as he barreled through the sea of grass, down the sloping skirt of the hill, limbs flailing, gasping for breath. The wooden haft of the boot knife felt glued to his fingers with dried blood. He glanced back over his shoulder. The lightning-fringed silhouette of Sentinel Hill loomed behind him, and the twister raked across the crest of the hill like the talon of a living thing. Debris stung his eyes, tearing them up, until his wild flight and half-blindness led him into a large rock hidden in grass and darkness. A sharp blow across his shin and he was flying, arms outstretched, landing face first in gravel and cactus.

He lay there for several moments before he could gather enough wind to swear. "Fuck!"

He gathered himself up, groaning. Blood streamed down his cheek, and the breast of his shirt was peppered with prickly little cactus bulbs. An itch at his ear brought a yelp as his fingers brushed across another cactus hanging lightly there. Gingerly, gasping with annoyance and pain, chiding himself for a moron, he plucked off the cactus.

His hands were empty.

Where was the knife?

"Fuck!"

The only light came from sporadic blasts of lightning, and his only weapon had disappeared into the thickening sea of grass.

"Keep your head, you stupid asshole."

Breathing deep to quell the frantic pounding in his chest, he began to search. Lightning flashed and boomed, blasting daguerreotype images into his eyes.

And in one of the successive flashes, a clump of grass had moved nearer to him, and then nearer.

"Fuck me."

Jimmy ran.

Blind and desperate and weaponless, he ran, and the grass dragged at his boots.

Breath huffed behind him, like a beast's.

In another flash, another glance, he saw the grass was hunched and low, as if the cannibal were running on all fours, and it was veering toward him.

And it was gaining on him.

"Fuck you!"

The ground away from Sentinel Hill had leveled out. He strived to redouble his speed, but he could not keep it up for long. His legs were already flagging, his breath overtaxed.

The cannibal rose onto two legs, still running, still gaining, and prepared to pounce.

A flash and a gunshot split the night, and a bullet zipped past, tearing an invisible tunnel through the grass.

Jimmy's glance backward revealed a dark figure astride a horse, a puff of smoke drifting away from the barrel of a pistol.

The cannibal dropped flat and disappeared like a northern pike submerging into its element.

The mounted figure spurred toward Jimmy.

In the uncertainty of darkness, the figure looked familiar, but he could not be sure. "That you, Hank?" Jimmy spun in circles, looking for the invisible pursuer.

Hank reined up nearby. "Where the hell did he go?"

Jimmy could not be sure, but he pointed. "He was over there! Right there!"

Hank trained his gun in the direction Jimmy pointed and cracked off two shots into the grass, with no visible effect.

Jimmy tried to blink the muzzle flashes from his vision.

Hank cocked his pistol again, but held the shot. "Cunning fuckers. Looks like you did for one of them."

Jimmy looked down at black-stained shirt. "I did, and smell was like to kill me."

"Get on. I couldn't find Charles. Or the girl. Or your horse." He offered a hand up. "Jesus Christ, is that cactus all over you?"

Jimmy took Hank's hand, slinging a leg up behind the saddle. "I'm so goddamn tough, I hadn't noticed." With a wince, he plucked another spiny ball from his armpit. "Let's get out of here. There could be more of them sons-a-bitches."

"Smartest thing out of your mouth all day." Hank spurred his horse into a run.

◈   ◈   ◈

The horse wearied quickly with two grown men on its back. A couple of miles from Sentinel Hill, Hank allowed the animal to slow to walk. Its breath was deep and hot and moist, its shoulders and flanks lathered, and its body shuddered with relief.

The thunderstorm had changed course, moved away from Sentinel Hill. It moved north now, toward the reservation.

Hank's innards were a taut, quivering mess, like holding a spring with too much tension. He still did not know exactly what he had seen up there. A bunch of grotesque, half-human cannibals that looked like they jumped out of a painting of perdition itself? A goddamn twister that looked like it *came for them?* And poor little Emily, goddamn poor little Emily. He hoped that goddamn storm had swept up all those things—he could not call them "people"—and spit them back out like so much pulp and gristle. But somehow he doubted that. They acted as if they knew it was coming. But how could that be? In a life as long as his, a man heard all kinds of crazy stories about voodoo and Injun shapeshifters and ghosts and mad tent-preachers who could supposedly turn real blood to real wine. Hank believed none of that shit, and some days he did not even believe God existed.

But if there was no intelligence or purpose behind what he just saw, he would check himself into the sanitorium tomorrow and for the rest of his days.

"Hey," Jimmy said, "I thought we were going to the reservation. Ain't it that way?" He thumbed over his shoulder.

"After what we just seen," Hank said, "we're headed to town to send some wires. My damn son was right."

"Them fuckers make Sioux look like Sunday service—"

"County sheriff, U.S. Marshal's Office, hell, even the Army."

"Ain't there Army at the reservation?"

"You saw what I saw. You think that handful of greenhorns stand a chance against cannibals who can hide like a goddamn

o prairie dog?" He tried to spit out the taste of bile, but it would not
go. "Goddamn cannibals. Can you believe it?"

PART 3

"What tribe or people has not had its golden age, before Pandora's box was loosed, when women were nymphs and dryads and men were gods and heroes? And when the race lies crushed and groaning beneath an alien yoke, how natural is the dream of a redeemer, an Arthur, who shall return from exile and awake from some long sleep to drive out the usurper and win back for his people what they have lost. The hope becomes a faith and the faith becomes the creed of priests and prophets, until the hero is a god and the dream a religion, looking for some great miracle of nature for its culmination and accomplishment. The doctrines of the Hindu avatar, the Hebrew Messiah, the Christian millennium, and the [Father] of the Indian Ghost Dance are essentially the same, and have their origin in a hope and longing common to all humanity."

—James Mooney, The Ghost Dance Religion and Sioux
Outbreak of 1890 (1892–93)

I

Major Wilson stood behind his desk, a slim cigar clenched in his teeth, glass of brandy in his hand, but Charles could not determine if it was anger or fear that made the glass tremble. Sergeant Weatherly and the quartermaster flanked him. Katie stood close at Charles' hip. Lightning flashed in the window, and a sudden clap of thunder made the roof shingles rattle. Small bits of wind-driven debris pelted the glass.

Major Wilson said, "You're saying they're atop old Sentinel Hill?"

Charles put his hands on Major Wilson's desk, leaning in. "My father and another man went up Sentinel Hill. There was a bonfire up there. There was a full-out gun battle. I don't know who might still be alive up there."

Major Wilson's lip curled. "And you ran away."

"A twister was bearing down on us! I was protecting the girl."

Major Wilson chewed on his cigar and scowled.

"Damnit, Major, innocent people have been abducted, white homesteaders."

Major Wilson yawned and checked his pocket watch. "I don't see there's much I can do. This is a civilian matter." Nevertheless, two droplets of sweat glistened on his forehead. "Besides, my men are hunkered down for the storm."

For a long moment, Charles stood speechless, unable to believe what he had just heard. "After everything you've seen in the last twenty-four hours—"

Wilson waved his hand dismissively. "I hardly think any of this is connected. Perhaps you should get some rest, doctor."

"It's *all* connected! Why can't you see that?"

The Major sipped his brandy with a trembling hand.

"My father is the only civilian law within forty miles. You have to do something!"

"You are hardly in a position to give me orders, Doctor."

Sergeant Weatherly shuffled between both feet, his face pale, and his eyes conveying quiet defeat. The quartermaster looked at Charles with ill-concealed disdain.

Charles raised his voice. "Can't you send out a patrol? A few men?"

Wilson stubbed out the cigar. "No force in god's creation will have me send my men off-post, into a thunderstorm—and we'll count ourselves fortunate if that cyclone misses us—to face an enemy of unknown strength. Your father fought in the war. He knows how to take care of himself."

"My father was a quartermaster." Charles had not intended so much contempt to seep into his voice, but he heard it as his words filled the room.

The quartermaster bristled.

Wilson *hmphed* with a smirk. "Hardly. Don't you know where he served?"

Charles realized suddenly how little he knew about his father's military career. His father had never, ever discussed it, never told Charles or his mother anything about his experiences. Charles had never asked, simply because conversations with his father had a long habit of going awry. He did not even know what unit his father had served in.

Wilson squared to face him. "Hank Zimmerman was a scout with the 117th Pennsylvania Cavalry. In 1863, one hundred and twenty-seven men from his regiment were captured, including him. One hundred and twenty-two of those died in Andersonville prison."

"How is it that you know this?" Charles said.

"My uncle was one of those who died. I have his last journal, written before he died of starvation. Your father was the toughest man my uncle ever knew."

Thunder rattled the window again.

"I was two years old then," Charles said. "He told my mother—"

"He was a soldier." Wilson's voice was as sharp as a cavalry saber. "He knew what going up Sentinel Hill meant."

The silence hung between them, smothering.

"So you're just going to do nothing," Charles said.

Wilson's face darkened. "You try my patience. If you were not the only doctor within a hundred miles, I'd have you in the stockade simply because I'm growing weary of your wagging tongue. But I'll send out a patrol to Sentinel Hill in the morning. You and the little girl can bunk in the infirmary until then. We're done here."

II

Red Horse paused when the Thunderbird's light revealed the two Bluecoat sentries ahead. All that filled his ears now were thunder and wind, and he had almost stumbled blindly into the Bluecoats and their rifles. He kept low, deep in the thigh-high grass, and circled them.

A match flared against a pale face, snuffed immediately. A muttered curse.

One of the Bluecoats spoke. "Damnation, that's a hell of a storm. Never seen nothing like that."

The other kept trying to light a match for the end of his ragged cigarette. "Never seen twisters before I came out to this Godforsaken country."

The wind bore their voices to Red Horse. He became the coyote, blending with the prairie grass on all fours, ears pricked up to listen, ready to run, but his steel tooth was in his hand. He could easily kill one of them if they spotted him; he was unsure about two. The wind brought him their scent of stale sweat and wool, tobacco and brimstone.

"When I was kid," the first one said, "we hid in the cellar while one took our barn and all our stock. Mama said it was like the finger of God come down and just wiped it away. Somehow back then it always made me think of wiping a booger off on your trousers."

As Red Horse slunk through the grass, the wind switched direction, and their voices were lost. For over a hundred paces he was the coyote, until they were far enough behind him to move more quickly. He prayed silently to the Thunderbird, that it would not see fit to reveal him to the sentries, and to the Father, that he might see fit to come soon.

III

Charles snarled, barely keeping himself in check. "Pompous half-wit!"

He stomped toward the infirmary with Katie just barely keeping up. He would put Katie safely to bed—she looked half-dead, eyes half-lidded, stumbling from exhaustion—see to the horses still tied outside the officers' quarters, and then consider how he would see that Wilson's superiors, General Miles in Rapid

City, maybe even the War Department, would know of his incompetence. Between that and thoughts of his father's welfare, Charles could not imagine encountering any sleep tonight.

The black clouds roiled overhead, flickering with lightning. Wind whipped dust around them.

"I hope the marshal's going to be all right," Katie said.

"If only he wasn't so goddamned hard-headed. Old fool!"

A face peeked around the corner of the infirmary, tentative, like a prey animal checking for danger. "Doctor!" Little Elk whispered.

Charles changed course and met her. Katie hung back, her eyes filled with awe and distrust.

"I heard you came back," Little Elk said. "Please. You must help us."

"What is it? Have you found the missing children?"

Even in the darkness, he could see the weariness in the lines of her face, the gauntness of her cheeks, the circles under her eyes. How beautiful she must have been before the terrible blow her spirit had received. "Something terrible is coming. I feel it. Red Horse found a blood trail. The blood trail might be from the missing children. But this is worse."

Charles snorted. "I doubt that it would have served you to speak to Wilson. I have never encountered a man so closely resembling a braying ass. In any case, it's not just here that people are disappearing. This girl's family was taken from their home last night. She saw it all." He glanced around, looking for guards. "Please. Let's go inside and talk."

Little Elk shook her head, trembling. "The taint of evil is in there." Her eyes glistened with fear, and something deeper, the kind of fear that coupled with knowledge. "Something terrible is coming, Charles. My people have gathered at the center of camp to protect themselves."

"All of them?"

"Yes."

Charles stopped to consider this. Then there were certainly no Lakota atop Sentinel Hill—hearing it from Little Elk made him feel vindicated—but that still left the mystery of who his father had been shooting at, and that strange chanting.

He brought Katie forward. "Tell her what happened, Katie."

IV

The circle of people had come together at nightfall in the center of camp. The women and children formed the center of the circle with men surrounding them, facing outward.

When Red Horse returned, he distributed his cache of weapons. There were not enough to go around, but some people produced their own. Some had a few scant rifle or pistol cartridges squirreled away, others brought out short spears or bows and arrows that had been disguised or hidden, others simply had knives, or had whittled spear points onto tent poles. They kept these efforts shielded in case of prying outside eyes, but as the wind rose higher and higher, no soldiers came.

Many of them wore their ghost shirts. The sight of the mystical images painted on them in red gave him a twinge of nostalgia for those times when Red Horse—Sunka Wakan Luta—had last danced with his people. They risked arrest for wearing the shirts now, but something told him that the white men were cowering in their barracks, afraid of the coming storm.

Lightning shattered the distant horizon like barrages of cannon fire, but unlike normal thunderstorms, there was no gray veil that indicated oncoming rain.

Red Horse stood with his people, and, for the first time in a long time, they all started singing together. Even Born-with-a-Smile sat with the women, and they supported her in her weakness. He smiled to see her out of the tent, out of bed. There was a warm flush to her cheek that he had not seen in a long time.

They sang the old songs to ward off evil, to entreat good spirits for protection. They sang songs of the Ghost Dance to lift their hearts, in the hopes that the Father might hear them, even though they did not dance. Even those who had never danced the Ghost Dance were so caught up in the spirit of the people coming together that they sang, too.

Born-with-a-Smile clutched her Bible to her chest as if using it to keep her body straight, and there were others who carried Bibles or wore crosses, but they sang the old songs, too.

The circle of people, the sacred hoop of his people. Tonight it had come together again, and they would fight to preserve it.

He looked for Little Elk, but did not see her there. She was his brother's wife. His brother was dead; her protection was now Red Horse's responsibility. He asked a few people if they might have seen her, but they shook their heads. Where could she have gone?

V

Charles watched Little Elk's face blanch at Katie's tale, but the Lakota medicine woman nodded as if her worst fears were confirmed. Her gaze kept turning toward the oncoming thunderstorm. "I did not believe they were real."

Charles said, "Who?"

Little Elk took a long, deep breath, watching the sky and storm as if in expectation. "Yesterday, I sought visions from the spirit realm. My visions led me in many directions, but kept coming back to my old friend, an Ojibwe girl who told me the stories of her people. She told me her stories but I did not believe them because they were not my people's stories." Her face took on an expression of wonderment and burgeoning fear. "She said that every seven generations they come from the bottom of the world. They walk in the footsteps of their evil god. It eats. It dreams. The cycle never ends."

"What are you talking about?"

Another long deep breath to gather the words. "The Black Wind People. They travel the world, from deep forests and ancient rivers, always moving. They hide, and they steal the young and the sick. And they ..." She swallowed hard. "... Eat them. They sacrifice blood to their god, who travels in storms and in dreams of storms. A terrible wind that eats the minds of weak and evil men. It makes them hunger. I thought the stories were just to frighten children." Her eyes turned to Charles, and the dark depths grabbed his gaze, clenched it tight. "Do you believe me, Doctor?"

His mind was a chaos of disbelief conflicting with what he had seen. He finally managed to speak. "I hardly know what to believe. But I believe this girl, and I believe what I've seen over the last two days. Something foul is afoot, and we are all in danger."

"We are always in danger. This time, the storm is here and the stories are alive."

An owl hoot almost passed by his awareness, until it occurred to him that any owl interested in self-preservation had long ago found shelter until the storm passed. A low shadow slid along the back of the infirmary, coming toward them with the glint of a knife in one hand.

Katie saw it too and jumped behind Charles; her own Lakota knife was in her hand.

Little Elk whispered something in Lakota, and Red Horse moved closer.

Charles said, "Red Horse, what are you doing?" He glanced about for sentries. "Put the knife away! You're scaring the child."

Red Horse sheathed his massive knife and said something to Little Elk in Lakota.

VI

Little Elk could see in Red Horse's expression the relief that he had found her.

Red Horse said, "The people are singing. We have all gathered, as you said, but you are not there. I do not want you to be lost like New Moon and Two Otters before the Father comes."

Little Elk wanted to embrace him for worrying about her, for the true concern in his voice, but there was too much to do. "This storm is not the messiah, Red Horse! Nor is it Iya! I had to hear the words of this little girl before I knew."

Red Horse's face darkened, hardened into something unreadable, and he drew back. "You know this beyond doubt?"

"Yes."

"How can you?"

"I am a Dreamer. You know I have been having visions. This child's story completes the puzzle, and changes it completely. Do you know of the Black Wind People?"

"Long ago, when I was a boy," he said, "at the gathering of the tribes. I got into some mischief, and an old Santee medicine man scolded me, told us children to behave or the Black Wind People would come for us, and eat us like rabbits."

"They are here."

She told the white child's story to Red Horse. When she was finished, waves of anger, sadness, and disappointment rippled across his face like the torn ribbons of a stormy sunset, a dark undercurrent of all these recent weeks threatening to rise to the surface.

"They might be coming here," he said.

She nodded solemnly.

Charles' English words reminded them of his presence. "What on earth are you talking about? Black Wind People? Tell me what you think you know!"

Little Elk swallowed hard and looked up at the sky. "It has many names. Some call it Wintekowa. The Ojibwe call it Wiindigu—an evil spirit—walking, half-formed, between worlds. It is drawn to suffering and starvation like a vulture to death, and it makes men hunger for the flesh of other men."

"I cannot believe what you're telling me. An evil spirit is driving these Black Wind People to abduct people and kill them?"

"The Wiindigu does not care what you believe, Doctor. The Wiindigu is hunger."

VII

A long minute passed while the pieces of events and stories and strange sights coalesced in Charles' mind. His gaze went from Katie, who stood now within her own darkness, quiet and full of unknowable thoughts, to Little Elk, whose eyes drilled their truth into him, to Red Horse's tense internal struggles.

Little Elk said, "There has been much suffering. All the wars, decades of war and death, the slaughter at Wounded Knee Creek, starvation …"

Charles swallowed hard. "Disease."

"There is a blot here on this land, a great unhealed wound," Little Elk said. "We are all still bleeding, and the scent of blood has brought the Wiindigu.

Red Horse clasped Charles' shoulder. "If Black Wind People come, they will eat. They will give white man's meat, Lakota meat, to Wiindigu. Wiindigu is death."

Charles opened his mouth to protest. This was surely all superstition. It could not stand against the face of the modern age, against science.

Red Horse's knife jumped back into his fist, and he pointed toward the darkness at the fringe of the camp, his voice a harsh whisper. "They are here!" He seized Little Elk's arm and hissed a command in Lakota. Then to Charles he said, "You go!"

Little Elk looked at Katie with a strange expression on her face, gave Katie a long, searching look as she touched Katie's blonde hair. She shook at her head at Red Horse.

Grassy ghosts appeared, darting among the buildings like smudges of menace.

Charles' and Katie's horses stood tied near the officers' quarters, where presided Major Wilson's office. And now three malignant shapes were stealing up from the opposite side toward the building's entrance, closer to the horses than were Charles and Katie.

Katie saw it, too. She snatched at Charles' sleeve. "Hide! Under here!" She gesticulated at the narrow crawl under the floor of the infirmary.

"Get in there!" he whispered.

Katie ducked into the opening and squirmed herself inside.

Charles took Little Elk's arm. "You too!"

She knelt and thrust herself into the opening.

Charles met Red Horse's eyes for a long moment. Red Horse nodded, then cast one last glance toward the silent intruders and disappeared into the night.

Little Elk's feet disappeared under the infirmary, and Charles followed her. The bare, moist earth was numbingly cold under his fingers. Three weeks ago had been the last hard frost of winter, but without sunlight this ground was still icy-cold. The rich scent of soil mixed with wood and mildew and cobwebs. The floor joists scraped his back, a nail ripped a long gash in his coat, and his straining breath echoed sharply as he wriggled deep into the narrow space. Katie and Little Elk were blacker blotches against the ribbon of dimness from outside, a mix of lantern light and oncoming lightning.

Filthy, naked feet shuffled through the ribbon of dim vision, the heads of obsidian-encrusted warclubs dipping into sight. Some of the intruders moved on all fours like great apes, abnormally long arms rippling with veins and hard muscle, whorled by scars and horrifically pierced by splinters of bone.

Katie started to whimper. Charles clapped a hand over her mouth.

A ragged scream tore through the camp, and chaos and carnage erupted in a frenzy. Sentries screamed in the distance.

A few soldiers, roused by the screams, stumbled out of the barracks. The cannibals fell upon them like wolves, tearing, slashing, pummeling.

A single gunshot rang out like percussion over a chorus of rising screams.

Charles whispered to Katie, "Close your eyes, honey."

He could see little from such a narrow field of vision, but the sounds turned even his hardened stomach. As a doctor, he knew well the sounds of rending flesh, crushed bones, the thick splatter of blood. Glass shattered. Wood splintered. Cries of fear and anger and surprise and evisceration.

Major Wilson's voice rose for but an instant. "What the devil is—" Until it was cut short by a sharp, crunching blow, then a long-drawn sickening gurgle.

Charles flinched with every wet, squelching blow that rained down on unseen bodies, death from every direction.

A cannibal warrior smashed a burning lantern through the window of the quartermaster shack. Flames bloomed within.

Katie gasped as the floorboards immediately overhead creaked with the passage of bare feet. Dust sifted from the above, tickling Charles' nose, threatening to launch a sneeze.

Private Spalding's voice came from above. "No! No! Stop, stop, st—!"

Charles clamped a hand over his own mouth as if to stifle the cries above.

The bodies of soldiers were dragged by the boots and stacked near the officers' quarters. A few distant screams punctuated the darkness.

Where were the Lakota? Had they fled away into the night? Were the Black Wind People slaughtering them, too? Or only the soldiers?

His breath sounded as loud as a locomotive venting steam.

Somewhere in the distance a chant rose over the sounds of carnage.

Ia-hey! Ia-hey!
Ph'nglui mglw'nafh Cthulhu R'lyeh wgah'nagl fhtagn!
Ph'ngha Wiindigu nogshogg.
Ia-hey! Ia-hey!

It all sounded like so many nonsense syllables, but while he had no concept of their meaning, the sounds imprinted themselves on his brain like a yellow-hot branding iron. If he lived to be a hundred, he would never forget them. A great yawning gulf opened within his guts, vibrating with the rhythm of the chant. A sensation not unlike hunger rose within him, almost like a growling stomach, but it was not *his* stomach growling.

As the wave of carnage crested, the quartermaster's office exploded into a conflagration of igniting fuel, glaring yellow-orange on black pools of blood that soaked the earth in all directions.

And all Charles could do was cower in silence, and pray not to be noticed.

VIII

Red Horse sprinted through the darkened camp toward the glowing center where his people were gathered. Fires there blazed a circle of light in vain efforts to keep at bay shadows of encroaching evil. Behind him, the screams of the Bluecoats rang out, gurgling, cut short like a blade through bone.

His guts were a sick mass of queasy waves, chopping over each other like whitecaps. Little Elk's words tore at his faith in the Father's return. All his hopes for a peaceful future free of the white man balanced on the edge of a knife, and if they fell wrong … But perhaps there was still hope. Perhaps it was a big mistake. Perhaps Little Elk's visions had been wrong. Perhaps this storm really was the Father coming to remake the entire world, but they had all misinterpreted his teachings.

What stories was he to believe?

A hundred or so paces from the circle of people and light, he stopped at his tent and lunged inside. The vacant interior smelled sour, of disease and despair. It had been good to see Born-with-a-Smile taking heart again within the circle of their people, even though something deep within him told him that it would be short-lived.

He cast about the dark interior, but he knew where it was, carefully folded and hidden in the bottom of a basket. As soon as his fingers touched the buckskin, he knew it. He dragged out the ghost shirt made for him by the medicine man Kicking Bear himself. Even in the dimness he could see the symbols of stars and birds, the red paint seeming black against the pale buckskin.

Kicking Bear and Short Bull had told them that the ghost shirt would protect them from the Bluecoats' bullets, but many at Wounded Knee Creek had been slaughtered wearing their ghost shirts.

What was he to believe?

Born-with-a-Smile had her book and cross of the white man's god. The white man's god would not save her.

Would his ghost shirt turn aside a bullet or a knife?

It did not matter. Perhaps the ghost shirt would not turn aside a bullet, but it might well ward off evil, and the air itself reeked of evil.

He put on the ghost shirt and raced toward the gathering.

Knowing how his people were standing at heightened vigilance, he announced his approach with an owl hoot, and was called into the light by Black Arrow.

Some around him, men and women, wore their ghost shirts, those few that had not been destroyed or confiscated, others like Born-with-a-Smile clutched their Bibles, still others clung to medicine bags and weapons, but all of them sang together. Here, almost two hundred paces from the Bluecoats' barracks, the singing masked the cries he had heard.

Red Horse moved to the center of the circle, climbed upon a crate and raised his arms. "Everyone, listen to me."

The song quieted.

Then a gunshot rang out. Three more in quick succession.

A tense hush fell over the throng.

Breaking the silence, a long gurgling scream in the distance.

"You hear the cries of the soldiers. They are not fighting among themselves."

"Then who?" a man's voice said.

"The Black Wind People."

His words filtered into their ears, into deep dark thoughts.

He continued, "We have heard the stories. The time for storytelling is later, after they have gone. If they come for us, we must fight. I have seen them. They are real, and they come as evil shadows to devour us, or to feed us to their evil god. Little Elk has Dreamed this. It is true."

A child began to cry.

"Where is Little Elk?" someone called.

"She is hiding. We must be vigilant. When the Black Wind People have finished with the *washichus*, they might come for us. If they do, we will fight them."

The women huddled together, dragged their children close. The men squared their shoulders and fingered their weapons. More distant cries, a gunshot. A flare of burgeoning flame.

"What about the white men?" said old Bull Bear, a man of over sixty winters. "The Black Wind People are evil made flesh. My grandfather told stories of them coming, long, long ago, stories that came from his grandfather. Should we help the soldiers fight them?"

Red Horse said, "We cannot help the soldiers. We must protect our women and children. And why would we want to help them?"

"Because the Father spoke of love for all creatures," said Two Knives.

"Not the white man," Red Horse said. "Nor could he have meant the Black Wind People and their evil god."

"There were Cheyenne who told me that Wovoka spoke also of love for the white man," Two Knives said. "We are all people of this world. We are the Human Nation."

Born-with-a-Smile met Red Horse's gaze, hugged her Bible, and nodded.

Black Arrow crossed his arms over his chest. "Let the Black Wind People and the Bluecoats kill each other. The Bluecoats do not deserve our help."

The distant flame bloomed and rose higher and higher, casting rags of smoke that were lost in the wind.

"There!" One of the warriors cried, training his rifle. The rifle flashed its thunder. Three others leaped to his side, pointing a pistol and two more rifles after the first bullet. "I saw one, sneaking between the tents on all fours, like a bear made of grass!"

"Did you hit it?" Red Horse asked.

"I do not know. It is gone now."

For long moments that stretched into lifetimes of thundering hearts, they barely dared to breathe, trying to listen for approaching enemies over the howl of the wind that drove their fires sideways, scattering embers into the sky like orange stars.

With each new scream in the distance, Red Horse felt a pang of satisfaction of justice done, lust for vengeance sated, but each scream hammered at this lust, battering it out of form and proportion. The Bluecoats were being destroyed, one by one, two by two, but when he thought about what the Black Wind People were doing to them, his belly turned cold, sour, empty.

The sky grew blacker and blacker, an immense shadow of dread looming closer and closer.

Finally, the distant screams fell silent, and all that was left was the wind.

IX

Charles waited an eternity before he gave the signal for them to emerge from their hiding place. Perhaps it was an hour, perhaps half that, he did not know.

When they emerged, the army camp had become an abattoir. The bodies of soldiers hung by their Achilles heels from the barracks roofs. Their slashed throats had spilled a moat of black blood around the blazing buildings.

Fear sweat drenched his clothes, and his hands trembled no matter how hard he squeezed them. Katie's pale face was a hollow-eyed mask.

"Don't look, Katie." Charles turned her away from the sight of Major Wilson hanging upside down from the roof of his office, just like his men, throat slashed, eyes plucked out and stuffed in his mouth. The major's viscera festooned the front of his quarters.

Little Elk's face bore a stoicism he could not fathom. How much horror had she seen that this did not seem to affect her?

A surreptitious birdcall from the shadows made the three of them jump.

Little Elk called out something in Lakota.

Red Horse and two more Lakota braves emerged from the darkness, weapons in hand.

Charles said, "Red Horse! Where did they go? Did you fight them?"

Red Horse shook his head. "We gather women and children, made circle and protect. But Black Wind People not come Lakota camp. Their bellies full of white man."

A crash of nearby thunder drew Charles' attention to the storm. It was approaching, its strength building again.

Katie whispered, "It's like the storm is following us."

"It *is* following," Little Elk said. "It is the Wiindigu."

Charles said, "What does that mean? You're saying that storm is this evil spirit? Come now, this is the 19th century."

"Can't you feel its hunger in your heart? Like a sickness!"

Charles opened his mouth to protest, but Katie whispered something that sent ice through his vascular system, "I tasted it. It was like death in my mouth."

Red Horse spat. "It *eats*!"

"Doctor," Little Elk said, "The Black Wind People eat to pay tribute. Their strange tongue has power. Their power stains the sky and the earth. They call to it. And they eat, and it eats, and its power grows over the generations until it becomes this." She pointed to the storm. "This one is powerful."

Charles could not hide his incredulity. "There's more than one?"

"The world is full of suffering. Everywhere men hunger. When that hunger grows too large, it turns on men and feeds upon them." She faced the oncoming storm. "This one is old, older than the mountains, older than the forest. It has eaten so much, it has become giant. Laughing Otter told me stories of men becoming Wiindigu. In times of hunger, if men eat human flesh—"

"Can we stop it?"

"Can you stop the wind? It is the beating heart of the black sky. It will stop only when its hunger is satisfied."

Deep down, the recognition of truth rang in him. "Or when there's nothing left to eat." Less than ten miles from here lay the unsuspecting town of White Pine.

Red Horse's eyes gleamed with vengeance. "We kill Black Wind People. They cannot feed the storm."

Little Elk nodded faintly. "Maybe then it will fade ... weaken."

Red Horse shook his Bowie knife at the storm. "We kill them all."

X

Amelia's eyes cracked open to admit the pale lantern light. Her head swam, and one of her eyes was half swollen shut. The memory of what had happened rushed back to her like a dash of cold water, and her muscles seized.

Where was Oliver McCoy?

A faint *skritching* sound came from beside her in the dimness. The lone lamp burned on the floor beside her bed—no, she was not on the bed, she was on the examination table—and Oliver's dark, hunched silhouette worked studiously at something, casting a monstrous shadow against the ceiling. With blurred vision and swimming awareness, she could see the scalpel in his hand, whittling with startling intensity at a piece of wood.

Then he doubled over with a ragged gasp and a spasm of pain, curling around his wound like a caterpillar.

In that instant, she thought she might escape. She attempted to sit up and found herself bound to the table with leather straps. She could not suppress her gasp of terror, but Oliver apparently took no notice, lost in his own agony. With each exertion, her head pounded like a fresh blow, and she writhed and wriggled, but to no avail. The leather was strong, and the knots were tight.

Oliver slowly uncurled himself onto his hands and knees and worked himself with excruciating, crawling slowness back into a sitting position, and his face resumed an expression of implacable concentration.

Amelia ceased her struggles lest she gain his notice.

The *skritch* of the scalpel continued for another few minutes, while Amelia's frenzied mind dreamed up one hopeless plan of escape after another, until with a last flick of splinters, he blew crumbs off of his handiwork. He held up a rough shape into the lantern light, carved of dry cottonwood, about the size of a hand, a spindly, vaguely human shape except that it had three legs and no head, clawed arms reaching upward. Somehow this small, crude image lent the impression of insatiable, ravenous hunger.

He stood, and she closed her eyes, trying to pretend senselessness. Through slitted eyes, she saw him place the figure on the tray near the head of the exam table. And then he turned to her and touched her with one hand. A whimpering gasp erupted from her. He did not react to the evaporation of her feeble ruse. The scalpel glinted in his right hand, and his left traveled up her body, sliding from her belly over her breast, but did not dwell there, traveling onward to shoulder, then down her arm, then back to her torso, sliding down to her thigh, but there was no lustful desire in his touch. His fingers appraised her, squeezing her limbs and flesh as if evaluating her tenderness.

Sobs burst out of her with fresh tears. "Please!" Her voice cracked. "Please don't hurt me! Please, Mr. McCoy. I've never done you harm. I want to help you! Please!"

His face leaned over hers, closer, closer, until his eye was a hand's breadth from hers, as though examining the inside of her head through a peephole. The full intelligence of his gaze, the volition, the full intention of what he intended to do, choked her scream dead in her throat.

XI

Hank was never so glad to see the dim lights of White Pine. His horse's breath huffed and gasped with the strain of carrying two grown men so far, its shoulders and flanks lathered.

In the last mile of the approach, he found his thoughts plagued by the knowledge that none of the residents of White Pine had the slightest notion of the horrors that existed in the world. It was bad enough that they built their town on land that twenty-years ago had been empty of aught but redskins, and that lingering sense of peril remained like a persistent scent in the air. Nevertheless, he had always felt right about it, had always felt that the tide of civilization could not be restrained, nor should it be. This nation was growing and needed some space. Where else to get it but from a bunch of heathens? Wouldn't be long and the states would stretch all the way to the Pacific coast and for as far south as they could beat back the Mexicans. It felt inevitable.

He had often wondered how many more decades would pass before South Dakota felt as settled and modern as the Pennsylvania of his youth. Would it ever? And if it did, would he have to leave then? He had seen too much darkness to ever feel completely right with a bunch of other folks around. He had no doubt those rebs who had tortured and abused his friends and comrades in Andersonville were all fine upstanding boys back in their hometowns. But the darkness had got in them, the darkness of war and hatred and fear. And all for what? A bunch of goddamn Negroes?

The war had been the first time he had seen "civilization," the everyday world, the world of suits and gowns and society and politics and schooling, all disappear like so much cannon smoke. A fragile veneer.

How could such things exist alongside the horrors he had seen tonight?

They couldn't, unless such things were a mere illusion, like a stage-magician's sleight of hand, like the world, or the Almighty, or the Great Spirit, or what-the-hell-ever, was saying *Look at this magic right here, but don't pay attention to what this other hand is doing.*

In spirals of contradiction his mind swirled, until he and Jimmy passed the boundary of town, and he reined up in front of the jail. Jimmy slid off the horse's rump with a sigh of relief, and the horse quivered and huffed with exhaustion.

Hank took a deep breath, rubbed his eyes, and dismounted, stretching the kinks from muscles that were too goddamn old and had ridden too goddamn far in the last two days.

Jimmy massaged his own backside. "Jesus Christ, I ain't had a ride like that since that whore in—" Then something caught his attention. "Say, ain't it kinda late?"

Hank followed his gaze.

A light burned from the window of Charles' office.

"On no account did Charles beat us here," Hank said.

XII

Katie sat on a bed of hay in the stable, shivering so deeply she thought her bones might flop out of her skin. But she was not cold, even though the chill of this awful night had long since seeped into her bones. There was a lot of activity outside. Charles and the Indians were busy with something, talking and such. Here she sat in the soft hay amid the scent of dust and mold, exhausted all the way to the quivering heart of her.

She clutched her roaring stomach tight. It seemed to her like a weird time to be hungry, what with all the killing and blood around. Maybe she was growing up. Or maybe it was the smell of blood making her hungry.

The first time she had watched Pa slaughter a hog, the great fount of foaming blood that poured out of its slashed throat had driven her away retching and heaving like a sissy to run away and hide behind the barn. Pa had laughed at her. Emily came along later and stroked her hair and told her that's just how things were. Katie liked bacon didn't she? And smoked ham? They had to kill the hog to eat.

A thick slab of greasy bacon, even half-cooked and dripping, sounded like a taste of heaven right now.

Lord almighty, that did sound good. She might even eat it raw. She thought back to the rabbit she had killed. Right now, she'd eat the thing raw, fur, guts, and all.

Her whole family had been hungry for a long time, just coming out of a hard, cold winter.

But she didn't have a family no more.

She hoped them Black Wind People had done for her pa. It would be justice on him. She imagined them stabbing him with spears and knives, all the while with him crying out like a baby. She never wanted to see his face again.

Ma had been the worst kind of coward. Katie couldn't remember a time when Ma had ever stood up to the piece of heartless, God-steeped leather that was Pa. He just slapped her and told her to shut her fool mouth. Did Ma know what Pa had been doing with Emily? Katie couldn't say that *she* knew exactly, just that every time Pa touched Emily, her sister looked sick to her stomach.

Something gnawed away at Katie's hope that she would ever see her sister again, like rats in the corn crib.

A hunk of corn bread sure would be good about now, dipped in bacon grease.

Even blood.

The doctor had covered her eyes to keep her from seeing that soldier hanging by his innards from the roof, but she had looked anyway. Who the hell was this doctor telling her what she could and couldn't see? She had already seen plenty. Wouldn't nobody ever tell her what she could see again, ever. And if he tried to make her, he'd better count his fingers afterward.

If she ever found Emily, the two of them would take off and leave and never look back.

And if she ever saw her pa again, she'd stick her Indian knife right into his foul belly and watch his guts fall out just like that hog's did.

XIII

The Lakota braves passed the ravaged corpses of the soldiers, their eyes glowering with horror and contempt. Twenty-four emaciated warriors—some with strong young limbs, too young to have fought in the last of the wars, some with legs and backs bowed and hair salted by air by age—had gathered outside the army stable, their faces smeared with soot as impromptu war paint. Little more than emaciated boys and old men, many of them.

Charles helped Red Horse and the other Lakota saddle the army horses. As the mounts were readied, the Lakota faces grew ever more fierce and resolute. The enormous bank of storm bearing down on them lent urgency to their efforts.

One of the ways the Army had subdued the plains tribes was to kill or steal their herds of horses, their chief form of wealth, their means of making war, and symbol of their strength as warriors. Without horses, they were nothing.

Tonight, once again, they were warriors.

Minutes flicked past as they loaded their guns and gathered ammunition. Dead soldiers were stripped of weapons, and the army magazine was emptied of all the ammunition they could carry. The air vibrated with the nervous agitation of imminent battle.

Katie sat on a pile of hay in the corner of the stable, wringing her hands, her eyes half-lidded as if struggling every second against sleep.

Charles knelt beside her. "Stay here with the women and children. I'm not taking you into further danger."

At the sound of his voice, her eyes snapped full open. She took a moment to absorb his words, then looked at him with hard eyes. "My family ain't here, sir. I got to go with you. Please."

"You cannot go into a fight!"

"If you try and leave me here, I'll just follow you. Ain't nobody going to boss me ever again."

The sheer determination in her face just then told him it was futile, unless he was prepared to tie her up. How could he be sure she would be safer here with the Lakota women and children?

"You got anything to eat, sir?" she said. "I'm so powerful hungry."

"I'm sorry, Katie, I don't." She looked so gaunt and pitiful that he had to turn away.

Outside, the wind howled higher and higher. Clouds swirled overhead. Was there a fluid, inhuman sentience to their movements, like tentacles of cephalopodan ink swirling in water?

In the frame of the stable door, a frail figure staggered into view, a Lakota woman clutching something to her chest. Red Horse saw her and approached with an expression of worry.

Born-with-a-Smile stumbled, but caught herself on a fence rail, looking marginally more hale and hearty than when he had seen her last.

Charles approached her and Red Horse. "Born-with-a-Smile, how do you feel?"

She peeled her gaze away from Red Horse and gave Charles a feeble smile.

"You must get your people to shelter," Charles said.

"Nowhere safe," said Red Horse, as he and his wife exchanged another long, pregnant gaze.

She said, "Many Lakota run away now. Maybe the Wiindigu not see."

"What about you?" Charles said, "You're in no condition to run."

Red Horse's face was grim. "She cannot run."

"I am … in God's hands," she said.

Charles opened his mouth to protest, but he knew his words would not matter.

Little Elk approached and embraced Born-with-a-Smile. *"Mitakuye oyas'in,"* she said.

With an anguished expression, Red Horse turned away, led his army horse outside, and threw a leg over its back. He raised his rifle and his voice. "Black Wind People pay with blood. Wiindigu dies today." He unleashed a terrific war cry, and the other braves took it up with him.

The wind wailed at them, gaining strength like a malicious beast working itself into a rage, with a deep rumbling undercurrent that vibrated in Charles' bones and turned his insides to water.

Little Elk hugged Born-with-a-Smile one last time, then turned to Charles. "We must go! Now!"

Charles looked at Katie again. Her gaze was fixed to him with implacable intensity. With a heavy sigh, he mounted up, and then offered her his hand.

She came forward and said, "What about Porky?"

"He's spent. He'll have to stay here. These horses are fresh, and I'm not letting you out of my sight."

She took his hand, and he helped her into the saddle behind him.

"Don't let go of me," he said.

The warriors whooped their defiance to the oncoming storm, rifles upthrust. With a cry and a gesture, Red Horse kicked his mount's flanks and led the meager band of warriors out of the burning camp, into the night, building speed and resolve as they went.

The Lakota war party thundered across the plain, sending chunks of sod high into the air, within minutes leaving the burning reservation encampment far behind them. Scarlet lightning crackled across the sky in great shuddering blasts, and the clouds boiled in a gigantic column lit from within.

The wind gusted at them from every direction, so strong at times that Charles feared Katie's grip in his coat would falter and she would be torn loose. And then a distant roar, akin to one he had experienced just a few hours before, came from behind them, and his heart went cold. He looked over his shoulder in time to see a writhing snake of tornado descend from the clouds and rip through the agency camp, raking like a black talon through fires and tents and structures. Lightning danced and struck. The ammunition magazine bloomed into a bouquet of thunderous explosions. Clouds of debris filled the air, silhouetted in the boil of fire and smoke.

For the moment, he was glad of the little hands desperately clutching his coat, but what dangers awaited in White Pine?

XIV

Amelia wept and begged and struggled. Oliver stood over her, contemplating, scalpel in his hand, oblivious to her squirming.

The scalpel slid underneath the fabric of her dress, parting her bodice like fresh gauze. Two more languorous slices through her undergarments and then her left breast and shoulder lay bare.

"No, please, Mr. McCoy, you don't have to do this. I'll give you anything you want!"

His calm, conscious eyes roamed her flesh, as if looking for just the perfect spot.

It was so sharp she felt surprisingly little pain; it drew a scarlet line from breastbone to armpit, long and slow. Maybe it wasn't so deep, maybe it was just a little incision, maybe just a few little stitches, maybe—then the lips of the cut parted and blood spilled out in a startling gush. And then her screams drowned all other sound.

An eternity later, some part of her felt the scalpel working through her flesh, and another part of her envisioned slicing through a steak she had prepared some weeks ago, the way the meat simply parted at the knife's edge, pieces of it coming away for the fork. And then the chewing sounds. She saw only the darkness and dancing stars behind her own squeezed eyelids.

A wooden crash shattered her blessed oblivion.

Hank stood in the doorway, shotgun in hand, with another man standing behind him. Why did they have such strange expressions on their faces? Why was Oliver McCoy grinning at them? Why were Oliver's lips and teeth and fingers bloody?

And then she remembered, and the screams started again.

Hank leveled the shotgun, and Oliver's head exploded into a red mist that sprayed across Amelia's legs. Oliver's body flopped floorward like a puppet with the strings cut.

Hank and the other man rushed to her side. Something warm and wet filled her left armpit, pooled under her shoulder.

The other man breathed a string of foul language.

A knife appeared in Hank's hand and made short work of slicing her free, but she was too weak to move. His mouth was a tight line as he tore a long strip from a cotton bedsheet, folded it, and held it over her wound.

The screaming trailed off to an incessant whimper. What a strange, discomfiting sound.

Hank said to the other man, "Hold this."

The other man laid a trembling hand on the bandage, but his eyes were fastened on where Oliver's body had fallen. She could hear a spasmodic shuffling against the floorboards.

Hank rifled through the cupboards, then returned with fresh bandages, removing the first—soaked through with a shocking volume of blood—and tossing it aside. With a large bandage pad applied to the wound, he wrapped her chest and shoulder so that the bandage was held tight.

The other man said to Hank, "You look like you done that before."

Hank gestured to where Oliver lay. "None of us have done *this* before." Then he finally looked Amelia in the eye. "Darlin', hang in there. Charles is coming to fix this."

The whimpering stopped, and Amelia began to weep.

The other man muttered to Hank. "He had her tittie almost off."

Hank jerked him aside. "Will you hobble that fucking lip?"

The man's attention was snagged by something near Amelia's head. He reached for it and picked up the figurine that Oliver had been carving. The instant her eyes fell upon it, a surge of nausea washed through her, and she wanted to retch.

The man held it up to Hank. "This look familiar?"

Hank's eyes narrowed. "What the hell?"

The man pulled Hank farther aside and spoke in a low voice. "Marshal, I hate to tell you this, but I'm getting a real bad feeling. I mean, *real* bad. Something's comin'. And it's got my guts all twisted up."

She hated when people spoke as if she were not in the room, as if she could not hear, as if she were not a thinking person. Men had been doing it around her all her life.

Hank's face was pale, paler than she had ever seen it, as if he had just seen the face of Satan himself. "The whole world's all twisted up."

"What are we gonna do?"

"First, we're gonna take care of that gash, then we'll cipher on our next move."

A few minutes later, when he finished binding her wound— she could feel the fabric of the bandages pressing between the lips of her flesh, into the meat of her breast—Hank said, "Amelia darlin', look at me. Stop crying for just a second and listen."

She had not realized she was crying.

"You're gonna be all right, you hear me? Just settle down."

She held back the sobs enough to speak. "I can't feel anything ... my ..."

"You'll be on the mend right quick."

"I'm not stupid, Hank. I felt him cutting into my ... I felt him cutting toward my heart ... Into the bone."

"Don't think about that now. I've seen folks survive a whole lot worse. Charles will fix it. Good as new."

The sobs rose again at the mention of Charles' name.

Hank said to the other man, "Get to the telegraph office and beat on the door until Ernest comes out. Then get his ass back here."

"I'll bring the rest of him, too," the man said as he departed. She did not like him. He had a wild and hungry look about him.

Hank said, "You stay put and relax for just a touch, while I haul out the garbage." He bent over at the side of the examination table, picked up Oliver's body by the bootheels and dragged it into the storeroom.

XV

Jimmy rushed across the street toward the Post and Telegraph Office. He stopped on the sidewalk. Right next door stood the livery stable. It wouldn't be no work at all to sneak in there and add horse-thieving to his list of offenses. He could be in Valentine by tomorrow afternoon on the next train for Denver. Maybe there were some prospectors up on Pike's Peak walking around with gold dust falling out of their pockets.

The office was dark as the inside of a horse's ass. He peered through the glass, but there was nothing but shadows. He raised his fist and beat on the door. "Hey! Anybody in there? Get your ass up! Get out here! Hey!"

He squeezed the latch, and the door swung inward. People out here were so trusting, they never locked their doors. That simple fact had made his life a whole a lot easier a few times. Maybe the telegraph operator had a room hereabouts.

Stepped inside, he called, "Anybody here?"

Lightning spilled in around him, but something in the flash looked wrong. He waited for another flash to confirm his fear. The hairs on his arms rose like the back of a porcupine. The next sputter of light revealed the smashed telegraph equipment covering the desk. He picked up the tangle of torn wires and smashed brass and copper.

"Damnit—!"

A fat, hairy man with porkchop jowls emerged from the shadows and clamped a meaty hand over Jimmy's mouth. His eyes looked up into Jimmy's with full intelligence and then something cold and hard pierced Jimmy's belly, biting deep, deep into his stomach. The strength left his legs like water from a punctured canteen.

Bile and blood rushed into his mouth. Another stab, and he was falling. Another.

There was no breath left in him.

A saddler's awl, smeared with blood, stabbed into his chest as his knees hit the floor. When it jerked out, he was falling sidewise, and it struck again.

If only he hadn't forgotten where he buried the money, he'd be halfway to—

Something was dragging him across the coarse wooden floor. Now he had splinters in his back to go with the cactus needles. Strangely there was no pain, just this strange muddle-headed feeling, and the sensation that a lot of him was leaking away. Having been around so many vicious fights—and nothing was more vicious than a knife fight—most always on the winning side, he had always counted himself lucky that he had never been stabbed before. A few cuts, but never stabbed.

Who was dragging him? The man with porkchop jowls.

He was in a tiny room now, with shelves and a lantern, a room smelling of dust and paper and blood. Or maybe that was just the blood in his nose.

His shirt—his favorite shirt!—was soaked.

He should kick this fat fucker's lily-white ass.

But his arms would barely move. He could not stand.

Mr. Porkchop dropped Jimmy's bootheels to the floor with a heavy thunk, then opened the back door of the room, gesturing through it toward someone else.

Jimmy tried to speak, but his mouth was full of blood.

Two more people came through the back door, a middle-aged bear of a man with a blacksmith's arms, and pretty little filly of no more than sixteen, blonde and freckled and full-bosomed and charming as she could be—had there been any soul left in her big blue eyes. There was intelligence there, but they were empty of any emotion except raw, ravenous hunger.

She had blood on her hands.

"Should we cut him up first, Papa?" she said.

"We should strip him first," said Porkchop Man.

The three of them stood over him.

Jimmy's lungs were full of blood, like his mouth, but he gathered a breath through the numbness and wheezed. "I hope you fucking choke!"

Then the three of them knelt and tore off his clothes.

Jimmy struggled against them, but he felt like a rag doll as his naked legs flopped.

His poor pecker had shrunk so small it was trying to retreat up inside him.

When they started to bite into him, that's when the pain came.

XVI

Hank covered Oliver's body with a sheet. Charles' office lay quiet except for the storm and the creak of the floorboards under his boots. Jimmy had been right; Amelia's wound was bad. Hank had seen men recover from worse, but he had also seen them die of infection from a whole lot less.

Hank returned to Amelia's bedside, and found her shivering, sweating, her flesh pale. What the hell does a man say to a near hysterical woman who almost had her breast sliced away by a cannibal madman? Comforting words had never been his way, not even when Martha had been on her deathbed; all he could do was watch, and sometimes he could not even do that.

Amelia's eyes glimmered toward his, begging for him to tell her everything was going to be all right. "We got the blood stopped. You're gonna be all right. Just brace up."

"Why does Charles hate me?"

The question, so out of place, so ridiculous, slammed into him hard. "What the hell kind of question is that?" He would never, ever, if he lived to be a hundred and fifty, understand women.

"If not for you, I would be dead right now, or else watching a madman …" Amelia bit down on a sob like a horse working its bit. "And while I thank you for that, I can't endure his hate anymore."

Maybe Hank had done his job too well. Maybe she was delirious. Why in the hell was she thinking about this when she could be dead by the next sunset? Her line of thinking was crazy, but her words were as calm as if she was teaching school. All he could do was humor her for now. "He don't hate you."

"Then why doesn't he love me?"

Hank bit down on his exasperation. Sometimes her waves of assumptions were so far out in the wilderness, it was like trying to talk to the Sioux. "That ain't for me to say, but a fella might ask the same of you."

"It's because he doesn't know how. And that's your fault."

He bristled at that. "What the hell are you talking about? I done right by that boy. I sent him to school."

"He got that scholarship in spite of you, to escape you, and then he came here to spite you, to prove to you that he's a man!"

"I done the best I could by him, by his mother. They needed more than I had." Hank's voice turned soft for a moment. Damn her.

"You gave nothing. You selfish son of a bitch."

His hand twitched with the urge to slap sense into her. Even an injured woman could only push him so far. But for now, he just narrowed his gaze. "Do you hear yourself? I thought you hated him!"

Fresh tears rolled down her cheeks. "I miss him."

Hank thought about how, after his granddaughters had died, he never saw Charles and Amelia together, except at Sunday dinner, and on those occasions he could have cut the tension with a buzz saw. That observation had been nagging at him for weeks, but it was not his place to say anything, or ask why that might be. People dealt with grief differently, each in his own way. "He loved them girls with all he had. So did you. I've seen a lot, but I never had to watch my children die." If he believed in angels, they would have been like his granddaughters.

"When they were gone," Amelia said, "there was nothing left. Nothing for me. Leftovers. Someone else gets the good Charles. Now he is a cicada skin with nothing inside."

Her eyes bored into him. "Just like you."

Hank got up and searched the room for a bottle of whiskey. She was just talking crazy, delirious. There was no whiskey; he had left a flask in his saddlebag. Charles should be the one listening to this, not Hank. It was not his place to make peace between his son and his daughter-in-law.

Amelia's voice followed him like an accusation. "Martha said that to me once, about you, before she died."

Hank stood at that window with his back toward her, his fists balled up white and stiff. His leathered hands pinched under the force of years of anger, simmering. Swirls of dust waltzed down in the street. Shutters clattered. The street lay dark except for a new night lanterns, and a lone figure standing silhouetted in a yellow-orange, second-story window. Who was that? What was that figure holding, something with a long handle?

Amelia's glare pressed against his back, and he said, "I left my insides in a Confederate prison. Martha never understood that." His voice was quiet, but she was driving him like a herd of buffalo to the cliff at the edge of his patience.

"Your wife was one of the loneliest people I ever met. Even on the day she died, with you hovering there like a ghoul waiting for it to happen. Couldn't come fast enough, could it, Hank?"

Stock still he stood, grinding his teeth. "You got no right. You got no goddamn right. You don't know a fucking thing."

"I have every right! I've watched my husband turn into you, buried in his work. Buried in his self-pity. I'm alone. And the silence. The silence is like drowning in a well."

She had no idea what real silence was, the silence that came only when the thunder of cannons and the pop-crackle of .69-caliber Springfield volleys had ceased and all that was left was smoke and blood and the ringing in a man's ears, when the last man in your tent was about to succumb to starvation and he'd given permission to … do what was necessary, said it was all right, that he didn't mind.

"Sometimes," Amelia said, "I scream at him just to shatter that damnable silence."

That was the first thing she had said that he truly understood.

The anger in her voice subsided into weariness. "It doesn't matter anyway. I'm leaving."

Hank turned from the window and eyed her. She met his gaze with eyes like flint chips. He said, "You're not going to die."

"No, I mean, I'm leaving White Pine. And I'm never coming back."

A scream echoed through the wind, breaking their impasse.

"What the hell?" Hank grabbed his shotgun and cracked the door. The silhouette in the window was gone; why did that tighten the unease in his gut? The stars above were long gone. That goddamn storm was coming here.

He rubbed his eyes and peered again where he thought he had seen a shadow flitting between two buildings across the street. Were the cannibals here? Or had that shadow been one of the townspeople? Or maybe his eyes were just fooling him.

There was no denying the sense of impending dread building in his guts. He knew not to ignore that feeling; it had kept him alive all these years.

Shades of electric blue threaded with scarlet flickered above, licking the underside of roiling clouds.

"Shit. Grab your things. Hate me later. We got to get somewhere safe."

Amelia tried to sit up, but fell back with a soft cry.

He crossed to room to help her off the examination table. "Damnit, let's go!"

She clutched the bloody bandages against her breast with her other hand, gasping at the pain. Her legs were wobbly but he hurried her outside.

Where the hell was Jimmy? Lit out? Bushwhacked?

With Amelia on one arm, and the shotgun in the other, Hank half-dragged her across the street toward the jailhouse.

Another scream tore from somewhere, impossible to discern in the swirl of wind, which threatened to tug his hat loose and send it spinning into darkness. He gripped the shotgun tighter. Reaching the jailhouse door, he fumbled for a moment with the latch before shoving inside, his shoulder punching the door open, dragging Amelia in behind him, then slamming it behind them, plunging them into almost pitch darkness. The only light trickled through the dirty window from outside. The lamp on the desk taunted him with its promise of easy light to drive back the fears slinking outside the door, sniffing around the back of his neck. The street was dark, and the window was too dirty for him to see a goddamn thing. He rubbed at it with his sleeve, but most of the grime was on the outside.

"What are you doing?" Amelia's voice whispered hollowly in the silence.

"Get in the cell."

Hank unlocked the gun cabinet.

"What—?"

"Get in the goddamn cell!"

Hank pulled a couple more shotguns from the cabinet and laid them across the desk, opened a drawer and spread out the ammunition. Shell by shell he started loading the shotguns.

Amelia had not moved, and her voice shrilled. "Don't talk to me like—"

"I am not Charles. You're not going to argue with me. Get in the goddamn cell, now!" He laid the first pump 12-gauge, loaded now, on the desk and took up the other.

Lightning crackled, heralding a tremendous crash of thunder, almost simultaneously, turning Amelia's face ghostly pale. Wet pink lips trembled. "Please, Hank. What's going on?"

Hank pulled a rifle from the gun cabinet and began loading that as well. "Do you still believe in anything, Amelia. God? The Devil? Hell?" Hank grabbed her arm—she gasped, but he did not relent—and walked her into the cell, shut the door, and locked it closed. He tossed the ring of keys inside to her. "What did your daddy tell you to do when evil is walking the earth, evil that ain't the human kind?"

"If he were here, he tell me to pray for the Lord's deliverance."

"Then you better get to it, but I don't think it's gonna matter."

The orange glow of a large fire bloomed in the window.

XVII

Charles, Little Elk, and the Lakota warriors reined up on the low hill overlooking White Pine. The wind and lightning had chased them all the way from the reservation, and now blew with an angry, ravenous howl over their shoulders, through their hair, tickling their scalps with invisible questing fingers. Flames engulfed a building on the edge of town, at the end of Main Street, the creamery. The flames were fierce with burning fat.

Malevolent shapes flitted through the shadows. Distant screams echoed through the night, fighting upstream against the wind at their backs.

The noise of the wind rose to almost deafening—Charles kept looking about for signs of a twister—but he pulled Red Horse and Little Elk close. "Katie and I will circle around the far side of town. There are weapons in the marshal's office."

Red Horse nodded.

"I am coming with you," Little Elk replied. She wobbled in the saddle.

"Is something wrong?"

She swallowed hard, and her mouth looked as if she were about to retch, eyes glistening. "We rode here ... and I saw things ... horrible things."

"What are you talking about?"

"I am a Dreamer. When I was a girl, I knew things I could not know, could not see with my eyes. I have always walked with one foot in the spirit world, so I became a medicine woman. We rode here, and I saw things."

Somehow the idea of clairvoyance seemed almost commonplace in light of everything Charles had seen in the last two days.

"What did you see?"

Little Elk glanced for a moment at Katie. "It was like having a dream, but I was awake." Her voice grew thick, as if the words themselves were too viscous to be spoken. "I saw what happened to this child's family. I will not say what happened, what her father did. But she saw it all, and I am so sorry for you, child. But I saw more, a group of wagons, white families, taken by the Black Wind People, eaten, picked clean, their bones left in a ditch beside a river, and I saw white men slaughtered by other white men they thought were their friends, and I saw white people in the town tortured by evil dreams, and I saw those people acting on the evil of those dreams. There is death down there. Only death." Her voice trailed almost to a whisper drowned by the wind, and her cheeks glistened with tears.

"So hungry," she said. "All so hungry."

"Enough talk!" Red Horse snorted. "We fight!" The other braves echoed his sentiment, raising their rifles.

Little Elk's words had unsettled Charles more than he cared to admit. Katie's hands twisted tight into his coat. He could not see her face, but her hands almost felt as if they were vibrating. "Are you all right, honey?" Charles said.

Several heartbeats passed before she responded. "Yes, sir."

The shadows seemed to be congregating near the burgeoning fire. Red Horse said to Charles, "We fight there." Then he raised his rifle and shouted, *"Hokahe! Hokahe!"*

The other warriors took the chant, and as a mass they charged down the hill.

"Good luck, Red Horse," Charles said, then turned his mount toward the other side of town and spurred down the hill, Little Elk close behind.

XVIII

Red Horse kicked the flanks of the Bluecoat horse, a fat, lumbering beast, and led the braves swooping toward the white man's town. Black Arrow rode close beside him with Bull Bear and Two Knives close behind. They kept silent to mask their approach, hoping to ambush the Black Wind People and with ferocity and surprise throw them into panic.

One of the buildings had become a towering bonfire, and as their horses pounded nearer, Red Horse could see the dark figures circled around it, arms raised. In his breast, his heart thundered with righteous battle fury, a sensation he had not felt since the Battle of the Greasy Grass when he was still a young man, when they had killed the Bluecoat General Longhair and all his men.

The Black Wind People would die tonight. Every last one.

Perhaps Red Horse would die, too, and that was good, because in his heart he knew Born-with-a-Smile was already dead. There was nothing left for him except courage and battle. Better to die with a weapon in his hand than to waste away like the old chiefs who succumbed to the white men's lies and became farmers or slaves to the government's handouts. The Wiindigu would never claim his spirit. He would die a warrior, and rejoin his people, and when the Father's prophecies came to fruition, he would rejoice at the Remaking of the world.

Half of the band peeled away to attack from a different direction, as they had arranged. Red Horse's group swung directly toward the bonfire. He cocked the Winchester and made ready, and it was good.

Their horses pummeled toward the town. How many times had he envisioned a massive war band destroying one of the white towns sprouting up like noxious weeds on land that belonged rightfully to his people?

His band rounded a corner, and the sight there at the bonfire tore cries of surprise and shock from the braves. Horses screamed in protest as riders hauled on reins. The massive bonfire belched smoke and embers, torn sideways by the wind. The smell of sizzling flesh filled the air. With his belly long empty, Red Horse's mouth burst with juices and his stomach roared, and then he saw the spits thrust upright near the heat. The bodies of white men and women, skewered into grotesque shapes and dismembered limbs, hung over the flames on posts.

Sizzling. Cooking.

The juices in Red Horse's mouth turned to shame and bile.

A woman in a horrid, wooden mask raised handfuls of raw, bloody meat outstretched in supplication to the sky. Surrounding her, Black Wind warriors stomped their feet in rhythmic unison. A small, hairy creature clung to her shoulder. Her small, filthy breasts hung exposed, and her flesh was pierced and distorted by bone rings and needles. Long tangles of filthy hair hung down her back.

The warriors of the Black Wind turned to face Red Horse and the shocked Lakota. The cannibals' eyes glowed white.

Red Horse unleashed his fiercest war cry, aimed his rifle at the nearest warrior, and fired.

XIX

Charles and Little Elk rode toward the opposite end of town. He hoped to reach the jailhouse from the darkened side and there retrieve his father's cache of weapons. Perhaps, if fate was kind, he might even find his father there. Some part of him still hoped against hope that Hank had escaped the tornado atop Sentinel Hill. Most likely, in that event, he would have returned to town.

His horse's weariness trembled into him. The ride thus far had been fast and furious, and they had all been lucky that none had stepped in a hole in the dark and broken a leg. The heat and sweat of the animal's muscles suffused his own weary legs. He was not accustomed to all the riding he had accomplished today.

Beside him, Little Elk gripped the mane of her galloping horse with one hand, the reins with the other, and leaned low over the army saddle. Her wild hair was a flailing tumult around her head.

The outlying buildings were within a few dozen yards when his horse stumbled and nearly fell. The saddle lurched under him as the animal kicked at something. Katie's grip slipped from his coat, and she flew through the air in a tumbling arc. She landed in the grass, rolled and bounced to her feet, apparently unharmed, mouth gaping and eyes wide.

The horse stumbled again and stopped, sinking to its knees as if all strength had suddenly gone out of it.

Charles bailed from the saddle; if the horse fell it would trap his leg under its bulk.

Little Elk spun her mount back. "What happened?"

Charles' horse struggled to regain its feet for a few moments more, then flopped onto its side with deep shuddering sigh.

A flash of lightning illuminated the dark quills embedded in its pale haunches. Not quills, darts.

Charles' throat clenched. "Come on! We have to go."

Little Elk leaped like a cat from her horse and landed beside Katie. "Are you all right, child?"

Katie nodded, still amazed.

Little Elk offered her hand, and Katie took it. "We must go!"

Charles frantically scanned the area behind them.

Mounds of grass were moving, shifting position in the sputtering lightning flashes, coming closer.

He took Katie's other hand, and they ran.

XX

Hank peered through the window at the distant bonfire. He could not make out what the cannibals had hoisted onto stakes near the fire, but after what he had seen on Sentinel Hill, he did not need to guess. If he could live to find out who the victims were, he would goddamn sure avenge every one of them.

"Hank, what's out there? What's going on?" Amelia clutched the bars of the cell.

"Bastards got some big fire burning down the street." Hank kept his eyes on the street.

"Who?"

"Woman, you'd better off go to your grave than hear about the shit we saw today."

"I'm not a child, Hank. A madman ... *ate* part of me. What happened to that man who was with you?"

"Jimmy's dead, I reckon."

A chorus of sharp cries threaded through the wind. Now *those* war cries he knew well. What the hell were the Sioux doing here? "There's a whole goddamn tribe of them doing the same thing to our neighbors."

"Are those Indians out there? Is the town under attack?"

"You might say."

"Are you trying to say the Sioux have turned cannibal?"

"No, these ain't like the Sioux. I don't know what the hell they are, and I don't know what in the hell the Sioux are doing here."

A loud thud against the door made both of them jump. Hank trained his scattergun on the door. Pounding commenced from the outside.

"Who's there?" he shouted.

"It's me, Dad! It's Charles! Let us in!"

A bucket of warm relief washed over him.

Hank threw aside the bolt and jerked open the door. Charles, Katie, and Little Elk rushed inside. After a quick glance to check if they had been spotted, Hank eased the door closed again and slid the bar down. He would never tell Charles how close he had come to the business end of a load of buckshot through the door.

Hank clapped Charles on the shoulder. "Jesus Christ, boy, it's good to see you. I thought you were a goner."

"I could say the same of you. When that twister came down—"

"Twister!" Amelia said.

"Amelia, honey, we've had a busy night," Hank said.

Inside the cell, Amelia looked Little Elk up and down, her face turning hard.

Charles approached the cell and reached through the bars. "Are you all right? What happened? You're bleeding!"

Amelia looked at his outstretched hand. "I'm alive. But your father won't tell me what's going on. Who's she?"

Charles slowly withdrew his hand. Hank shook his head. Goddamn. The boy looked like he'd just been switched. When Charles finally mustered some words, he could not raise his eyes. "This is Little Elk. She is a medicine woman at the reservation."

Little Elk stepped toward the cell. "Are you Doctor Zimmerman's wife?"

"I am." Amelia's voice was a hard as her jawline, as cold as her eyes.

Hank rolled his eyes. Impatience turned his jaw to stone, and he peered out the window again, hoping to shut out the conversation he knew was coming.

Little Elk said, "You are lucky to have such a good husband."

A sizzling pause hung between the two women.

This was not the time for a catfight. Hank tried to cut the tension. "I'm glad to see you got the little girl back here safe and sound." He tried to give Katie a smile, but the hollow look in her eyes, half-lidded as if she were about fall dead asleep where she stood, killed it. "On the other hand, you might have been better off just heading for Nebraska. I can't see shit about what's going on down there, but after what I seen on Sentinel Hill, I got a pretty good idea."

Charles hugged Katie to his side. "Where's Jimmy?"

"I sent him to the telegraph office, but he ain't come back. I'd imagine he's dead now."

"The wind took him," Katie said.

Charles said, "What—?"

Gunshots outside cut him off.

XXI

Swarming from the darkness came snarling, hideous warriors, wild-eyed and talon-fingered, filed teeth gleaming. A hurled warclub brained Red Horse's mount, sending him crashing onto the earth. He managed to keep his grip on his rifle, rolling to his feet, firing from the hip at a cannibal hurtling toward him. From less than a horse-length away, the bullet tore through the cannibal's face, and he fell twitching.

Everywhere, the battle was joined. Horses screamed and thrashed and fled. These Bluecoat geldings had no spirit. A Lakota steed and a warrior worthy of him would fight as one.

Gunshots cracked and bullets whizzed and ricocheted.

Black Arrow spurred his horse into the nearest Black Wind warrior, screaming a war cry, and spitted his adversary with a lance made from a lodge pole. Other enemy warriors converged on him, and he launched himself into them. Lakota war clubs and knives slashed into Black Wind flesh. The sharpened claws of the Black Wind warriors dug the meat from Lakota bone. Bull Bear fired arrows from horseback at the dark shapes flitting at the fringes of the bonfire light. One of the Black Wind warriors stole up behind Two Knives as he reined up his mount, dragged him from the saddle, and brained him with a single vicious stroke of a warclub.

Red Horse raised his rifle and dropped Two Knives' killer with a single shot, found another target, fired again.

A foul, charnel reek washed through the melee.

A shrill, rhythmic chant suddenly rang in his ears, through the clamor of battle.

The Black Wind witch raised her bloody hands, chanting in supplication to the storm. The small creature clung to her neck with tiny hands, squealing and croaking and hissing, its furtive, man-like face fixing on Red Horse. When his eyes met those of the little beast, those tiny, little eyes so sharp and full of intelligence, he felt a revulsion like he had never experienced.

"Ia-hey! Ia-hey!" the witch chanted. "Ph'nglui mglw'nafh Cthulhu R'lyeh wgah'nagl fhtagn! Ph'ngha Wündigu nogshogg. Ia-hey! Ia-hey!"

The horrific syllables bored into Red Horse's mind like maggots. The Black Wind warriors seemed to take strength from the sound of her voice and fought back with renewed vigor. Their weapons, both deadly and bizarre, crushed Lakota skulls and severed Lakota limbs.

Red Horse levered fresh cartridges through the rifle at the nearest knot of the enemy, as fast as his arm would manage. He tried to manage a shot at the witch, but too many warriors stood between them.

And then his ammunition was gone.

With a howl of rage and glee, he drew his knife and charged.

XXII

Hank peered out the window, queerly fascinated as the silhouettes around the bonfire joined in some savage dance to the percussion of gunshots. "Good lord, something's going on out there."

"We brought some help," Charles said.

"Tell me you brought the army."

"No soldiers left, Dad." Charles lowered his head.

"All of them?" Hank asked.

"All of them."

Charles stepped to the jail cell bars again. "Amelia, what happened to you? I need to look at that."

Amelia clutched the bloody bandage tighter to her chest. "Your father already saw to it while you were … off somewhere else."

Charles mouth worked but nothing came out.

Hank gritted his teeth again. Good lord, would that boy ever grow a backbone?

"What happened to you? Where's Oliver?" Charles said.

Amelia's knees buckled, but she regained her balance before she fell.

Hank said, "Oliver didn't make it."

Charles stood there, and Hank could see that his mind was trying to fill in the gaps, but Amelia certainly was not prepared to talk about what happened. Hank did not much care at this point. The whole world had gone to shit. He turned his attention back to the distant fight outside but could see frustratingly little from this angle, and he was not about to stick his head outside without good reason. "Hmph. Damned if I ever thought I'd root for redskins to win."

Voices in the room fell silent, and only the wind spoke, building its chorus of dread just above the rafters, just outside the walls, broken only by distant shouts of pain or fury or terror. Eyes traded glances. Some of those sounds were coming from closer than the battle.

Goddamn, Hank hated waiting for the other boot to drop. And he sure as hell didn't like sitting here like a sluggard while a bunch of redskins did his fighting for him.

The medicine woman glanced from person to person, as if expecting something. She had the look of someone who had lost everyone dear. She was awful pretty, for a Sioux, in a powerful, mournful way, even with her hair hacked to bits. Hank had heard that her husband had been a warrior who died at Wounded Knee Creek. There were so many stories and rumors about what really happened out there in the snow beside a frozen creek. There had been so much fighting in the last twenty years, so much killing, white settlers butchered, entire villages of Sioux slaughtered in return.

It had never bothered him before, the thought of an entire settlement wiped away, women, children, old folks and all. Until now, now that he knew what was coming for White Pine, this town that he had helped build. That *thing* and its subhuman toadies would offer no quarter.

"So how many did you bring?" Hank said, when he could stand the silence no longer.

Charles said, "Not enough."

Little Elk stepped forward, eyes wide with urgency. "Take your guns, Marshal! Help my people! Help *your* people!"

A lump formed in Hank's throat. "After what I saw up there …" If he lived to be a thousand years old, he would never forget the sight of what they did to Cyrus Delacroix, much less Clara and poor Sean.

Vague shapes struggled and screamed in the flame-rippled distance. His fingers trailed over the handful of shotgun shells in his pocket.

"Amelia, gimme them keys!" Hank said.

Amelia handed the keys to Hank through the bars. He opened the cell door, grabbed Katie's arm, and thrust the girl inside.

"Safer in there, girl," Hank said, but some strange sensation raised his short hairs when he touched her, when he looked at her pale face smudged with grime. "Hey, you feeling all right?"

"Yes, sir."

Hank gestured toward Little Elk, bidding her to enter the cell.

She pulled away. "I will die before I ever go into a cage again."

Hank shrugged and shut the door, locked it, and tossed the keys to Amelia.

A scream cut the air from outside, too close by. He ran to the window.

A wild figure, arms flailing in desperate flight, a pale flannel nightgown painted orange by the distant blaze. Olga Teague running down the street, mouth agape with terror, glancing with platter-sized eyes over her shoulder, away from her husband Robert, who chased her with a double-bitted axe. In between pants for breath, she screamed and screamed.

"Son of a bitch! Whole goddamn town's gone deranged!" Hank froze with his hand on the door bar. Goddamn, Robert was going to catch her. That New England Nancy hadn't lifted an axe in all his born days, but he looked like an old hand at it now. Flinging open the door came too late for Hank to stop the axe from rising and swooping down, striking Olga a glancing blow in the back, knocking her onto her face in the dirt.

"Stop, Teague!" Hank roared, but the man ignored him.

The lawyer's face was a twisted mask, like the faces on a totem pole. Or a wooden Devil-mask. He was laughing.

Hank raised the shotgun. "Teague! Hold it right there!"

Olga rolled onto her wounded back, raising her hands in supplication and defense.

Grinning with pleasure, Robert raised the axe over his head for the final blow.

"Teague, goddammit! What the hell are you doing? I don't want to shoot you!"

Robert turned his face to Hank, axe held high. "Feeding God, Hank. Can't you taste it?"

Charles and Little Elk had followed Hank outside, and Hank caught sight of the muzzle of the double-barrel 10-gauge in Charles' hands.

Olga's body heaved with sobs.

Charles stepped forward. "Robert! You don't truly want to hurt your wife do you? Olga loves you! What about your children? Where are they?"

"God has already embraced them. Black breath for all."

Olga forced words out between hysterical sobs. "Please, Robert, no!"

Robert looked down at her. The axe head sagged a little.

"You don't really want to hurt her!" Charles reached out to him.

Robert grinned. "Yes. I do. I always wondered what her pussy tastes like."

The axe began to fall, but Hank's shotgun roared, blowing a fist-sized hole through Robert's ribcage. He tumbled sideways as if struck by a sledgehammer.

They ran to Olga's side. She lay on her back, weeping, gasping.

Charles knelt and said, "Don't worry. We'll get you fixed up at my office." He eased her onto her side to look at the wound.

Hank stood over them, scanning the nearby area for signs of more attackers. "I'd advise against that, son. Your office is that way." He pointed toward the bonfire and its nearby melee.

"Then where?"

"Jailhouse. It's a fort. One way in."

"And only one way out."

Hank brandished his shotgun. "Anything comes through that door gets cut in h—" Something flickered in the darkness at the corner of his eye. "Oh, fuck."

Four cannibal warriors emerged from the shadows, two on each side of the jailhouse. The warriors bared their sharpened teeth, laughing and hissing. Eyes blazed white.

Hank swiveled the shotgun.

A warrior drew back an arrow and fired.

Hank squeezed the trigger and a blast of orange sparks roared from the muzzle. The warrior screamed and fell, his face a buckshot-peppered mess.

But the arrow kept coming, and the obsidian point glinted with firelight the instant before it sank into Hank's left shoulder. The point sprang out his back. The shock and impact nearly dropped him like a buffalo. The world reeled around him, but he kept his feet.

Charles was shouting something.

Hank's left arm was ablaze with fire and numbness, but he levered another shell into the chamber with his remaining arm. The cannibal warriors faded back into the alley shadows. "Get Olga up, son. Get her out of here." His words burned like Kentucky moonshine in his throat.

Charles helped Olga into a sitting position. "Can you walk?"

Olga coughed, blood reddening her lips, but she nodded. Little Elk and Charles helped her to her feet.

"Cover us, Dad."

Hank hoisted the shotgun up higher into his armpit, trying to rest it on an arm that would not obey him. He roared into the night. "Come on, you devil sons-a-bitches!" Then he let loose another blast into the blackness where the cannibals had disappeared. He levered in another shell one-handed.

One of the warriors darted through the open jailhouse door.

"Son of a bitch," Hank muttered.

"Dad—!"

"Get a move on, boy, before I tan your hide!"

Hank ran back across the street, but he was gasping for breath before he covered half the distance. An arrow was sticking out of both sides of him, but he managed to reach the shadows of the opposite alley. Amelia and Katie were still inside the jailhouse, and he'd be goddamned if he was going to let the cannibals have them. He'd kill them himself first. But he wasn't going to walk into an ambush either.

From the corner of the alley, he watched Charles and Little Elk half-drag Olga down the wooden sidewalk toward Charles' office, her bare feet stumbling on the uneven, splintered planks.

Charles paused to give Hank a forlorn glance, until the medicine woman touched his arm and returned his attention to the task at hand.

Hank could only let them go and concentrate on his.

XXIII

Amelia jumped at the gunshots outside, at the shouting, but the angle of the open door prevented her from seeing what was happening. She clutched little Katie Delacroix to her—the girl's face pressed against the same patch of belly that Eva had favored to lay her cheek, just above her womb where a new life waited for its time to be born. Fear streamed down her cheeks.

"Don't worry, darling," she said. "I won't let anything hurt you."

"I'm hungry," Katie said.

"Don't worry, darling, we'll get you some food as soon as all this is over."

Amelia's eyes fell on the last shotgun resting on the desk. All she knew was to point and pull the trigger, but she could not reach it right now. To get it, she would have to open the cell door.

A dark shape darted and rolled through the door with a sound like rustling grass. Amelia suppressed a gasp and clutched Katie tighter. The figure rolled to its feet, reaching a terrifying height, swathed in a cloak of prairie grass as it pressed its back against the front wall of the jail just beside the door. A man wearing a miasma of filth and decay and blood. The stench twisted her stomach into a sudden knot.

Amelia pulled Katie into the darkest shadows of the jail cell and clamped a hand over Katie's mouth. Katie did not struggle, showed no tension of fear. Only calm.

What kind of man was this enormous creature? He was not dressed as a Sioux, and in his hand he carried some sort of strange, twisted warclub that somehow glittered with shards of night. He took long, slow, quiet breaths, as a hunter waiting for prey.

Should she scream a warning to Charles and Hank? As yet, he did not seem to have noticed her and Katie's presence. She glanced again at the shotgun on the table, longing for an extra eight feet of reach on her arm.

The intruder cocked his head, sniffing the air. He turned and looked into the darkness, narrowing his gaze.

Sobs burst into Amelia's throat, but she held them in. A sound came from Katie's mouth muffled by Amelia's hand. It could have been sobbing. Or a plea for help. Or an innocent child's whimper of terror.

But it wasn't.

Something pierced deep into Amelia's belly, something cold and hard and so, so sharp.

Katie's hand was wrapped around the bone handle of a knife. The red lips of Amelia's belly closed around the base of the blade, and a trickle of blood oozed from the corners.

The point pressed deeper, into her womb, and started to saw, to cut. A hot gush fell down her legs, and her strength left her.

"My poor baby my poor child my dear poor baby," Amelia was saying as she sank to the floor.

The intruder's hoarse laughter echoed within the brick confines of the jailhouse.

Katie giggled with him as she continued to cut.

XXIV

Olga's weight sagged against Charles' shoulder, and he paused to re-situate her. Her blood leaked over his forearm from the gash across her back, and every step brought gasps and sobs from her. If not for the wind, he would have worried that the enemy would hear them.

But it did worry him that his office was halfway to the scene of the bonfire and swirling melee. He could only hope that the shadows of the eaves and sidewalk and the chaos of the melee would allow them to remain unnoticed. He clutched Olga Teague in one arm and the shotgun in the other. Little Elk supported Olga on the opposite side, and even in this morass of fear and death, the touch of her arm against his carried warmth, drew warmth from deep within him, that he had not felt in … years.

The look of icy contempt on Amelia's features when she had seen Little Elk was something he would never forget. And that made his jaw clench so tight his head hurt. He had just wanted to help her, but she had spurned him out of jealousy. He had done nothing improper. Nothing. He could not help the emotions that washed through him like conflicting tides. Was she likening herself to God, judging him for the deepest, darkest of his impure thoughts?

At the first opportunity, he led Olga and Little Elk out of the firelight of the street, into a dark rear alley where he could approach his office from the back door. Gunshots and screams echoed throughout the town, and screams came from directions where there was no obvious battle. How many sleeping homes had become nightmare charnel houses akin to what happened between Olga and Robert Teague? Shouts of anger, consternation. The laughter of madness. If Hell existed, this was what it would sound like.

There was the back door of his office, a shadow of illusory comfort.

Then he heard that roar.

And saw it.

The swirling mass of cyclone descending from the lightning-dappled chaos of sky.

On Sentinel Hill, it had been a finger. Here, it had become a fist.

He shoved open his back door and dragged Olga and Little Elk inside behind him. A soft, heavy mass on the floor tripped him, and he fell, his palm landing in a thick wet puddle, sliding from under him in a black smear. The stench of blood lay thick in the back storeroom. He had fallen over a corpse covered in a sheet. The blanket was soaked with blood where the head was—where the head *should* be.

This must be Oliver McCoy. His heart clenched at the futility of everything he done. All of it, everything, clenching into an agonized thorn of sheer despair.

Olga staggered and almost fell on him, but Little Elk righted her.

Charles jumped back to his feet and ushered them through the storeroom. A blast of wind slammed the back door open against the wall.

The office lay pitch-black save for fireglow and lightning flash through the front windows. Nevertheless, he knew the space like his own hands. Rushing to the supply cabinet, he fumbled through bandages and bottles.

Olga's wound would need cleaning and sewing, but it was not immediately fatal. The axe blow had been only glancing.

He lay her on her side on the blood-stained examination table, gently as he could.

The locomotive roar of the tornado grew, with a horrific crunching, splintering, clattering, shattering roar as it began to eat through the town itself.

He folded a wad of bandages and placed them over Olga's wound. She flinched against the contact, leaking fresh sobs and tears. "Oh god why Robert why Robert why Robert why why ..."

Little Elk stood near him. "What shall I do?"

Her hand was warm and alive as he took it and placed it on the bandage. "Hold this here."

He ran to the front door, locked it, wedged a chair under the latch.

"What are you doing?" she said.

"I have to go back for Katie and Amelia."

Her hand reached out for him as he passed, clasped his arm. Pausing beside her, feeling the warmth of her touch, feeling it spread to his face, he stood transfixed. Her hand rose from his arm and touched his face.

White heat surged through him, lust such as he had not felt since … ever. Instantly his manhood swelled and pressed against his trousers, throbbing with his heartbeat. He turned away, simultaneously thankful of the darkness and chiding himself for his body's betrayal of all integrity. His body ached to take her right there, against the examination table, against Olga Teague's body.

The shapeless syllables of the chant he had heard while hiding under the infirmary glowed inside his skull like yellow-hot iron, smoking and metallic and thrumming with desire made corporeal. He felt Little Elk's heat surging through her body, across the space that separated them, smelled her, musky and sweet and earthy.

He took her wrist, yearning to feel her naked flesh pressed against his, enveloping him, moist squeezing and muscles supple under his grip, until he exploded into her, pulled her closer, sank his teeth into her throat and—

Charles snatched his hand away and drew back. Little Elk faltered as if she had been struck a blow, hand clutching her heart, recognition flickering as if she had seen his thoughts.

Without another word, he fled.

XXV

Threaded jags of lightning curved along the swirling contours of the clouds.

This Red Horse saw, as he heaved off the body of the Black Wind warrior who had just impaled himself on Red Horse's knife. The foul, black blood of these … creatures reeked like living Evil. They could not be of Creation.

Red Horse's blood-slick hand still clutched the knife, and his assailant had torn a chunk of meat from his shoulder with its vile teeth. Around him lay the dead and wounded. Gunshots and war cries were swallowed by the howling hiss of the wind as the storm bore down upon them. The gasp of weariness that escaped him revealed how his strength had been sapped by age and starvation.

Black Arrow straddled an enemy on the ground, strangling him with his bare hands.

Bull Bear lay dead from a split skull, with several arrow-pierced enemies lying near him.

This storm was not born of the Thunderbird. Like the Black Wind People themselves, it was a corruption, a blot of congealed hunger on the face of the sky, a canker. Its evil had found its way into Red Horse's belly. For a handful of heartbeats, he looked at the dead warrior and saw only food, food enough for several days. So long since he had tasted buffalo roasted over the fire, great chunks succulent red flesh, dripping with juices, sizzling with fat and blackening, shoulder and haunches and hocks and fingers and tongue.

His stomach roared, but he shook his fist and screamed defiance at the black god swirling above.

This was where he belonged, in battle, weapon raised above his head, slaying an enemy that could not be slain.

Before him stood the witch, haloed by flame, her hideous little man-beast clinging to her neck. Slowly she peeled up the wooden mask that obscured her hideous face. Her nose was a single empty black pit in her face. She smiled, and her grotesque fangs gleamed yellow, her eyes burning with an inner light like charcoals at midnight.

Here before him stood the beating heart of the Black Wind People. Kill her, and their will would be broken.

Red Horse charged.

XXVI

Hank leaned against the wall of the jailhouse, gasping, shivering. The arrowhead grated against the wall, sending pulses of electric flame into his shoulder, up his neck and down his arm. He bit down hard on his lip to suppress the grunt of pain until he tasted blood.

Where had those other two bastards gone? One dead, one inside the jailhouse, and two still out here in the dark.

Clouds of wind-driven grit peppered his face and eyes. The twister ravaged the other side of town, coming closer. Boards spun through the air overhead. His legs felt empty, hollow, like empty sausage casings, barely able to support his weight. Only the steel and wood of the shotgun in his hand felt real, that and the wooden shaft piercing his shoulder.

He had to get the goddamn thing out. Grabbing the shaft sticking out of the front of his shoulder, he snapped it off, and the shock of it sent fresh pain through him. To reach the other half of the shaft, he would have to lay down the shotgun, and this was not the time.

While he waited for his breath and heart to slow, he reloaded his weapon with rock-steady fingers.

XXVII

Planks and dust and trees spun through the deafening, screeching roar. The bonfire guttered amid showers of sparks and fluttering embers. Splintering wood and shattering glass filled the air.

The witch dodged Red Horse's knife thrust and then tore into him with her claws. The creature clung to her neck, chattering and squealing with sounds that could have been language.

He closed with her again and plowed his knee into her belly. She doubled over, giving him opening enough to kick her in the face. She staggered back, and he went for a final knife thrust, but the little beast leaped with shocking agility from her shoulder straight toward his face. Tiny claws ripped into his cheek and ear, and its tiny too-human face squealed and bit at his eye.

The shock of the beast's attack drove Red Horse backwards. He clutched at it with his free hand, but it was preternaturally quick and seemed to sense his grab before it came, darting to the rear of his head and tearing at his hair.

The witch was recovering, blood drooling from her broken mouth.

The creature darted over Red Horse's pate and bit into his brow with sharp, tiny teeth. This time, he managed to snatch its furry body in his fist and peeled it off him, tearing away a chunk of his eyebrow in its teeth. It squirmed and flailed in his grip, and he squeezed with all his might as blood poured into his eye from the open wound.

He flung it into the bonfire.

A tiny repellent scream echoed for several heartbeats from the depths of the crackling flames, but it was not a bestial scream of pain; it was the scream of the being that knew full well that its death had come.

Red Horse wiped at the blood in his eyes, recovering in time to glance the witch cocking her arm to throw a war club. She let fly, and he flung up his arms and knife in defense. Her aim was true. The twisted wooden weapon would have brained him a heartbeat sooner, but it just knocked his knife out of this grip, and shards of black glass embedded in its contours tore fresh gashes in his forearms.

The witch leaped upon him, driving him back with slashing claws, a frenzy of whirling arms and rending rage. A powerful kick to his groin doubled him over, and she pressed her advantage, slipping her claws inside his guard and closing them around his throat. The force of her assault knocked him onto his back. She fell upon his chest, blood dribbling from her mouth into his face.

Through the haze of pain and blood and asphyxiation, Red Horse heard her chanting again.

"Ia-hey! Ia-hey! Ph'nglui mglw'nafh ..."

Her claws squeezed deeper into his neck, cutting off his air. Her strength exceeded that of any man he had ever fought.

He smashed his fist against the side of her head, but she did not relent. He looked about for aid, but saw only Black Arrow's dead eyes staring through a mask of gore.

"... Cthulhu R'lyeh wgah'nagl fhtagn! Ph'ngha Wündigu nogshogg ..."

Eyes full of blood and darkness, he fought against her powerful wrists, but to no avail. His strength began to ebb.

Her chant continued with gleeful laughter. *"... Ia-hey! Ia-hey!"* She spit blood into his eyes, her own face a rictus grin.

He scrabbled and strained against her, but she clung to him with ferocious strength.

Then something hard and cold bumped into his arm as he strained for purchase against her. He dropped his hand and hope sprung alive; his fingers closed around the blade of his knife. A moment of desperate fumbling, and the hilt was in his hand. In one sudden, forceful upward stab, he drove the blade up under the witch's jaw. Her hands convulsed and released him, her jaw worked up and down on the blade, and one of her eyes went askew. Her body tumbled off him, stiff and twitching.

Drenched in gore, Red Horse jerked out his knife and fought to his feet, coughing, gasping fresh breaths.

He snatched a handful of her filthy, bone-woven, blood-crusted hair, jerked it taut, and with the edge of his knife, peeled her scalp from her skull.

The lost Lakota children were avenged. Through the taking of her scalp, the spirit of the Black Wind People now belonged to him.

A great shudder went through him, deep and booming. He spotted two Black Wind warriors staring at him, their mouths agape, their eyes white with fear. He gathered a ragged breastful of breath, threw up his arms in triumph and defiance, dripping scalp thrust upward toward the mouth of the descending cyclone, and screamed the ancient war whoop of his fathers.

A scarlet burst exploded down from the sky, down onto where he stood.

A blast of heat and sparks flung him into the air, sending him crashing through the glass window of the nearest building. Blackness descended over him.

XXVIII

The thunderous lightning strike so near made Hank flinch, bringing a fresh jolt of pain. A silent curse as he collected himself, then he snuck down the alley. He peeked around the corner, and found himself face-to-face with a snarling cannibal warrior. The warrior raised his warclub, but Hank's shotgun blasted a three-inch hole through the cannibal's torso.

Levering another shell into the chamber, he said, "Two to go."

One was still inside, but what about the last? The alley stood empty but for himself and the dead heathen at his feet. Perhaps the last still lay against the far side of the jailhouse. He crept along the thick wooden wall toward the opposite corner, cold sweat pouring down his face. His hands were shaking now; if they got much worse he would not be able to hit the side of Sentinel Hill.

Pausing only a moment at the corner of the building, he took a deep breath, and then spun around the corner with his shotgun leveled.

And found no one there.

The hairs on his neck jumped to attention, and he spun behind him. Creeping silently up behind him, the cannibal raised his club, eyes blazing with fury.

Hank's shotgun blast tore a meaty crater in the cannibal's chest.

XXIX

Charles ran down the street toward the jailhouse. The report of his father's shotgun was muffled by the wind, dwarfed by the power of the thunder, but the sound was unmistakable. He cocked both barrels of his own shotgun and tried to forget that two hundred yards behind him, a tornado was chewing through White Pine. He tried to forget the sickening, grotesque urges that had billowed through him, urges that had been real and born of his deepest longings. He tried to tell himself that they were born of the Wiindigu's influence, but their convincing reality turned his insides to a sea of bile.

When Charles stood fifty yards from the jailhouse door, a dark, amorphous shape emerged from within, a low, slinking shape. He cocked back one of the hammers, raised the shotgun, and took aim. The muzzle of the shotgun swayed in rhythm with his hammering heart, until he held his breath and squeezed the trigger as his father had taught him.

The butt kicked against him, and the barrel roared smoke. A wind gust snatched the smoke away and revealed a cannibal writhing in pain on the ground.

Charles ran closer. He had one shot left.

The wounded cannibal thrashed and flailed like an enraged badger, grasping for something, anything to kill, roaring in a language that grated across his ears like fingernails on a blackboard.

Charles halted ten feet from the unnerving spectacle, leveled the muzzle, swallowed the hatred in his throat as he took careful aim, and splattered half of the cannibal's head across the sidewalk.

A figure lurched out of the alley, instantly familiar but unsteady on his boots. Hank fell unsteadily upon Charles' shoulder. Charles could not speak, and his hands were shaking.

In all his life, he had never felt comfort from his father's hand. Must he have had to kill a man before he gained his father's respect? Must he have had to kill a man before he wanted it?

Hank pointed toward the exploding destruction at the far end of town, then pushed Charles toward the jailhouse door with his good arm.

Once they were inside, Hank slammed the door closed and threw the bar down with the butt the shotgun.

Charles looked for Amelia and Katie in the darkness, but the lightning had disrupted his night vision. "Katie? Amelia?"

The only response was a sound his mind could not grasp. Wet sounds like a dog chewing on a fresh steak. Something was moving, but he could not see.

"Katie? Amelia?"

Hank edged forward. "You two all right?"

They waited for a reply, but when none came, a fresh chill of dread fell into Charles stomach.

Hank said, "Amelia, throw me the keys."

The only response was more loathsome mastication.

Hank snorted a curse and lay down the shotgun, fumbling with a box of matches and the lantern, snapping a flare of matchlight and applying it to the wick.

In the burgeoning light, Katie's face was a blood-smeared mask. Ropes of Amelia's entrails dangled from her hands. She grinned at them.

Hank snatched up the shotgun. "Fuck!"

Charles cried out. *"No!"*

Hank swung the shotgun and pulled the trigger, spraying lead and pieces of Katie Delacroix across the back wall of the jail cell.

Charles fought back a retch and turned on his father with a snarl. "Dear God! You shot her! You shot a little girl!"

Hank's face was carved of wood with matchstick for a mouth. "She wasn't one of us anymore."

Charles grabbed Hank by the shoulders and shook him. "How could you?"

Hank cried out in pain from the arrow wound. "That little monster just killed your wife! What is wrong with you?"

The 10-gauge was still in Charles' hands. He wanted to smash the butt of it across his father's face. "What if we could have helped her? What if this madness is all going to pass? She was trapped in that cell. She was just a little *girl!*" She had needed his protection, and he had failed *again*. He slumped to his knees.

Hank dropped to one knee beside him. "Don't do this, son. Not now. Not this. We got work to do. There's a twister coming."

"Let it come."

Charles rested his head against the cold, iron bars.

The thunderous screeching howl of the cyclone intensified. Debris pattered against the windows in larger and larger chunks, some threatening to shatter the glass. The rafters rattled and creaked. Planks clattered and flew, glass shattered, a dog howled and whined somewhere nearby, tree boughs splintered and fell.

Hank laid his hand on Charles' shoulder again. "Charles. Son. It's not what it seems. This is not your life. You didn't ask for this, but you inherited it. It's goddamn circumstance. Circumstance put me in a Confederate prison. Circumstance took your mother from me. From you. Circumstance goddamn killed your babies and there wasn't a thing you didn't do to save them. I ain't gonna apologize for being hard on you. But I'm fucking proud of the man you are." He stopped, as if realizing what he just said.

Charles had never heard such words from his father before. He pressed the heels of his palms against his eyes to block the tears.

"I am sorry you lost your little girls. And now your wife. But this little girl here ... she wasn't one of us no more. You didn't see what was on that hill, what I saw. You didn't see *them*, what they *did*." He cocked the shotgun. "You were right about the Sioux. But *these* animals need to be put down. We're all the law that exists now. You and me. And circumstances gave us one more job to do."

Charles could barely hear Hank's voice at the end over the shrieking tumult of the storm. He could not be sure if the scream of the wind was not mingled with screams of White Pine's townspeople. The street outside was a black mass of flying dust and debris, strobed by scarlet lightning.

A voice came through the door. "Marshal, open up! Let us in!"

XXX

Olga Teague groaned as she shifted, but her weeping had stopped.

Little Elk held the bandage against Olga's wound, feeling it grow ever heavier as it absorbed blood. She ignored the white woman's frantic sobbing and closed her eyes to fight against what had almost just happened with the doctor.

Charles had not been alone in his desire.

Every fiber of her being had become a searing ache of lust. Her groin was still wet with it, almost dripping against her thigh. She would have thrown him down on the floor and coupled with him and let the white woman die as she watched. Little Elk's face burned with the shame of it, and now her belly was a cold, cavernous ache, clenching with hunger. Somehow the lust and the hunger were tied together within, like caverns of need unlocked by the touch of the Wiindigu's tendrils.

If they had succumbed to their urges, if they had coupled, together they would have eaten Olga Teague.

Even now, all Little Elk's efforts were focused on containing how hungry she was.

Olga's frantic sobbing subsided and she glanced over her shoulder at Little Elk. She sniffled. "Are you ... from the reservation?"

"Yes."

"Why are you here?"

"That is a long story."

"Am I going to die? I don't want to die!"

"No, you will not die."

Little Elk wondered what the "Heaven" of white people was like. When Lakota died, they went to the Happy Hunting Grounds, there to be reunited with lost relatives and friends in the spirit realm where game was plentiful and the land was peaceful, bountiful, beautiful. It was something to be looked forward to, unless the person had been scalped, in which case their spirit was trapped with the scalp here in the earthly realm in the possession of the one who kept the scalp.

Lightning flashed in the windows, and thunder roared over the tumult of the cyclone.

The booming tumult outside spattered the wooden face of the building with flying debris, and the building creaked as if a great hand pushed against the side, moaned in the crevices.

A girl of twelve emerged from the darkened corner of the room, head bowed, shoulders slumped as if in great sadness. Two dark braids hung before the shoulders of her pale cotton dress.

Lightning flashed through the windows, through the gauzy dress, silhouetting a form within that was not—

"Laughing Otter!" Little Elk gasped.

The girl stood beside Little Elk now, without having crossed the distance between them.

Olga was speaking to Little Elk, oblivious to the girl's presence, but the white woman's voice was lost in the wind.

Little Elk stepped back. "What do you want?"

"Everything."

"What are you? Are you Iya? Are you a Wiindigu? Are you Satan?"

"How can a thing so vast be contained in only one name, one puff of wind?" said the girl that was not a girl.

"Leave us alone!"

"You called us here. All of you. So we came."

The girl raised her face, and looked up into Little Elk's face with eyes as fathomless as the night sky, gulfs of infinitely cold stars glittering within those depths. The girl's mouth opened, wide, wide, impossibly wide, and a great howling cyclone emerged.

XXXI

Something bumped against the door, then spoke.

Charles jumped to his feet, but he could not make out the words.

The voice had had a strange, reedy quality, but the distortion could have been from the noise.

Hank peered out the window. "I can't see a goddamn thing!"

Charles called, "Who's out there?"

The voice came again, thin and wind-tossed. "Is that the doctor? We got somebody hurt out here!"

Charles glanced at his father. "I don't recognize that voice. Do you?"

Hank shook his head.

The voice came again, "Please, Doc! Please!"

Screams filtered in on the wind's hiss, growing louder, closer.

The impulse to help surged up in Charles' muscles like a reflexive twitch, but he stopped himself. He met his father's skeptical gaze. Neither of them moved to open the door. The screams continued, growing louder, until it sounded like a cacophony of voices were in the jailhouse with them. Blows fell upon the door. The window was a black morass, revealing nothing. The rafters groaned.

Charles clapped his hands over his ears.

The screams silenced.

As quick and sudden as if a switch had been thrown, leaving only the incessant howl of the wind and the shuddering groan of the jailhouse.

From outside, a feeble voice, "Oh, God. I can taste it in my mouth. The darkness wants you!"

Eternal moments raked over them as the storm raged.

Charles said, "Hold still, Dad, let me pull the arrow out."

Hank turned his back to present the blood-smeared obsidian arrow point. Charles took the point in his hand and braced himself to pull the arrow through.

Then a great crackling wrench tore through the structure and a section of the roof spun off into blackness. A sucking blast of air stole the breath from Charles' lungs.

Rafters fell, and more of the roof peeled away. Part of the front wall collapsed. A tremendous blow and a crushing weight smashed Charles to the floor.

Dazed, dizzy, half-blinded by darkness and stinging dust, he looked up in time to see his father's boots leave the floor. His ears were a tumult of deafening noise.

Above him, his father clung with his good arm to the splintered end of a rafter as the immense sucking maw of the storm dragged him up toward the abyss.

Charles gasped for breath, trying to drag himself free of the wreckage. "Dad," he said, but the wind swallowed his voice.

His father's fingers clung to the splintered wood, boots hanging above him, his face a mask of sheer, solemn will.

Charles pushed himself up with all his dwindling might, trying to shift the beam just enough for some purchase to free himself. "Dad!" One last surge of strength through his arms and he heaved himself onto all fours, shifting the mass of collapsed wood.

With another shuddering crack, Hank's rafter let go and he spiraled upwards, into the sky.

Charles reached for him, in vain. He could only watch as his father disappeared into blackness.

Through the shattered face of the jailhouse, illuminated by the lightning, Charles glimpsed what was left of White Pine.

Nothing.

A wasteland of shattered timbers and debris.

Scarlet lightning crackled and sighed.

One last burst of effort, and he heaved himself free of the wreckage and struggled to his feet, buffeted by wind.

He looked up into the face of the eldritch vortex. "Take me, goddammit! Take me!"

The swirling thunderous abyss looked down onto him, into him, an emptiness that could never be filled, and Charles sensed that it *saw* something, and came to a decision.

The vortex pulled away.

Charles reached with both hands. "No! Take me!"

The mouth of the funnel receded upward into the swirling clouds, and as it pulled away, Charles felt a strange, tearing sensation that grew sharper and deeper until he felt one or all of his organs must be ripping free of their moorings, an agony that dragged a wail of pain and despair from the depths of his being, and as the vortex drew away, whatever part of him it took receded with it.

The lightning diminished. The wind weakened.

"No."

He sank to his knees.

Something sticky was in his hand. The bloody tip of the broken arrow. For a long time, as the tumult ebbed and storm clouds moved away, he could look at nothing but the arrow and feel nothing but the emptiness within him.

XXXII

A sliver of dawn sliced across the horizon, under the clouds. As Charles knelt in the wreckage, he thought that he should be weeping, but no tears would come.

Amelia's savaged corpse lay behind him, half-buried in the debris of the shattered jailhouse. Should he weep for her?

He could not think about what remained of Katie. Should he weep for the child she had been or the monster she had become?

The blood on the broken arrow had dried it to his hand, until in the burgeoning dawn he had to peel the arrow loose and cast it away.

His ears still rang, muffling all sound. He did not know if he would ever hear properly again.

What did it matter? He was not certain he should see the next sunset.

The storm had moved away to the east. Would it dissipate before it reached Sioux Falls, or St. Paul, or Chicago? Would it change direction? Would it slumber in evil dreams until some unknowable summoning brought it forth again?

Charles' clothing was covered in dust, blood, and debris. His face felt like nothing more than caked mud and white dirt. For a moment as he stood, his posture mimicked a double-bent savage, dragging his fingers through the dirt.

Near the ruins of the jailhouse lay the bodies of the cannibals he and his father had killed. There could be more prowling around town, seeking stray meat.

Within minutes, he found his father's lever-action shotgun in the wreckage. A ready shell awaited in the chamber. A deep gouge scarred the wooden stock, and the lever was slightly bent askew, but it still functioned perfectly.

He contemplated the weapon, this thing that could erase life so effortlessly. Such a small thing, so easy, a mere finger twitch to pull the trigger and end a person's existence.

He shambled through the devastation. The Long Horse Saloon sign stood upright, embedded a foot deep into the earth. Horses lay crushed under the weight of bricks and wood from the Post and Telegraph Office. A few sheep and goats lay ripped apart and splattered across the street.

If he forced himself to look closely, he could see motionless human limbs protruding from wreckage in every direction.

His office was a ragged tangle of splintered wood and shattered glass. In the center of the debris stood a lump where his heavy metal examination table had stood. Close beside, a pale, limp-wristed arm protruded, the elbow bent the wrong way.

On the wrist was a bracelet of wood, beads, and dark polished stone.

Should he weep for Little Elk, who had gone to join her husband and the rest of her people?

Still no tears came. Had he no heart at all?

At the far end of the street lay the remains of the enormous bonfire. Spitted, half-roasted corpses still stood above the blackened mound. Bodies of Lakota braves lay among dead cannibals, all strewn like scattered cordwood.

He should call out, seeking survivors, but he knew that there would be no answer. Perhaps there were a few townspeople who had fled to their storm cellars, only to fall prey to the entity's ravenous influence.

White Pine was dead.

Back at the jailhouse, he stood over Amelia's body. A beam of dawn slid across her pale, dead face, frozen in horror and anguish and blame.

A shudder went through him, and he knelt to shut her eyes, brush the debris from her face, her cold lips, the lips he had once, long ago, kissed with fervor. He tucked her back together. Slowly, methodically, he dragged away the wreckage until he could lift her free.

Shotgun cradled under his arm, he carried her to the far corner of town where their house had once stood, now nothing more than a mass of smashed timbers, much of which had been scattered to parts unknown.

Somehow, two wooden crosses still stood beside the graves of their daughters.

He laid Amelia on the ground, then grabbed a splintered board, and scratched out a fresh grave. It would not be deep enough, but he had no other tools. His hands were bloody by the time he was done tearing through the tough sod to the earth beneath.

On another board, he carved the words "Loving Mother" with a bent, rusty nail, and then laid her there in the shallow groove. He had not even a sheet to cover her.

With the shotgun butt, he pounded the cross into the ground at the head of the fresh mound of soil. He thought he should say a few words. Custom demanded that he say a few words, but he could not muster any that mattered, and there was no one to hear.

Then a horrid scream of brutal rage and madness filtered through the muffled ringing in his ears. He snatched up the shotgun.

XXXIII

Sunka Wakan Luta heaved himself onto all fours, his arms trembling from exertion, the pounding in his head sapping the last of his ebbing strength, just as the weight of the fallen building was stealing the last of his breath and pinning his legs. His only thought was to breathe free again. But it was all too heavy, the wood and pain and weariness. His strength was gone.

No.

Sunka Wakan Luta would not die like this. His blood was the blood of warriors going back to the Beginning.

He gathered his strength into a cry, then a scream.

The weight on him shifted.

His scream built with all the power of his ancestors.

Splinters and nails tore furrows in his flesh as he pried himself from under the wreckage.

Then he stood up into the silence of dawn and desolation.

He raised his fists to the sky and roared with exuberance, and then with despair that his wish to die on the battlefield had not been granted. A rattling, tangled mass of hair and bone and beads hung from his fist. The witch's scalp, still wet with the foul stench of her people's corruption.

He clutched it tighter, twining his fingers deeper into the filthy, matted mass.

The Black Wind People were no more.

Washte yelo. It was good.

He staggered into the street. His foot would not work right. Blood ran from a deep gash along his anklebone. There in the street, near the scattered remains of the great bonfire, lay the wreckage of battle. Weapons, corpses, dead horses, blood pools mixing with the sickening ichor that flowed in the veins of the Black Wind People.

The silence of death shrouded the wreckage of the white man's settlement, silence like that which must have hung over Wounded Knee Creek as the smoke of rifles and cannons drifted away on the wind.

A lone figure drifted through the wreckage, perhaps a hundred paces distant, blurred by blood and aging eyes. He wiped the crusted blood from his eyes and searched about for a weapon. A warclub encrusted with the razor-sharp black glass lay encrusted with blood and Lakota hair. He would not touch such a foul instrument. A shattered rifle lay nearby, useless.

There.

His Bowie knife. He picked it up, straightened, closed his eyes, and waited for the dizziness to pass.

XXXIV

A strange voice drifted into Charles' attention, the strange, familiar, singsong chant, crawling, squirming into his ears, through the walls of his muffled hearing.

Ph'nglui mglw'nafh Cthulhu R'lyeh wgah'nagl fhtagn ...
Ph'ngha Wiindigu nogshogg ...

He looked about but could not find the source. It was as if the syllables wriggled from between the splintered timbers, out of the blood-soaked ground into the soles of his feet, inching like worms up his legs, cold leeches over his genitals, up his back and belly, his neck, his cheeks, splashing like blood-dripping symbols into his mind.

It was a song of feeding, a song of reverence, a song of power, a song of ancient names that carried more weight can any collection of English noises.

The remnant wind disappeared, and perhaps for the first time since he had arrived in this territory, the world lay becalmed. Blood-colored streamers crossed the sky. Scarlet tinged the sunrise.

A cannibal stood over there, facing him, drenched in blood and ichor from head to toe.

But not just any cannibal. A woman so hideous and bestial that he could not count her as human. Her hair was a matted mass of filth and bones and blood, her breasts and naked flesh pierced and scarred in ways unimaginable to any sane human being. This could be none other than the chieftess of these monsters.

A severed head hung by the hair from her fingers.

Red Horse's head.

The whites of her eyes shone from within the ravaged mask of congealed blood that was her visage.

She smiled, a vicious baring of needle-sharp teeth.

Sunka Wakan Luta staggered forward. He could see now that it was Charles who approached him, shotgun in his hands. Charles' face was that of a man who had stood at the brink of the deepest evil and looked within.

The wind still whistled around him, and the morning sun was warm and bright on his face, a blue sky emerging from the shreds of blackness.

What would they do now, he and his white man? Where could they go? What life was left for either of them?

They were, each of them, now utterly alone. There was nothing to do now but embrace this white man as a brother. Together they had defeated the Black Wind People and their evil god. They would loft the witch's scalp onto a pole and sing the old songs.

On trembling legs, he advanced toward Charles.

The cannibal witch charged with a ragged shriek that sent ice through Charles' veins.

As if the world were mired in tar, he raised the shotgun.

The bloody whites of her eyes gleamed.

Red Horse's slack mouth dribbled blood beneath her fist, lifeless eyes rolled back.

Such an easy thing to pull the trigger and unleash the bucking fire and end this once and for all time.

The nearly headless body fell forward.

Charles shambled like a ghost through a graveyard, looking for what, he did not know. Biding his time until starvation took him and he did not have to do anything anymore? The dead faces and lives erased, as if they had never been, meant nothing to him.

In the middle of the street, a glint of metal caught his eye.

He stood over it. The Town Marshal star of his father. A single spot of blood marred its dusty surface.

He picked it up, polished away the blood and dust with his sleeve, and pinned it to his vest.

Surrounded by a town of dead things, Charles sat in a creaky chair on the stoop of what was once the jailhouse, checked his father's shotgun to see if it was loaded, and placed it thoughtfully into his lap.

He would never weep again, and an emptiness yawned within him that would never be filled.

The wind whistled through White Pine.

ABOUT THE AUTHORS

Freelance writer, novelist, award-winning screenwriter, editor, poker player, poet, biker, roustabout, Travis Heermann is a graduate of the Odyssey Writing Workshop and the author of *The Ronin Trilogy, The Wild Boys,* and *Rogues of the Black Fury,* plus short fiction pieces in anthologies and magazines such as *Apex Magazine,* the *Fiction River* anthology series, *Historical Lovecraft,* and Cemetery Dance's *Shivers VII.* As a freelance writer, he has produced a metric ton of role-playing game work both in print and online, including the *Firefly Roleplaying Game, Legend of Five Rings, d20 System,* and the MMORPG, EVE Online. He enjoys cycling, martial arts, torturing young minds with otherworldly ideas, and zombies. He has three long-cherished dreams: a produced screenplay, a *New York Times* best-seller, and a seat in the World Series of Poker.

jim pinto is a 20-year veteran of the gaming industry, with numerous credits in about a dozen categories, including writing, design, development, art, and editing. He's written everything from gaming adventures to board games to comics to screenplays to hot tub catalog copy. His latest fiasco involves a gondola, 87 conspirators, and a 19th century Masonic voting box. A multicultural savant, he knows "hello" in twenty languages, as well as most of the world's capitals. His first book in the gaming industry was about Japanese culture, favorite novel is French, favorite movie is Chinese, favorite country is Romania, favorite food is Indian, and favorite wife is Korean. He might have also won a few ENnies, an Origins award, a Player's Choice award from Inquest magazine, and $50 from a college fiction contest. He's not sure. He has no children, pets, or lice. jim pinto is allergic to capital letters.

IF YOU LIKED ...

If you liked *Death Wind*, you might also enjoy:

City of the Saints
D.J. Butler

Blood Ties
Quincy J. Allen

Best of Penny Dread
Quincy J. Allen

OTHER WORDFIRE PRESS TITLES

Our list of other WordFire Press authors and titles is always growing.
To find out more and to see our selection of titles, visit us at:

wordfirepress.com

67879527R00155

Made in the USA
Charleston, SC
23 February 2017